One Kind of Hero

Also by Rob Bauer

Fiction

The Depth of Midnight

Against the Oncoming Night

Dreams Lost & Found

Theodora

The Nightmare Kingdom

The Long Way Home

Darkness in Dixie

The Buffalo Soldier

The World Traveler

My Australian Adventure

Nonfiction

Outside the Lines of Gilded Age Baseball: Alcohol, Fitness, and Cheating in 1880s Baseball

Outside the Lines of Gilded Age Baseball: Gambling, Umpires, and Racism in 1880s Baseball

Outside the Lines of Gilded Age Baseball: The Origins of the 1890 Players League

Outside the Lines of Gilded Age Baseball: The Finances of 1880s Baseball

One Kind of Hero

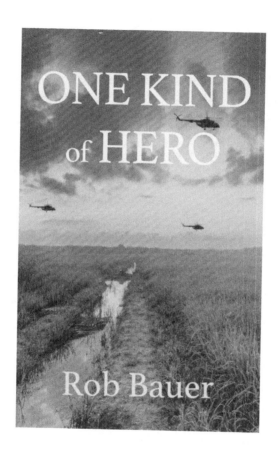

Rob Bauer

This is a work of fiction. Names, characters, places, and incidents either are the product of the author's imagination or are used fictitiously. Any resemblance to actual persons, living or dead, events, or locales is entirely coincidental.

For any inquiries regarding this book, please contact Rob at Rob@robbauerbooks.com.

No part of this book may be reproduced in any form or by any electronic or mechanical means, including information storage and retrieval systems, without written permission from the author, except for the use of brief quotations in a book review.

Copyright © 2023 Robert A. Bauer
All rights reserved.
ISBN-13: 978-1-948478-27-4

For Jim and anyone still struggling with the aftereffects of Agent Orange and similar chemicals. Most of the world has forgotten about you, but I haven't.

Contents

1	My Bird Takes Flight	1
2	Homecoming	9
3	Trying to Enjoy Myself	19
4	Back at Home	31
5	Vietnam Through Lisa's Eyes	42
6	Visiting Ted	54
7	Compassion Becomes Weakness	63
8	On My Own	76
9	I Wish it Would Rain	87
10	The Williamson House	93
11	The Days After	103
12	Elaine's House	116
13	My Latest Mission	126
14	Disaster	132
15	My First Anniversary	137
16	The Sierras	148
17	Changes	156
18	I Try to Bounce Back	165
19	Three Strikes	172
20	A New Hope	181
21	Sabotage	192
22	Misery Loves Company	202
23	I Try Diplomacy	208
24	A Finesse Mission	217
25	Secret Plans	221
26	The Mission	229
27	A Final Visit	232
	Scott's Postscript	234
	Sandra's Postscript	240
	About the Author	246

Chapter 1

My Bird Takes Flight

November 30 of 1967 was my final mission in Vietnam. My Freedom Bird took off from Tan Son Nhut Airfield in Saigon on December 1 of 1967. I became a civilian the same day.

It's true. On the last day of November, I completed my final combat mission, and a day later, I stand on the sunny tarmac at Travis Air Force Base in California, no longer a member of the United States Army.

I've done nothing wrong. My discharge was honorable. But when one leaves Saigon for the States (via the Philippines and then Guam), one crosses over the International Dateline. Thus, I mustered out of the Army the same day I left Vietnam.

The Pan American Boeing 727 that brought me home rests behind me. I sling an olive-green duffle bag over my shoulder while I head toward the terminal. It's only a few days before my twenty-first birthday.

No crowd cheers my arrival, nor do any hecklers jeer me. Travis Air Force Base is a military installation, after all. I walk aimlessly into the terminal while the sound of jets taking off and landing continues around me.

I left a few things behind when my Freedom Bird departed Saigon. The guitar I'd bought and learned to play tolerably was the

One Kind Of Hero

one I missed the most. Well, make that the second most. I left a number of friends behind as well. Some remain on active duty, their tours still with a few weeks or months to go. A handful will remain soldiers forevermore, the departure of their Freedom Bird eternally delayed.

My friend Ted Williamson walks beside me. Ted is a graceful man who stands six-three and looks like he should be an athlete. But, although I've seen him play basketball, Ted isn't much for sports. What he really likes is building model cars and model airplanes. Naturally enough, he'd started as a helicopter mechanic for some of the Chinooks that flew in Vietnam. He'd been so good at it that our maintenance officer promoted him to crew chief before long and flight engineer shortly after that. If Ted said a chopper wasn't ready to fly, it didn't fly.

Ted is also Black while I am White. The thing that brought us together, besides Ted being the crew chief of the Chinook on which I was a crewman, is that both of us come from the Los Angeles area. Ted and I met at Fort Eustis, Virginia, where we learned to fly Chinook helicopters. After finishing our training, we began our tour and fought together. Both of us tend to the quiet side as well, at least by military standards, and the friendship developed from there.

One final thing we did together was to extend our tours in Vietnam by two months once our year overseas was up. Believe me, we didn't do it because we like fighting or enjoy Army food. Rather, we extended our time in Vietnam because that left us with eighty-nine days remaining to serve once we got back to the States. The Army has a policy whereby it discharges soldiers returning from Vietnam with fewer than three months to go in their enlistment. I guess the Army figures that is cheaper than equipping us and transferring us to a new base. That's how Ted and I became civilians the same day we left Vietnam.

My Bird Takes Flight

The next leg on our journey home is the bus ride from Travis to the Oakland Army Terminal. At midnight, we're shoved out the door, no longer members of the United States Army. Neither Ted or I took up the Army on its inspiring offer to serve a second tour.

Like most guys we flew home with, Ted and I take a cab from the Oakland Army Terminal to San Francisco International Airport, sleeping in a hotel nearby. The rest of the guys have to catch a flight to wherever their hometown is, but since Ted and I live in Southern California, we won't fly. We only went to the airport to say goodbye to some of our buddies and because it's a convenient location for my father to pick me up.

"You said your dad was driving to get you, Sticks?" Ted asks me while we meander through the pickup area. My name is Scott, Scott Reynolds, but in Vietnam everyone called me Sticks. I got the nickname because I'm one of those lucky guys who can eat and drink all they want and never get fat. Even though I'm six-one, I doubt I've ever weighed above one hundred-sixty pounds.

"Yeah, he's gonna pick me up. How about you?"

"My parents bought me a bus ticket home."

"Damn, I should've asked you about that sooner. You could've ridden with us."

"It's okay. The ticket's bought and paid for. Might as well use it."

"Still, it's a long bus ride. You sure?"

Ted nods.

"What's the first thing you want to do now that we're home?" I ask him.

"Stretch my legs. That flight from Guam was *long*, and the bus ride won't be much better, I'll wager. Then I'll take a hot bath. After that, we'll see. How about you?"

"I don't know," I admit. "Funny, isn't it? I spent a year in Vietnam, and all I could think of was not getting killed so that I could be somewhere else when that year was over. Now I'm somewhere else, and I have no idea what I should do."

3

One Kind Of Hero

Ted chuckles lightly and nods. "There it is."

As we speak, we near the spot where my father said he'd meet me. The sunlight washes through the airport windows as if the sun, too, wants to welcome me back to the States. I shiver anyway. Two days ago in Saigon, the temperature topped ninety-five degrees, and heaven only knows what the humidity was. Even though it's just as sunny in San Francisco, the air is at least thirty degrees colder than what I've become used to. Without the humidity, the difference feels more like forty or fifty.

"I know what you mean," Ted says after a moment. "You'd think that after surviving a year in the Nam, I'd have a grander plan than a walk and a bath, but hell, I don't know. Two days ago we were looking for Charlie, and now I'm looking for the bus station. It's hard to go from one life to the other so fast."

"That's how I see it, too. I spent the whole plane ride thinking how lucky I was to live to catch my Freedom Bird. That's practically all I thought about the whole way here. I could've been Todd, or Shane, or Gordon, or one of the other guys I went to boot camp with who aren't coming home at all. Now I'm home, and it's like, damn, I've got so many choices of what to do, which one do I choose? Kinda like the first day of summer vacation when we were in school, you know?"

"Except we don't have to go back to school. We don't have to take orders anymore, either. That'll be nice."

"You know what, Ted? I do know what I'm gonna do first. Sleep in. That's what I'm gonna do. I'm gonna sleep until my body feels ready to get up. Even if that means I sleep for twenty hours straight."

Ted laughs again. "Dig that, man. I dig that."

"You've got my family's phone number, right? I wanna get together after a week or two, check in on how things are going."

"Absolutely," Ted responds as we reach the parking lot.

I look around. There he is. My father's timing is perfect. He rolls up in a bright blue Buick Electra that he bought right before I left for Vietnam.

"Well, this is it. For now," I say to Ted.

My father puts the car in park and gets out, slowly walking over until he's right in front of me. "Welcome home, Son," he says, shaking my hand firmly and flashing his warmest smile. "It's good to see you." Then he turns to Ted. "You must be the friend my son mentioned in his letters, Ted. Welcome home to you, too," he says over another handshake.

"Thank you, Mr. Reynolds."

"Just call me Darryl. Anyone who's done what you men have done can skip the mister."

Ted smiles. "Thank you, si—sorry, Darryl. It's gonna take some time to get used to not addressing people as sir," Ted says tentatively.

"Yes, it will. If you ask me, people should be calling you sir."

Ted relaxes and smiles, but then glances down at his watch. "I don't have that much time before my bus leaves. I guess I'd better go find it."

"I told Ted he could ride with us, but I suppose his family will be waiting for him at the bus station," I say to my father.

He nods. "That's probably true. We'll see you again, I'm sure, Ted. Let's get moving, Scott."

We drive east and south on our way home. The trip is more than four hundred miles, so I figure Dad and I will have plenty to discuss on the way. But for a long time, he drives in silence while I stare out the window of the Electra.

Something doesn't feel right to me.

"Aren't we going a little fast?" I ask Dad while we motor down Highway 99, the sunny hills and fields all around us. It seems like the landscape is flying by.

"We're right at the speed limit."

I glance over at the speedometer, and Dad isn't pulling my leg. I shake my head. "It seems fast compared to Army jeeps, I guess."

"You'll get used to it again. I was going to ask if you want to drive for a while, but maybe not."

"I haven't driven a vehicle in months," I confess. "Maybe I'll leave it to you this time."

On the flight home, I imagined that Dad would pepper me with questions, but while I gaze at the scenery, he looks ahead calmly, one hand on the wheel, while the miles stretch onward and the morning turns to afternoon.

Although I have a hundred things I want to say to him, I know we have time, so I feel content to reacquaint myself with what the Central Valley of California looks like. It's mostly brown at this time of the year. Although the rainy season in Central California begins in December, "rainy season" is a relative term. The whole valley is rather dry except for where irrigation ditches from the Central Valley Project bring water.

Finally, I shift in my seat and look over at my father. "What are you hiding, Dad?" I ask with a cautious smile.

"Hiding?" he replies, his expression revealing nothing.

"You're awful quiet. I thought you'd have a million questions for me."

"I do."

"Then what are you waiting for?"

"You."

This is typical of my father. Calling him a man of few words might be generous. At my sister's twenty-first birthday party, a friend's mother teased him by claiming she had a bet he wouldn't say three words all night. She had to strike up a conversation to win the bet. His answer was, "You lose." And then he said nothing for the next hour. It was all in good fun, of course, and he had plenty to say before the party ended, but that's how he is. It's why I suspect he's hiding something now—his sneaky sense of humor works in exactly this way.

The only exception is when he runs his bakery. Dad loves talking to every customer, and he knows many of them by name. Some people have patronized his bakery for years, which makes it an institution in the small commercial district where he works. My father is the perfect person to put customers at ease—average height, average build, dark hair parted on the left, a slightly rounded face, and a genuine smile.

But when he claims he's waiting for me, that catches me off-guard. "Why are you waiting for me?"

"I figured I'd let you talk when you felt ready."

"Why wouldn't I be ready?"

"You've barely spoken since we got on the road. I figured you weren't ready yet."

Another thing about my father is that he's always got a reason for everything he does.

"It's been two years since I've seen California. I mean, I visited on leave, sure, but I knew that would only be temporary. Now, it's my home again, and it's so different from Vietnam."

"That's not what I meant."

"Come on, Dad," I say with a smile, even though I'm a little confused. "What do you mean, then? I feel fine, and all this quiet is awkward."

"I want to ask you all about Vietnam, of course. But when I left Germany in 1945, it took me days before I could talk with a civilian again. I didn't know if it'd be the same for you. Once you've been in war, a man has certain things he can only talk about with other soldiers. Some things will never make sense to people who haven't fought, and when I came home from Europe, it took me a long time to realize that."

"It's a good thing you had a lengthy sea voyage back to America, it sounds like."

Although my father fought in Europe during World War 2, he rarely speaks of it. He's never been one to tell war stories as a method of claiming respect or attention. As a result, I know only a fraction of what he did while overseas fighting the Germans.

"Yes, and that's the key point," he tells me. "I had many days to let go of the tension, stress, and fear before I ever set foot back in America. You haven't. I didn't know how much that might affect you. Every man is different. That's also why I told your mother I'd get you alone. If she were here, she'd have talked both of your ears off already. Your sister Lisa would've done the same. I didn't want you to experience that without time to prepare yourself."

I laugh. That describes my mother and sister perfectly. Both can talk for days when so inclined. But I also see my father's point, and it's one I'd never considered during the flight home. I think I'm ready to see the rest of my family, but what if I'm not? It's a thought I come back to several times while Dad and I talk about Vietnam the rest of the way home.

That homecoming turned out rather different than I anticipated.

Chapter 2

Homecoming

"Let me get that for you," Dad says when I shoulder my duffle bag in the driveway of our home.

I pause a moment. People doing things for you isn't a regular feature of Army life. But Dad has already taken the bag from me and headed toward the front door as if nothing could be more natural. I follow.

Like many houses in the Los Angeles suburbs, ours has two stories with a token front lawn, a two-car garage on the ground floor, and the bedrooms upstairs. Unlike both neighbors, however, no pink flamingos decorate the front yard. It took Mom years to convince Dad it was okay to have palm trees flanking the driveway and that painting the house yellow wasn't too pretentious and showy. But he would only agree to dull yellow rather than bright yellow. A man's principles can stretch only so far, I suppose.

"Go on in," he says while gesturing me to precede him. "Your mother and sister are anxious to see you."

It's dark outside now, but the porch light is on. So are the lights inside the house. Everything looks as warm and cheery as my imagination hoped it would on this day.

I stop at the front door, a beautifully stained, heavy oak door, and close my eyes, hand on the knob. Each day for the last fourteen months I thought about this moment, wondering how I would feel when it arrived. A hint of a tear wets the corner of one eye, but it's a tear of happiness.

I'm home.

"Go on," Dad says again, smile in place. "Everyone wants to see you."

Holding my breath, I turn the doorknob and step inside. When I look in the living room to the left, I see no one. The house appears empty. I'm about to look to Dad for an explanation when several familiar voices shout, "Surprise!"

My sister jumps up from behind the sofa, my mother walks in from the kitchen, and my girlfriend, Elaine, bounds down the staircase. Other family members follow.

I reach for my rifle, roll to my left, and take cover behind the edge of the sofa.

Everyone laughs and claps. But they don't see that I'm breaking out in a sweat. I happen to glance back at my father from my position behind the sofa's sky-blue arm. His smile fades immediately as he sets my duffle bag next to the door of the hallway's coat closet and closes the front door. Clearly, my reaction surprised him.

"Bravo! Bravo!" I hear my mother, Susan, call. "Come on out, Scott! We didn't expect a demonstration of Vietnam on your first night home, but that was great! Climb out of your foxhole, young man, and give your mother a hug."

For a split second, I lean my head against the sofa's arm, still out of view of everyone but my father, and close my eyes. I realize that I've balled my fists while a shiver comes over me. I take one deep breath, and I tell myself to let the tension go.

Rising, I put a smile back on my face. Once I'm up, Elaine leaps into my arms and kisses me in front of everyone.

"I've waited two years for this day," she says through her beaming smile. "Aren't you going to kiss me back?"

My smile gets a little more genuine when I do.

"That's better," Elaine grins. "I've missed you so much. Welcome home, Scott."

"It's great to be home finally," I remember to say as I set Elaine back on the floor and try to regain my emotional balance.

Homecoming

Elaine looks perfect. Her brown hair is in a chin-length bowl with her bangs touching her eyebrows and a blue ribbon headband in her hair. She's wearing a white cotton dress that contrasts beautifully with her dark hair and brown eyes.

Elaine Collier is my sweetheart from high school. We started dating our junior year. The chance to see her again is one of the things that kept me going day after day in Vietnam.

We met in the school band. Elaine was a great trumpet player. I was, well, I was an okay trumpet player. But I spent my freshman and sophomore years practicing hard so that I'd be good enough to sit next to Elaine and play the first trumpet parts. My motivation for improvement may not have been typical, much less out of a pure love of music, but it worked. By the spring of our junior year, we were a couple.

Next, I see Pete trot toward me. Pete was my dog growing up, my best friend. Even in high school, I'd let him sleep on my bed beside me. He's about ten now, and I missed him almost as much as I missed Elaine for the past two years. I kneel down to receive a lick while I give the chocolate lab a big hug and a scratch. "Hi, Pete. It's good to see you, old friend." Pete's tail wags furiously. It's a relief that he hasn't forgotten me. I didn't think he would, but I don't know how a dog's memory works compared to a person's memory.

"I said I need a hug from my son," my mother proclaims again while striding up to us, a grin spread across her face. "How's my little Eisenhower, my young Patton?"

"Geez, Mom, that's overdoing things just a little, isn't it?"

"Not to me, it isn't. You're a hero, and you always will be a hero in this house," she says while enveloping me a hug. And when I say envelop, I mean it. Not only is my mother Susan six feet tall, she's always been heavy, and it appears she got a bit heavier while I was away. Unlike Elaine, who has the same hairstyle as when I left, Mom has changed hers into the flipped bob that Jacqueline Kennedy made so popular. This surprises me—Mom hates the Kennedy family.

Finally breaking the embrace, she declares, "I barbequed ribs and mashed some potatoes for dinner. I know those are two of your favorites."

"You haven't eaten yet? It's past eight."

"Of course we waited for you. You didn't think you were getting warmed-up leftovers for your welcome home party, did you?"

We both laugh, and I relax a little more.

In her personality, my mother differs vastly from my father. While my father never uses two words when one will do, my mother never uses two when she can get away with a dozen. She makes three acquaintances for every one my father does and never misses a chance to join a new church social group, women's club, or civic league. In any given week, she's bouncing back and forth from Santa Monica to Burbank to Pasadena to attend all her social events. Heaven only knows what drew my parents together to begin with, since their personalities are so different. I sure don't know what it was.

After some more hugs and handshakes from a few uncles, aunts, and cousins who live nearby, my mother ushers us into the dining room.

She gestures to the head of the table. "That's your place today, Scott, at the head of the table. For our guest of honor."

I smile again. My family doesn't have formal chairs at the table, but Dad usually sits in one spot, facing away from the living room and toward the dining room window, and Mom refers to that spot as the head of the table.

When I approach the chair, though, something doesn't feel right. I say, "That's okay, Mom. That's Dad's place. I'll sit over here."

I choose a chair in the corner of the dining room where I have two walls to my back and I can see the kitchen, living room, and out the living room window.

"But I set that spot special for you."

"I know, but I feel better over here. Thank you, but I'll just sit down on the side of the table."

Homecoming

"You never used to sit there."

"It just feels right for today."

"Well, okay, suit yourself. It's your party."

We start in on the food, but I sense tension. The reason is obvious enough. Everyone wants to ask some version of the question *What was it like over there?* Maybe even *Did you ever kill anyone?* But, each person waits for someone else to say it.

At least the food is good. My mother is a fine cook, and Dad brought fresh bread home from his bakery this morning. I eat quickly, like people who must do everything on a military schedule tend to do.

"You can slow down, Scott," Elaine whispers from beside me once my food is nearly gone, her broad grin still in place. "You aren't in boot camp anymore, honey."

She's right, of course. Looking around, my plate is nearly empty whereas everyone else has eaten only half their food, if that. I try to pace myself, but I still clear my plate well before anyone else. I place my hands on my thighs and wait for everyone to catch up.

"More ribs, Scott?" Mom says presently. "I cooked extra because I knew you'd be hungry."

It shouldn't, but the question takes me by surprise. In Vietnam, one doesn't generally get second helpings. The taste of Army food typically isn't conducive to wanting a second helping, either.

"Here, have some more," my mother says, not waiting for me to respond and dropping another rack of ribs onto my plate. "You finished so fast, you must be famished. Eat up."

"Thanks, Mom," I remember to say at last.

"Once you've finished that, you can tell us a little bit about being in Vietnam. I've read all the letters you sent home, of course, most of them three or four times, but it's always different to hear things firsthand."

"Letter writing isn't something I'm very good at. I never had to do it until the past two years."

"Well, tell us how things were over there! I'm sure everyone wants to know how it felt to fly around in a helicopter on your adventures. None of us have ever done that."

Adventures isn't the word I'd choose for our missions, but I let it slide. "It wasn't as exciting as most people probably think. Most of the time my helicopter didn't fly combat missions. We did what was called combat-assist. That means we moved supplies around and so forth. I also spent some time spraying this chemical called Agent Orange. It kills vegetation. We sprayed it so that Charlie would have less cover."

"No one wants to hear about that part, Scott. That doesn't sound very glorious. Tell us what it was *really* like in that helicopter."

"That *is* what it was like most days. I spent a lot of time loading and unloading equipment. Then, on the days that we sprayed, we'd fly around and spray this chemical on the trees to kill the leaves. Some days I'd come home soaked in the stuff. When we sprayed and the spray got caught up in the propellers of the helicopter, a mist surrounded the chopper until we finished. And it takes a while to empty a five hundred-gallon rubber bladder of Agent Orange."

To be honest, spraying Agent Orange and moving supplies isn't the only thing I did from my helicopter, but it's the only one I'm supposed to tell civilians about, so I leave it at that and hope my mother drops the subject. Not only did my officers discourage me from telling civilians about some of my other missions, but those memories aren't ones I like to think about. No one likes to admit to breaking international laws, after all, even when they did so under orders and a superior bears the responsibility.

"Why do you call the Vietnamese 'Charlie'?" Elaine puts in. "I've always wondered where that word came from."

I thank Elaine for changing the subject by squeezing her hand below the table. Then I say, "The people I was fighting are known as the Viet Cong. The VC. The way the Army does it, 'Victor' is the word for V and 'Charlie' is the word that goes with C. 'Victor

Charlie' is a mouthful to say each time, though, so it got shortened to 'Charlie.'"

I see the hint of a frown on my mother's face. It's clear she isn't satisfied with what I've told her. "But you wrote in your letters about the time your helicopter took fire and went down. Tell us all about that. That must have been so dramatic!"

I sigh and close my eyes for a moment, rubbing my temples lightly. I don't want to spend my first night home telling war stories to people who can't understand how it felt to be in the Nam. But maybe if I do it once, that'll satisfy my mother for now.

"Mostly I was scared the whole time. The hydraulic system of the helicopter took some hits, and we lost pressure. You can't fly without that. So, me and some other guys had to feed hydraulic fluid into the reservoir by hand. That's why we had to touch down and radio for help. But plenty of other helicopters were part of that mission, so we had air support until an evac team rescued us. I'd like to say I did something heroic while all that was going on, but I didn't. I handled the hydraulic fluid to keep us from crashing while other guys fired back with the machine guns mounted on the sides of our ship. Before ten minutes was up, we were on our way out of there and back to base."

"That's more like it!" my mother crows. "Someday, you'll have to tell me about every little adventure you had over there."

I know I can't do that. I wonder how many conflicts that fact will cause?

"Can't you just let him eat, Mother?"

I look across the table at my sister, Lisa. Her face is red, which contrasts sharply with her blond hair and blue eyes. Lisa shakes her head. "I swear, can't you let my brother eat without asking about something that might've killed him? Let him enjoy the food before you badger him with questions about the horrible war he was forced to fight."

"Why, of course, Miss Accountant. I forget, you hate the war your own brother was involved in. The war he fought to keep *you* safe and free so that you could go to college and get such an impressive education."

My father clears his throat. "Perhaps we should let Scott decide what he'd like to talk about. It's his party, after all."

Like he did so often while I grew up, Dad's suggestion defuses the budding argument between Mom and Lisa. My sister has always been just as headstrong as my mother. I see that hasn't changed.

After receiving a number of letters from Lisa while overseas, I also know she's a firm opponent of the war, whereas my mother backs it unconditionally. And because of her self-righteous streak, Lisa struggles to understand why other people don't see the war's flaws in the same way that she does. Because Lisa was a driven student who got nearly straight A's in college and certainly is the smartest and best-educated person our family has ever produced, she expects everyone to take her seriously, even though she's only twenty-three.

Still, once I know my mother is distracted for a moment, I wink a thank you to my older sister.

Because of my dad, the conversation stays on neutral ground for the rest of dinner. I try to throw my mother a bone by talking about how poor the food was in Saigon compared to her cooking. Afterward, the wine corks pop, the beer bottles clink, and the party gets livelier. My cousin Freddy chats for a while. We're the same age, and he'd been drafted into the Army like I had, but Freddy failed his physical and consequently never went to boot camp.

I have one beer, but that's all. Over in Nam, my buddies sometimes gave me grief for being a lightweight with the alcohol, but at least I never had to fight off a hangover the next day.

Once I realize I'm not the focus of the party anymore, I drift outside to the back porch. It's nearly ten at night, and the air is decidedly cool. Immediately, I'm reminded that one can never really see stars in the Los Angeles night sky because of the light and smog. That's different from being in the field in Vietnam, where some nights it seemed like I could see them all. Elaine follows.

Homecoming

"You're a little quiet tonight, aren't you?" she asks while putting a hand on my shoulder.

"Maybe. I don't know. After two years away from home, I'm not sure what to compare myself to."

"To me, it seems like you're being quiet. You know how much work your mother did to put this party together, right?"

I nod.

"I think she's feeling a little underappreciated. You don't seem that happy."

"It's uncomfortable for me being a civilian again. A couple days ago I was in the field, and now I'm in Los Angeles."

"But you're happy, right? You aren't in danger here. Shouldn't that be relaxing?"

"It should, yeah. But I'm still used to being in Vietnam. People know that, don't they?"

"They'd know it better if you said so."

I shake my head. "Isn't it obvious? Besides, you heard my mother. She doesn't want to hear about that."

Elaine frowns. In the semi-darkness of the back porch, I'm not sure if it's a frown of concern or of disapproval.

She goes on. "Like I said, I think she's disappointed that you don't seem more excited about your own party. I'm a little disappointed too, to be honest."

My shoulders droop. I didn't expect my girlfriend of over three years to say she was disappointed in me on my first night home. "I told you, I don't feel like myself yet."

Elaine rubs my shoulder. "Look, I'm on your side. You know that. I'll always be on your side. But try to act a little more thankful when you go back in the house, okay? I'm so happy that you're back, and I want things to be wonderful between us. Most of all, I want to see you joking and carefree, like you used to be. That's what I want for you. We've got happy lives ahead of us. Vietnam is the past. California is the future. The sooner you remember that, the happier you'll be. Right?"

Elaine puts her arm around my shoulders and gives me a squeeze, followed by a kiss on the cheek. "Trust me, things'll be fine. Just relax and enjoy yourself a little more. It's so wonderful to have you home."

She's right. I hope.

Chapter 3

Trying to Enjoy Myself

I spend most of December adjusting to being back in California. Trying to adjust, anyway. I know I need to find work soon, but my parents insist I wait until January.

So, one week after my return home, I'm sitting on the sky-blue sofa in the living room, watching television by myself on a Tuesday morning. It's a sunny day. I watch birds fluttering in the tree outside the window while I yawn and sink deeper into the corner of the sofa. My cup of coffee, still untouched and now quite cold, rests atop a wooden coaster on the glass coffee table where Mom left it.

Dad's at his bakery, and Mom has gone to one of her church meetings. Or maybe she's at a women voters meeting. Mom's in so many groups, I have trouble keeping them straight.

At first, I dislike the delay in looking for work, but the holidays are on the way, so I don't argue the point. My objection stems from the fact that in the Nam I always had things to do, and the quicker I did them, the more time I had to myself. I feel uneasy about sitting on the sofa and watching television while knowing I can do that all day if I so choose. But after a week of regular sleep and meals featuring food worth eating, I table my objections and ask myself, what's the rush to get work, anyway?

But I'm too restless to sit and stare passively at the screen all day. So, even though the television is on, my mind wanders, and I think back on various parts of my time in Nam.

One Kind Of Hero

I saved considerable money during my tour. The amount of up-front pay that soldiers get isn't that much, granted. But I got an extra fifty-five dollars per month for "hazardous duty" pay, since I flew in a helicopter. I always thought that calling it hazardous duty was the wrong term because in Vietnam nearly everything was hazardous. But I suppose the Army figures that flying in a helicopter is even more dangerous than usual, and who's gonna complain about getting more money?

The other reason my savings are in good shape is that while on active duty, soldiers have few options of what to spend their pay on. Meals, housing, clothing, and medical care don't cost anything for soldiers. So, I keep telling my parents I can help with groceries, but they won't hear of it.

Even though the first night home was awkward, my family truly is happy to have me back, and it's hard to stay mad at anyone for long during the holidays. It's harder still when someone can bake pies as well as my mother can.

Although I feel like I should be busy doing something, I also contemplate why I'm worried about money. Something I learned in Vietnam is that bullets don't care how much money a person has. Rich or poor doesn't matter to bullets. When a machine gun sweeps a field of fire, a guy with a full bank account is as vulnerable as anyone else. When your number's up, it's up.

That's partly why a number of guys in Vietnam develop a fatalistic, "Who the hell cares?" or "Don't mean nothin'" attitude about life. When we arrived, many of us believed that we were real-life John Waynes—young, tough, and thus indestructible. But after we'd been in-country for a while, we learned that even the biggest and toughest guys got killed sometimes. After that realization, for some soldiers it seemed pointless to calculate the odds or spend time worrying about tomorrow.

Likewise, that's how a lot of veterans get the stereotype of being guys who live in the moment and struggle to think through the long-term consequences of their choices. That might be true of some of us, I suppose, but for guys like me, it's more that we get out of the habit of thinking about the future because that's counterproductive in war. Anytime a guy in the field gets distracted by his thoughts, he's only increasing the risks to himself and his buddies.

That's also why military guys frequently have reputations as heavy drinkers and risk takers. It's not that soldiers don't know drinking lots of beer is bad for our health. But if a man could be dead tomorrow, or in a week, who cares about having a gut at forty-five? I didn't adopt this attitude personally, but I understand it.

I'll admit that I didn't know exactly what I was getting into when the Army drafted me. Like a lot of guys, I figured that if America could beat Germany and Japan at the same time in World War 2, fighting a puny, undeveloped country like Vietnam couldn't be that hard. I believed we'd go over there, turn loose our firepower on the patsy Viet Cong in their thatched huts, and the war would be over before long.

Not only that, but the Viet Cong are communists, and communists are evil. Before long, I learned about the Domino Theory. This holds that if the U.S. doesn't prevent Vietnam from falling into the hands of the communists, all of Southeast Asia will follow the example of Red China and the Soviet Union, and then America will be in danger. Japan might follow Southeast Asia, and who knows what might happen after that?

All my life, I've been taught to hate communists and shun them should I ever meet one. When I played basketball in middle school, my coach would reprimand poor passing by yelling out, "Don't make that pass! That's a communist pass!"

From how much people talk about the threat of communism, one might think that communists are everywhere in the United States, hiding around corners and in dark alleys, plotting conspiracies and stealing children. Fact is, I've never met a communist in Los Angeles. Leastways, I've never met anyone who admitted to it.

I'd never heard of the Domino Theory before I joined the Army, however. And although I was drafted, it didn't bother me because the country was at war and I wanted to serve the United States like my father had when he fought the Germans. Serving in the Army seemed like an honorable thing to do, so I didn't mind. Even though a great many of my preconceptions about Vietnam turned out to be wrong, I still don't regret being drafted.

Since I don't have to worry about a job interfering with my schedule, for New Year's Eve, Elaine suggests we go to a party some of her friends from work have organized. Elaine waits tables at a local burger joint, and she's friends with a few other waitresses about her age. I'm not sure if I feel up to a big gathering, but I go to make her happy.

The party is more fun than I'd anticipated, though, and most of the people there have never met me, so they don't ask too many questions about Vietnam. I'm sure Elaine told some of them her boyfriend was a soldier, but after a few rounds of drinks, most people have forgotten. So, we party to records of the Doors, the Rolling Stones, and Jefferson Airplane. Balloons are strewn about the room, the punch bowl gradually diminishes, and the lava lamps are doing their thing. The smell of burning tobacco hovers in the air, the smoke from the cigarettes giving the lights a hazy filter. I drink two beers, and in between dances, I socialize a little with the people around me.

After a while, I find myself talking with Mary Anne. She waits tables with Elaine and is also a girl I remember from high school.

"It's been so much fun to see you again, Scott," she tells me. "For the past three months, Elaine has done nothing but talk about what it'll be like to have you back. Even when she had those fevers for a while, she couldn't stop talking about you."

I smile. "Her letters were one of the main things that helped me get through my tour. She wrote more often than ever after she got sick."

"You two are *so good* together, you know that? I don't think I could've waited fourteen months for a boyfriend to get back if he went into the Army, but she has. You're really lucky."

"I know. She told me she'd always be here for me when I left for Vietnam. Maybe I shouldn't admit this, but I don't know if I believed it at the time. A bunch of guys over there told me about how their girls said they'd wait for them to come back, but after a few months they got letters saying she was dating a Jodie."

"Dating a Jodie?"

"Sorry, military talk. That's our term for another guy whom we've never met. I thought maybe that would happen to me, too, but it never did."

"You'd better not tell that to Elaine. She'll be angry that you doubted her commitment. She is *so* devoted to you, it's unreal."

"It's not a knock on her for me to say that, believe it or not. I never doubted her intentions. But people change sometimes, you know? Sometimes you don't even realize how much they've changed until you look back and see where they started from. The change isn't always for the worst, either, or because the other person has bad intentions. It just happens."

"Wait, what are you saying? You haven't lost interest in Elaine, have you?" Mary Anne looks at me very intently, blinking her bright blue eyes and gently biting her lip.

"Of course not. I love her as much as I ever did. I meant what I said in a general way. Sometimes people just change, and it's no one's fault. But I'm happy that hasn't happened with us."

She exhales audibly and smiles. "Whew. You had me worried for a minute there. If you ever did ditch her, it might be the end of Elaine. You know that, right? She's put so much hope into your relationship, I don't know if she could take it if you walked away from her."

"Well, I'm not going to walk away, so she'll live to see the new year," I joke with a smile of my own. "But what about you, Mary Anne? What do you do these days besides wait tables?"

"Not that much," she replies while pulling out a cigarette and lighting up. She offers me a smoke, too, but I decline with a wave of the hand. "I'm still waiting for the right man to come along. He will. I'm only twenty, you know. I've got some time."

Although I like Mary Anne, I fear she may have to wait a while. She still has her hair with a side part and deep curls on the side opposite the part. It's the same look one saw on lots of 1950s movie stars. But it's the last day of 1967, and the glamor look doesn't really suit her because her nose is huge and overshadows the rest of her face. Add to that some teeth that never quite grew in straight, and Mary Anne's looks are not her best feature. I'm not saying I judge women solely on looks, of course, only that looks help get men interested in women in the first place.

In her defense, Mary Anne is a dove who's compassionate and thoughtful. And she was smart enough to learn both German and French in high school, so maybe I should give her better odds than I do.

"Did you ever think about starting a career at something?" I ask her after a moment.

"I don't know. One of my high school teachers suggested I go to college. But my parents are against the idea. They said if I want to go to college, I'm on my own. I'm not really thinking much about college at the moment, to be honest."

"I dig that," I reply, borrowing one of my buddy Ted's favorite phrases. "I always thought you were a real whiz, though. How come your parents don't want you to get more education?"

"They're pretty traditional, my dad especially. He believes a woman can't be a good mother and work at the same time. Mom never had a job when I was in school. My parents also think it'll lower my odds at marriage if men think I'm too smart for them."

I laugh. "In Vietnam, we appreciated smart women, let me tell you. The smart women were the ones who kept guys from dying when they were in the hospital recovering from being wounded."

Across the room, a champagne bottle pops, and somehow, I'm no longer in Los Angeles. Without warning, my mind is back in Vietnam, or, more precisely, back in Laos on the Plain of Jars.

The mission was a humanitarian one. My Chinook helicopter was supposed to jump the fence into Laos, land on the Plain of Jars, and evacuate some villagers. The village was a target not because of anything the villagers had done wrong, but because the Army feared the village might fall under the control of the Viet Cong passing south along the Ho Chi Minh Trail. Recently, the military brass had received reports that a new branch of the Ho Chi Minh Trail had opened and that the Viet Cong had targeted this village as part of their new supply route. The brass determined that relocating the village was preferable to allowing Charlie to infiltrate it. We had to destroy the village in order to save it.

The trouble, besides the timing, was that the United States was not at war with Laos, and our troops had no business being on the Plain of Jars or anywhere else on the Laotian side of the border with Vietnam. My CO warned us not to tell civilians about being in Laos. He was one of those guys who felt like the less civilians knew about what soldiers actually did in the field, the better. I have no idea how many guys in our platoon listened to him and kept their mouths shut.

The Plain of Jars is the most unique and beautiful place I've ever seen. While my big Chinook flew in, we passed over a verdant countryside of rolling hills, farmland, pasture, scattered trees, and small lakes. Modest villages, the homes clustered together, completed the scene.

The place takes its name from the large stone jars that dot the landscape everywhere. From the air they look tiny, but when one lands and sees them up close, one finds that some jars are ten feet tall and must weigh tons. Many feature images of people or animals graven in the stone. Someone told me the jars were two thousand years old, but I can't verify if that's true. Nor do I know what they're for. I only know the Plain of Jars resembles nothing I've ever seen in America, and it's beautiful.

Suddenly, I feel a hand on my arm. I look up and see that Mary Anne is still sitting beside me, staring at me expectantly. "You okay there, Scott? Any bats in the belfry?" she asks with a nervous smile. "You had a strange look on your face just now. And you didn't answer my question. Did you have a bad memory or something?"

I'm not even sure what Mary Anne's question was. "Thousand-yard stare," I tell her while shaking my head to clear the images.

"What's that mean, 'thousand-yard stare'?"

"It's an expression we had over there. I'm sorry, can you repeat your question for me?"

"I wanted to know if you were ever in a hospital with an injury. You were talking about smart women as nurses, remember?"

"Oh, yeah, that," I chuckle, trying to downplay the fact I have no idea how long I'd just spent reliving one of my unofficial missions. And because the mission to the Plain of Jars is unofficial, I give Mary Anne the answer that one would find in Army records. "No. I saw combat a few times, but I was one of the lucky ones."

"I'm so happy about that. Gordon Williams was a friend of mine in high school, you know, and he was killed several months ago. He grew up right across the street from me."

"I knew Gordon, too. We went to boot camp at the same time."

Gordon Williams would be Exhibit A in my earlier statement about the bullets not caring who they hit. In high school, he was a marvelous athlete at anything that involved running—track, cross country, basketball, you name it. If physical fitness was the key to avoiding being shot, he could've stayed in Vietnam for a decade and come home without a scratch. But he didn't. Gordon died in the Central Highlands just five months into his tour.

"Do you think you'll work for your father in his bakery?" Mary Anne asks, breaking the lengthening silence following the mention of Gordon's death.

"I'm not sure yet, but I think I might try something else. I learned a fair bit about engines and repairing them while in Vietnam, so maybe I'll do that instead." Much of my knowledge is thanks to being friends with Ted.

"That doesn't sound bad at all. Can I ask one more thing, Scott, or have you had enough questions?"

"I suppose one more won't hurt. I haven't seen you since our high school graduation, after all."

"Was it exciting to be in a fight, or were you scared?"

I pause. To be honest, I'm not sure how to tell Mary Anne that it was both at the same time in a way that will make sense to someone who will never fight in a war. I start to stumble into my answer when Elaine comes over, bottle of Schlitz in hand. Come to think of it, this beer is probably the fifth or sixth Schlitz she's had in hand tonight. She also looks a little skinnier than I remember. It must be because her black party dress shows off her form. Or maybe the fevers caused her to lose a little weight.

"Hey ya, what ya talkin' about?"

Since I'm still stumbling for what to say, Mary Anne speaks first. "I was telling Scott about how much you missed him and how you always talked about him for months on end, wishing he was home."

"And now he is! You two wanna join the rest of the party? The countdown to the new year is gonna start pretty soon."

As midnight approaches, we gather around to listen to the last few seconds of 1967 count down on local radio. I'm enjoying myself once again, a second beer of my own in hand, when the fireworks begin in the neighborhood.

I'd forgotten that New Year's Eve featured fireworks. When the first ones go off, I crouch in a corner immediately and turn my head rapidly, scanning for trouble.

Elaine notices. "Scott, what's wrong, honey? It's just fireworks," she says with a smile while walking over. When she takes me by the arm and helps lift me to my feet I can smell the beer on her breath mixed with her perfume. Looking around, it doesn't appear anyone else witnessed my reaction, thank goodness. They're busy toasting and drinking from beer bottles and champagne glasses, chanting the numbers down to one as 1968 arrives.

When it does, a big boom of fireworks rends the air. For the second time that evening, my mind is no longer at a party in Los Angeles.

I'd thought our mission would be easy. Our task was to land, inform the people that they were in danger from the Viet Cong, and take them with us to new homes where the war couldn't reach them. We had several interpreters who spoke Laotian. The people we evacuated would receive ample food until they could plant new crops as well as help building new homes.

One thing had escaped the minds of the brass who ordered the operation, however. Not everyone would leave their homes voluntarily. I remember watching our interpreters, some of them Laotian themselves, plead with older people and nursing mothers to grab their most valued possessions and come with us promptly. As the time stretched on, pleading turned to begging and efforts to force the villagers toward our helicopters.

The evacuation plan that had seemed so straightforward and logical on paper soon turned chaotic. Some of the villagers interpreted "prized possessions" to mean goats and chickens, herding their animals toward helicopters the animals could not board. In other cases, some family members proved willing to leave immediately while others vowed to stay behind, come what may. I saw children crying because their parents made them leave their homes without time to explain why.

I also realized another problem had arisen that our evacuation plan did not account for. Because we'd flown over some of them on our way in, I knew that several villagers were in their fields or roaming the hills herding animals. How were we supposed to get those people out?

As our big Chinooks pulled away, I watched a pair of brothers, no more than six or seven years old, stare tearfully at their parents below, the wind from our Chinooks whipping their hair about behind them while their children flew away.

When you're flying in a Chinook, you can't talk that much because everything is so loud. But when we got back to base, I overheard a couple guys talking about what we'd seen.

"Damn gooks, what's wrong with 'em?" one GI twanged in a thick Southern accent. "We're trying to get them out of the shithole they live in, and some of 'em wouldn't come with us."

"Hell, man, it's their home," another member of our crew replied. "What would you do if someone kicked down your door in the middle of the day and said you have thirty minutes to pack up and leave forever?"

"That wouldn't happen to me because I don't live in a shithole," the first GI responded.

"You're from goddamned South Carolina. What's the difference?"

"Fuck off, Yankee."

"I'm from California, dude."

"Like I said, a fuckin' Yankee."

The exchange continued like that for several minutes. I didn't pay it much mind—guys talked like that all the time. Plus, if the guys arguing are like me, this mission had them on edge. Jumping the fence into Laos meant we were pretty far from base. If anything had gone wrong, we'd have had to get out of trouble ourselves.

Before we took off to begin the evacuation, I asked my CO if going into Laos was safer than a mission in Vietnam. After all, we weren't at war with Laos.

"That's the type of thinking that gets grunts killed, Reynolds."

"How so, sir?"

"All these gooks are the same. They all hate us. You've gotta assume that all of them are enemies. You forget that, you go home in a body bag."

"Understood, sir."

It was only my first month in the Nam, so I took his words to heart. Not many things get a new guy in the doghouse quicker than questioning orders, or having his CO think he *might* be questioning orders.

"No joke, Reynolds. You forget that, and your parents'll be real sad because they'll never see their son again."

"Yes, sir."

"Scott? Scott?" I feel someone shaking and pulling at my arm. "Scott! What's wrong?"

Slowly, I look up, my eyes unfocused. I blink a few times at the haze-shrouded lights overhead.

"Scott? What happened?"

Finally, I realize it's Elaine's voice. I've taken cover once again, and this time, some of the other partygoers are looking my way. I squeeze my eyes shut for a moment before looking up at everyone. "I don't know what happened. One minute I was here, and the next I was back in . . . Vietnam," I tell her, remembering at the last moment that I'm not supposed to talk about Laos because that mission never officially took place.

"What do you mean? You've been right here at the party dancing and talking with me the whole time. We just saw in 1968!"

"I know. It's hard to explain, but for a moment, I was back there."

Elaine looks at me for several seconds. She has a quizzical expression, and I can tell she's struggling for what to say. "But you're right here with me. How can you be over there?" she stammers at last.

I stand up and take her by the hand. "It won't happen again, I promise. Let's have another dance."

"That's the spirit," she says while taking another sip of beer. "Happy New Year, sweetheart! Here's to 1968! Who knows what amazing things this year has in store for the two of us?"

Chapter 4

Back at Home

I drank only two beers, so I drive Elaine and two other partygoers home in my dad's Buick after things wind down. It took a couple days after my homecoming, but I got behind the wheel again, and driving came back to me in no time. Still, I take it slow while I cruise around dropping people off. No one's said anything to me about what happened during the fireworks. If my time in the military is any indicator, they've had enough to drink that by tomorrow morning, it'll all be a haze, anyway.

While I drive, I finally put a finger on something that was nagging at me. I embarrassed myself with my flashbacks, for sure, but something else has been eating at me all evening. The people at the party were too carefree. No one even concerned themselves with how they would get home that night, much less with what might happen tomorrow. They partied like they had no cares at all.

In Vietnam, that was an approach that got people in trouble. Sure, a few guys lived every day on the edge, but most of us realized that our odds of survival went up along with our awareness of our surroundings and attention to details. The people at the party tonight didn't care. Shouldn't they be more serious? Or am I nuts for taking the war back to Los Angeles with me?

I drop off Elaine last. Before getting out of the Electra, she asks me, "Scott, do you know what happened to you during the fireworks tonight? You don't need to act like you're still over there, you know. You're in Los Angeles, and everything is okay."

I wince because I still feel embarrassed. "I don't know what to say. I don't have an explanation for what happened, either."

"Try to figure it out quickly, okay? I love you, but I didn't like that at all. It kinda scares me, to be honest."

Although I want to repeat that I don't know why I'm having flashbacks, I decide not to say anything that might upset Elaine right now. A guy always hates to disappoint his girlfriend, especially one who waited so long to see him.

"I had a really fun time tonight," I tell her instead. "Forget about it. I think it'll be okay before long. Maybe I need more time to forget about being overseas. I'm sure that's all there is to it."

She hugs me deeply. "I love you so much, and I just want you to be yourself—to be the Scott you were before Vietnam."

"I'm trying."

"I know you are. And I'm here to help you. Just forget the bad memories, so we can make new ones together from now on. I'll see you in two days, okay?"

"That sounds great. I'll call you, and we can pick a place to meet," I say while giving Elaine a long goodnight kiss. When we part, though, I see bags under her eyes that I hadn't noticed during the party. Are they from worrying about me? Is Elaine losing sleep because my behavior frightens her? If so, that's one more reason to figure out what's wrong with me.

After another short drive, I pull into the driveway of my parents' house. The lights are on, and Lisa's car, a red Ford Falcon, is there. Being an accountant must pay decent money because the Ford is only a couple years old. Lisa's probably saying goodnight to my parents. Even though I'm not a macho guy, especially by Army standards, I do take a little pride that I stayed out partying later than my folks and my sister did.

I don't get out of the Buick right away, however. Instead, I think back on the party. Why did I instantly find myself in Laos when the fireworks began? It scared Elaine, and it scares me, too. That shouldn't happen. She was right when she told me things will be fine, but I'm not sure they are. Is something wrong with me? Gently, I lean my forehead on the steering wheel and shut my eyes.

My face colors with shame as yet another memory from Vietnam surfaces, although this one has nothing to do with Laos. Not directly, at any rate.

We were on a mission to extract a Special Forces unit from an operation near the demilitarized zone that separated North from South Vietnam. Although no one said so, I'm pretty sure they'd been in North Vietnam, either as saboteurs or assassins, because these were bad looking dudes. One of them wore a necklace with four human ears on it. Another, his uniform rotting off his body, had a pair of human scalps dangling from his belt. Altogether, the squad carried enough firepower to clear an entire village—grenade launchers and heavy assault rifles. One even had an anti-tank rocket, just in case. Like I said, bad dudes. One look at them, and you knew these men did not fuck around. And that's not a word I use lightly.

Once the pilot found a place to drop below the canopy and get these guys into the Chinook, Charlie opened fire. We responded with our M-60 machine guns while lifting off and pulling away, and the Special Forces guys opened up, too. It was something to see. We returned fire with so much heat that small trees were falling over. A civilian probably can't imagine what it looks like to watch a wall of vegetation get shredded by 7.62-mm machine guns.

The problem came when one guy in our helicopter crew, Shawn, took a hit in the exchange. The wound was bad—real bad. Some of his guts spilled out through the entry wound while we gave him medical attention.

It wasn't the first time I'd seen a man hit, of course. By the time of this mission, I'd already been in-country for months. But Shawn and I always flipped a coin to see who'd operate the M-60 mounted on the front door of the Chinook. He'd "won" the toss that day.

One Kind Of Hero

Our coin toss was one of those silly and superstitious things that soldiers do. Yet, as we climbed into the sky, I realized that the chances were fifty-fifty of me being the one dying with my intestines smeared on the floor. I vomited out the side of the helicopter once as we flew back to base. A couple of the Special Forces guys gave me scornful looks, like I was soft. Normally, soldiers hate any sign of weakness, but for once, I didn't care.

By the time we got to base, Shawn was dead. I couldn't shake the feeling that it might've been me flying home in a body bag except for random luck. It might've been my parents and sister weeping when someone handed them a folded-up flag. Another guy in my crew, Sammy, saw me and came over.

"You look terrible, man. You thinkin' about Shawn?"

I nodded. "Every day we flipped a coin to see who manned the gun. Today happened to be his day."

"Damn, man, I didn't know about that. You know it ain't your fault, though, don't you? Charlie did that to Shawn, not you."

"It's not my fault, no, but it's only luck he's dead and I'm not. How do you do it?"

"Do what?"

"You've been in-country for, what, about ten months now?"

"Ten months and eight days," Sammy replied.

Some guys start counting down how much time they have left sooner than others. Other guys think it's bad luck to count down the days and won't do it at all.

"How do you see guys you know get shot without letting it get to you?"

"It's war, man. There it is. You just accept it."

"That's hard for me to do. I mean, I know guys are gonna die, but how do you deal with it when they're guys you know?"

I must've looked really shaken because Sammy's face softened. Soldiers are supposed to be tough, so one doesn't see that very often.

Sammy lowered his voice. "I've got something that might help when you hit a rough stretch."

"What are you talking about? I don't think I can drink this memory away."

"That ain't what I mean. I've got something special for the bad days. I can hook you up, but it ain't for everyone."

I narrow my eyes. This sounds bad. But I can't shake off the grief, so I keep listening.

"You ever dropped acid, man?" he asks.

I shake my head. Dropping acid was one of those things people joked about doing in high school, but no one ever actually did. At least, no one I knew.

"If you want to escape the pain for a while, tell me, and I'll set you up."

"What's it like?"

I'm not sure I want to know, but I don't want to look weak or scared, either, and I feel depressed on top of that.

"It's different for everyone, but it'll make you forget your problems for hours. I can guarantee that."

"You've done it before?"

"Only on the worst days, but yeah, I've tripped a few times. It's not addictive, though. You won't get hooked."

It took me a long while to make up my mind. I couldn't erase the image of Shawn, drenched in blood from his chest down, trying to push his intestines back inside his body on the floor of our Chinook.

"Ah, forget I mentioned it, man," Sammy said after a while. "Acid ain't for everyone. You're probably better off without it."

"I'll try it once."

Once became four times. Sammy was right that acid doesn't hook you. I never craved it—except when I needed to forget something horrible that I'd seen.

The first time I tripped, I learned why taking acid is known as tripping. I heard the color red while I saw the wind whispering around me. My green hat was the size of a tent, and the sound of my shouts echoed for miles inside my head.

A few weeks later I heard the Bob Dylan song "A Hard Rain's A-Gonna Fall." I remember some of the lyrics. He described a highway of diamonds with nobody on it. A black branch dripping blood. Bleeding hammers, and a ladder cover with water. Ten thousand people with broken tongues.

Doubtless, Bob Dylan meant those lyrics symbolically, but taken literally, that's kinda like what my first trip was like.

When my trip ended, I found I was sweating profusely and breathing hard. Sweat soaked my clothes in places.

I turned to Sammy. "That was heavy. How long was I out, man? It felt like, I don't know, five or ten minutes is all."

"Four hours."

"No way."

Sammy flashed me his wristwatch, and I conceded I'd been out for four hours.

Despite that, I felt better. At least, I thought I did. The images of Shawn dying from his gutshot wound still came back now and again, but the horror those images generated wasn't so intense.

I don't know that I ever truly felt guilty that he'd died when it might've been me. Some soldiers develop something called survivor's guilt in situations like mine. That's not how I felt, though. With me, it was the utter loneliness of knowing I could've died ten thousand miles from home without my family around me. If someone has never faced that possibility, they'll never understand why my fear felt so debilitating, or why I dropped acid a second time some weeks later.

Even though I wasn't an addict, after my third trip I realized something Sammy hadn't warned me about. I kept the dosage the same for my first three trips, but the third one was much shorter and less intense than the first two had been. Consequently, I barely felt any different at the end. So, for my fourth trip, I upped the dosage considerably.

The next seven hours are difficult to describe, even now. Instead of seeing sounds or hearing colors, happy images from my past became grotesque, devilish parodies of my memories. My dog Pete became a giant beast whose mouth dripped poison as it tore at the carcasses of other dogs. I leaned in to kiss Elaine only to see her face wither and crawl with maggots as I did so, but her grip on me was so tight that I couldn't pull away. Instead of my father teaching me how to swing a baseball bat, he became a giant who used the bat to club harmless birds from the clear blue summer sky. But the birds never fell to the ground because crows swarmed them and tore them apart as they fell.

Some of my visions were even more terrifying—dead, rotting corpses of children singing nursery rhymes while they gnawed on each other, black blood spurting and dripping from their faces. Blocking the memories works when I'm awake, but at night it doesn't, and some nights they come back to me as nightmares.

My body shudders violently, slamming my forehead against the hard plastic of the steering wheel, and I open my eyes, blinking rapidly. How long have I been sitting in the driveway with my eyes shut?

I'm not sure. What I do know is that after my fourth time dropping acid, I never did it again. Seeing those horrors for hours and not being able to wake up was just as bad as what I saw with my eyes open. The mental images felt so intense, so real, that it took me days to convince myself they truly were my imagination.

I wish I could say that fear of being dishonorably discharged for using drugs was the reason I stopped dropping acid. But damn, if that were true, about half the guys in Vietnam today would be at risk of dishonorable discharges. I had flown over entire fields growing nothing but marijuana in South Vietnam.

Truth be told, some officers distributed amphetamines to their men like candy to children. Guys wanted amphetamines to stay alert when fatigue set in on long missions. I tried them myself a few times, including when we had to hop the fence and fly into Laos.

One Kind Of Hero

Some soldiers got creative with their efforts to get high. I still recall one time when some guys in my unit made a hookah out of an empty artillery shell and a beer bottle. The one thing I wouldn't do, however, was use some of the hard drugs that appeared the last couple months of my tour. I never tried heroin, especially after my last acid trip spooked me so badly.

These memories are the source of my shame. Growing up in the Los Angeles suburbs, I never used a drug stronger than aspirin. I couldn't even have described what an amphetamine looked like before I went to Vietnam. On the rare occasions when the topic of drugs came up at home, my mother described them as something only weak-willed losers used. I doubt that she's changed her mind in the past two years, either. What would happen if she ever learned what I'd done?

Even worse, I fear that my father will learn the truth somehow. What if he overhears me say something during one of my nightmares? He went to Germany and fought the Nazis, and he never needed drugs. My father was stronger than that. I'm not sure I could look him in the eye and admit that I had been a drug user. He'd lose his respect for me, I have no doubt, and what kind of son can stand to look pitiful and weak to his father?

I close my eyes and rub them. Maybe I'm just tired tonight, and that's why all the bad memories want to crowd in on me. Whatever the cause, I need to go inside. My parents probably heard the car in the driveway, and they'll be wondering why I've been out here for so long.

My plan is to greet them and wish them a happy new year if they're still awake, and then crash. January 1 is a big day for college football, and my father will probably want to watch all the games he can—Cotton Bowl, Rose Bowl, Sugar Bowl, and Orange Bowl—so I hope he's gone to bed already. January 1 is among the few days when he closes his bakery. In high school, I watched the games with him, even though I'm not a big football fan, so I suppose I will this year, too. It became a tradition, I guess you'd say, and I see no reason to break this tradition.

When I approach the front door, however, I hear an argument in progress. Mom and Lisa are shouting at each other. I palm my forehead. Can't the two of them even let up on New Year's Eve? But I guess that explains why no one came out to check on me.

I stand at the door for a moment, trying to decide what I should do when I go inside. Try to skirt the argument? It sounds like they're in the kitchen, and I can maybe sneak down the hallway and get upstairs without either noticing. The back door is no good—it's right next to the kitchen, so I'll have to use the front door. The last thing I want is to have one of them drag me into their disagreement by insisting I take one side.

Not relishing that possibility, I stand for a moment longer, hoping the argument will end if I give them a minute. Mom and Lisa are shouting about the same things they always do.

"I can't believe you're still dating that guy," Mom yells. "His hair is longer than yours!"

"What does that have to do with anything? Stephen's brain still works fine, unlike yours."

"He looks like a hippie or a tramp! Did you meet him at the local homeless shelter? And why does he wear that fatigue jacket? Those are for real soldiers like your brother!"

"Those aren't sacred. He can wear what he wants," Lisa states flatly.

"It's an insult to the people who love their country. People who hate America have no business wearing that jacket."

"Stephen doesn't hate America. He's tired of seeing young people get shot for no reason."

"No reason? No reason! They're fighting the Reds! Our soldiers fight to keep ungrateful brats like you safe," my mother shouts.

"Our soldiers are fighting peasant villagers. The Vietnamese peasants have been oppressed by their own landlords and by imperialist nations like France for generations. They want to live free of outside interference. Who cares if they live by a different economic system than we do? It's not our business. The world isn't going to end based on what happens in Vietnam."

"That's easy for you to believe with all your college book smarts. But those books you read have nothing to do with how the world *really* works. Young men like your brother are putting their lives on the line for you, and you're stabbing them in the back!"

"It's better than getting them shot in the face," Lisa says with a tone of resignation. "Who feeds you all that propaganda, Mom? And why do you believe all of it without question?"

"My 'propaganda,' as you call it, comes straight from our leading generals. If they say something is true, I believe it. So should you."

"Are those the same leading generals who told the president that the *Maddox* was fired on by the North Vietnamese in the Gulf of Tonkin?"

"Yes. Because it was."

"Ugh!" I hear my sister groan. Then I hear her footsteps stomping down the hallway toward the front door. Momentarily, it flies open. Lisa's face is red and her jaw is set. She's about to charge out with her head down when she sees me standing there.

"Oh, geez, Scott, I didn't know you were home."

"Sounds like I missed a whopper this time," I respond quietly.

"You have no idea. I can't get through to Mom no matter what I do. Facts bounce off that woman when it comes to Vietnam."

"I don't have much to say about that. It'd be nice if the two of you argued less, though. Especially on New Year's Eve."

"Yeah, maybe that's true," Lisa admits with a resigned sigh, her shoulders slumping and some of the color draining from her cheeks. She takes a moment to shrug her navy blue jacket over her shoulders.

"Most of the evening wasn't that bad," she continues. "I came over for dinner before going to my party, and things were fine. The argument didn't begin until Stephen and I stopped by to wish Mom and Dad a happy new year. After Stephen left, that's when the sparks flew. Mom couldn't resist badmouthing him behind his back."

Stephen, Lisa's current boyfriend, hates the Vietnam War even more than she does, if that's possible. He's a few years older than her and writes articles for an "underground" newspaper as well as flood the *Los Angeles Times* with letters to the editor about the immorality of America's presence in Vietnam. We've only met once, and he was a little cold to me, but not rude. I suppose he didn't know how I'd react to him, being a soldier myself, so he kept his distance. Most likely I'd have done the same in his shoes.

"I've got an idea," Lisa says to me. "Wanna meet for coffee or doughnuts later today after we've had a chance to sleep? I've got a few things I'd like to talk with you about. Things that will be easier to discuss when our parents aren't around."

I take that as code that Lisa wants to ask me things about Vietnam. "Sure," I reply. "I'm probably gonna watch some football with Dad, but I think four games are on, and they go all day. I'll have plenty of time to meet you. Where?"

"How about the café down the street from Dad's bakery? You remember the one, right?"

"Sure. See you there around noon?"

"Right. Sounds good, Scott."

I just hope Lisa doesn't try to ambush me with anti-war crossfire.

Chapter 5

Vietnam Through Lisa's Eyes

It's a few minutes after noon on January 1, and my sister and I sit sipping coffee across from each other in a local coffee shop. The smell of fresh coffee wafts up to me while I look around. From our seats near the cash register, we can see out the large glass window fronting the street. Today is overcast but warm for January, almost sixty-five degrees.

"I'm surprised you drink coffee now. You never used to," Lisa tells me.

I can't hide a bit of a sour face. "Honestly, it's still not my thing, but since you said you're buying, I'll drink."

She smiles. Lisa has on a dull red, light cotton sweater, flower-print white miniskirt, and high leather boots, her lightweight attire a testament to the benefits of living in Southern California in January.

"Do you want to talk about last night's argument?" she asks hesitantly after a moment.

"Not really, but I suppose that you do. That's the reason you wanted to meet me here, right?"

"How much of it did you overhear, anyway?"

"Only the last minute or two."

"Ah, the bad part. I get so frustrated talking to Mom whenever Vietnam comes up, and neither of us are any good at letting something drop when we're convinced we're right."

I nod. When it comes to talking, Lisa is more like my mother than my father—never at a loss for words. I'm about halfway between my parents in that regard. At least, I was before Vietnam. Now, I'm not sure what I am.

Lisa goes on, her voice tentative, "I want you to know, though, that when I criticize what's going on over there, I'm not talking about you. I'd never criticize you because I know you're one of the good guys who tried to do the right thing. You had to follow orders, after all. You know that, right?"

"Of course. We argued enough as kids that I know your tone of voice when you're trying to get on my case."

Lisa laughs, and I see her posture relax. "I'm glad. Sometimes, I'm not sure what to say around you. I think the war is bullshit, but I don't know how you feel about it, or if you'll get upset when I say that."

I pause, considering how to respond. "It's hard for me to describe my feelings about Vietnam sometimes. It's so recent. I mean, when you're a soldier, you aren't supposed to have opinions about what you're doing. You get orders and you follow the orders. Thinking too much can get a guy killed."

Lisa keeps her eyes on me while I continue thinking about what to say.

"But at the same time, a soldier can't help wondering about what he's doing after a while. Most of the guys I fought alongside were average guys like me. We didn't study the reasons for the war before we volunteered to fight or got drafted. Our country needed us. We answered."

"But don't you think you've been used, Scott?"

"In some ways maybe we were. But a soldier can't think like that. You can't pass complaints up the chain of command too often, or else you spend your days scrubbing toilets."

That was supposed to be funny and lighten the conversation, but Lisa continues right away.

"But I meant don't you think the government was using you for a purpose besides keeping the country safe? What does it matter if a few million Vietnamese peasants live in communes? No one can say that's a real threat to the United States, as much as Mother wants to believe it is."

"I know what you meant. But I'm proud of my service in Vietnam. A soldier has to be if he wants to perform at his best in the field. If a guy goes around saying how the war is all wrong and starts believing it, he gets careless, and a GI can't afford that. Being careless gets you and your buddies in trouble."

"You aren't in Vietnam anymore. How do you feel about it now?"

"I know what you want me to say," I reply calmly, looking Lisa in the face earnestly. "You want me to say the goals of the war are wrong, all the villagers in Vietnam hate Americans, the South Vietnamese government is a sham, a puppet of the U.S., and so forth. And those things are true. Sometimes. But not all the time.

"It's also true that a lot of guys I served with were brave men willing to sacrifice for a cause the country believes is important. That means something, at least to me. I was never in North Vietnam, so I can't tell you if the people there live better, worse, or about the same as the people in South Vietnam. I suspect they live about the same, though. Compared to Americans, most of the people in South Vietnam are really poor. Introducing our way of doing things would probably make their lives better, even if it takes a while. That's worth something to you, isn't it?"

I expect Lisa to get angry and start arguing with me, but to my relief, she smiles again and pats my arm. "My little brother has grown up a lot in two years. I don't know if I agree with everything you said, but at least you were there, and you have reasons for saying those things. Mother just parrots whatever nonsense her favorite politicians are spouting at the moment. It drives me crazy."

"She probably feels the same about you."

"Maybe. But I try my best to get the facts. I don't take everything I hear at face value because I want to agree with it. That's part of how the war started in the first place."

I realize Lisa hasn't said anything about Dad and how he views Vietnam. Come to think of it, he's never spoken much about that to me, either. In the weeks after I came home, he asked some questions about my experiences overseas, but I don't recall him ever offering his view on whether the war is a just one. Maybe he's accepted that he won't convince anyone as stubborn as Mom or Lisa, so it's pointless to start the debate.

"I have one other thing I wanted to ask about Vietnam. Is that okay?" Lisa says.

"Sure."

"Do you hate the Vietnamese? Or hate the Viet Cong, I should say?"

I pause for a long while.

"That's an interesting question. To the extent that the VC were trying to kill me, yeah, I hated them. They're the enemy, so I treated them like an enemy. I mean, on the one hand, I know they're people, and a lot of them probably don't want to be fighting a war any more than I did. The notion that because the VC are communists, that makes all of them inherently evil, well, I'm not sure I agree about that. That's one question on which Mom and I would differ.

"But on the other hand, it was war, and in war it's kill or be killed. A soldier can't forget that. You have to hate the people on the other side trying to kill you and assume that they hate you just as much. That's how it is."

"I'm not sure I could ever bring myself to shoot a person."

"That's one thing that boot camp is for. You drill, and drill, and drill, so that in combat you'll respond from memory rather than thinking about what you're doing. Like I said, you learn that it's kill or be killed, and I didn't want to get killed."

"I still don't think I'd be any good at that."

I'm about to reply when I notice the person to my right at the cash register sighing loudly and muttering under her breath. I probably shouldn't look, but I do, expecting that the woman has eavesdropped on our conversation and wants to put in her two cents about the war.

That isn't the case, however. Instead, she's fumbling for something in her purse. "Oh, no. I forgot my wallet," she mutters.

Then the woman turns to the employee at the cash register, a young woman about my age, with an apologetic look on her face. "I'm so sorry, I seem to have forgotten my money. I feel so awful, and I've already had my coffee, so I can't give it back. What do I do? I'd be happy to go home and come back and pay you, but I suppose you don't trust me to come back."

The woman stares at the cashier, fidgeting with a nervous smile.

I glance at the young woman behind the register, who doesn't seem to know what to say. She's rubbing her forehead, and her eyes dart about like she's looking for someone to ask for advice. Without knowing why, I reach into my pocket and hand the lady a quarter. "Here. This should cover it."

"Oh, thank you so much," she replies, eyes briefly looking to the sky with hands clasped in front of her chest. "Thank you so very much. I promise to come back and return your money if you'll just wait a little while so that I can go home and find my wallet."

I wave away her offer. "It's only some spare change. Don't mean nothin'. Happy new year."

"Are you sure?"

"Absolutely. No need for you to come back."

"Bless you," the lady replies before walking out the door.

"That was very kind of you," the woman at the cash register tells me. "I've only been at this job two days, and I didn't know what I should do when a customer can't pay for her order. But I have a feeling the owner would be upset if I let her walk out without paying."

"Like I said, it's nothing. A person can't go wrong with being nice to people, can they?" I say to her.

I give the cashier another look while I talk. She has long blond hair, a little button nose, and hazel eyes. She isn't very tall, probably not more than five-one or -two, and wears a few extra pounds. She's rubbing her hands on her work shirt while she talks, and her hands shake slightly. That's when I notice her fingernails are purple, which I find an unusual choice.

The woman starts to reply, reconsiders a moment, then says to Lisa and me, "Pardon me for saying this, miss, but that was a real fine gesture on your boyfriend's part. You're very lucky," she finishes quickly.

Lisa laughs, which causes the cashier to blush badly. "I'm sorry, I meant that as a compliment. I just came on shift a little while ago, and, well, like I said, this is only my second day at this job. The person who usually is the cashier during the day couldn't work today; otherwise, I wouldn't even be here."

The woman's voice shakes, and she brushes a few strands of hair behind her right ear. "The owner told me to be nice to the customers. That's all I was trying to do."

I look at my sister, who's still smiling broadly. "It's okay . . . Sandra," she replies after leaning forward to read the woman's nametag on her deep-blue work uniform. "This lovable gentleman here is my brother, not my boyfriend."

Sandra's blush reddens further. "Oh, my goodness. I should've thought of that. I'm so sorry. It's just that what he did was so nice. Maybe I need to learn to keep my mouth shut a little more."

"It's okay," I tell Sandra, trying to find the most reassuring laugh I can. "Really, it is. You said this was only your second day at work, though. Did you mean at this job, or in your life?"

"This is the first job I've ever had. Well, the first real job. I also babysit a lot. It appears I'm not much good at this job yet."

"Nah, you're doing fine, I'd say. You live around here?"

"Yeah, I live close enough that I walk to work. I don't know how to drive a car yet."

"What else do you do when you aren't working?"

"I like to read books," she says quickly. Some of the red has left Sandra's cheeks. "And I sing, too. Choir was always my favorite class in school."

To myself, I try to guess Sandra's age. It appears she's out of high school based on what she just said, but not by much. We might even be the same age.

"Well, I used to play the trumpet," I tell her to keep the conversation going. She's starting to relax, finally, and since no customers are paying for their orders at the moment, I'm not preventing Sandra from doing her job. "I wasn't that good at it, but I learned to play guitar a little while I was in Vietnam."

Sandra's mouth forms a little "o" and then she says, "You were in the war?"

"I've been home for a month."

She stares at me for several moments, then swallows like she's trying to clear a lump from her throat. "The owner wants us to be nice to veterans. Even more than usual, I mean. But you're the first one I've met."

"Well, it's nice to meet you. I'm Scott."

"And I'm Sandra. But wait, you already read my nametag. Sorry again."

While I speak with Sandra, I notice that Lisa's begun staring at me while tilting her head to the side slightly.

"I love the ribbon you've got in your hair. It looks real nice," I say to Sandra. When she brushes back her hair again, she smiles, and I notice how cute her smile is. Her face is a little pudgy, but her smile is very cute.

Lisa clears her throat while looking at her wristwatch. She hands Sandra another quarter as she stands to leave and then says, "Scott, I'm meeting Stephen pretty soon, so I'll have to go. I need to ask you something first, though."

"Just a minute. I'll be right back," I tell Sandra before joining Lisa on her way to the door.

Once we're outside the café, she asks me, "What the hell are you doing?"

"What do you mean?"

"If I didn't know how much you love Elaine, I'd swear you were flirting with Sandra."

I frown and scowl. "Come on. I'm doing nothing of the kind."

"I'm just saying how it looks to me."

"Sandra's at her second day of work. She's nervous. I'm trying to calm her down by asking her about things she's comfortable discussing."

"You asked her what she does outside of work, and you complimented her on her looks. If I were Elaine, would you have done either of those things?"

"Probably," I say with a shrug.

"Come on. Really?"

"Yes, really. Don't get bent out of shape. Over in Vietnam guys talked to the off-duty nurses like that all the time. Some of the nurses had boyfriends, too. It doesn't mean anything except that I'm trying to be friendly."

"You aren't in Vietnam anymore, Scott. You might keep that in mind. Elaine's a nice woman. I like her quite a bit. Seeing her together with you is one of the few things Mother and I seem to agree on. Don't mess that up."

"I'm telling you, it's nothing. Look, I'm gonna go finish my *innocent* conversation with Sandra, and then I'm going home to watch more football with Dad. Nothing for you to worry about. We'll talk later, okay?"

"All right, then. I hope you know what you're doing."

"Elaine trusts me. You should, too."

I walk back inside and say a bit more to Sandra. She asks what I did in Vietnam, so I tell her about spraying Agent Orange from helicopters, moving men and supplies in my Chinook, and explain the difference between a Chinook and a Huey. Then she inquires if I'm from L.A. and makes other small talk. After five or ten minutes, she's smiling and laughing a little, and I think I've accomplished my goal of making her feel more at ease. I drive home feeling pleased because a little generosity has helped three people have a better day—the woman who forgot her wallet, Sandra, and me.

"Hi Dad, has the Rose Bowl started yet?" My father has a beer open on the coffee table and his Southern Cal Trojans sweatshirt on.

"Just barely."

"You still want to keep our bet from yesterday?"

"Yep. If Southern Cal wins, you owe me two car washes. If Indiana wins, we put two plastic pink flamingos in the yard for a month."

Honestly, I don't think that Indiana's odds are too good. Southern Cal is the number one-ranked team in college football for 1967, and they have a star running back named O.J. Simpson. But I've always been more of a UCLA guy, to the extent that I care about college football, mostly because I like their light blue and gold uniforms. The Bruins had been number one until losing to the Trojans the weekend before Thanksgiving. I couldn't listen to the game on Armed Forces Radio because I was flying a mission that Saturday, but I found out later. I have to content myself with the knowledge that it was UCLA's quarterback, Gary Beban, who won the Heisman Trophy for 1967 while Simpson finished second.

"How was your sister? Your mother told me they got into it last night after I'd gone to bed. Has Lisa calmed down today?"

My father must be a heavy sleeper. Their argument was loud.

"Yeah, she was fine. Lisa doesn't understand where Mom gets her ideas about Vietnam from. I told Lisa that Mom probably feels the same about her."

"You're right about that, I'd guess."

"I didn't say much to her about it, except that I wish she and Mom would get along better. New Year's Eve seems like a strange time to start an argument, doesn't it?"

"Your sister's boyfriend set her off."

I nod. "And how do you feel about Stephen? From what I heard Mom say about him in their argument, she'd like to strangle the guy."

Dad laughs briefly. His eyes are on the game, but I know he's paying attention to what I say. "I haven't made up my mind yet about Stephen, to be honest. He doesn't know everything he thinks he does, but I suppose that's true of most any young person."

"Mom seemed angry that he wears an M-65 fatigue jacket sometimes."

"Yeah, he probably shouldn't do that, but he thinks it's part of his identity. Lots of young people use clothing to broadcast their identity, which isn't always a bad thing. At least I never have to guess where they stand on something."

"And did you ever broadcast your identity?"

"Yeah. By wearing my baker's apron," he responds with a grin.

I laugh. "And how is business?"

"About the same as ever. Some days it could be better, but most of the time I do okay."

"Speaking of, I've been thinking I should get work of my own soon."

"Your mother and I spoke about that while you were gone. She said I should let you join me at the bakery. I told her I didn't think you wanted to be a baker. But if I'm wrong, you're welcome to give me a hand."

"Thanks, Dad, but I was thinking about something else. You aren't disappointed about that, are you?"

"Son, I want you to do a job that gives you satisfaction. I get satisfaction from baking food that people enjoy. But if you don't, then you should do something else. I'll admit I've dreamed about handing you the business when it's time for me to retire, but if that's not what you want, I won't force it on you just to keep the bakery in the family. I doubt your sister has much interest in baking."

It's good to know my dad never changes. A more matter-of-fact, straightforward, and honest man was never born.

"Maybe someday I'll give baking a try, but I want to do some other things first."

"Such as?"

"I got a little experience with fixing things while I was in Vietnam. I think I want to try working on cars."

"That's sensible. As long as Americans drive cars, we'll need people who know how to fix them."

We stop talking to watch the game for a while, but then I gather my courage to ask my dad a question I've been thinking about often lately.

"Dad, how do you feel about the war? I know you're proud of me, but I've never asked you if you think the war is a good idea. I assumed you supported it since you were a soldier yourself once. But you don't get into arguments with Lisa, so I guess I really don't know."

Dad pauses for a while, clearly thinking over how to answer. Finally, he says, "How much did I ever tell you about fighting against the Germans?"

"Not that much that I remember. You told me that you fought in the Battle of the Bulge and then advanced on Berlin in 1945, but I don't remember much more than that because I was a dumb teenager and didn't pay close enough attention."

He smiles at my blunt admission. "The Battle of the Bulge was the coldest thing I've ever felt. Day after day, the snow and wind tormented us. I saw snow, freezing rain, freezing fog, hail, all of it. Later, I found out that some of those days were the coldest on record for that part of Belgium."

"Sounds like the opposite of what I saw. I knew a few guys who said the heat, humidity, and the bugs were harder to deal with than Charlie was."

"Well, the point I'm getting at is that when the Germans made their attack in December, all that cold and hardship would've made a good excuse for the men to fall back or fight without enthusiasm.

But most of the men I fought beside didn't want to do that. We stood our ground. You know why?"

"Because the Army trained you to be stubborn?"

"Well, yes, that's one reason. No soldier likes to lose ground because they only have to fight again later to regain the same piece of ground. But the thing that stood out to me is that our men in the Ardennes Forest felt like we had a purpose for being there. We believed that the Nazis were bent on world domination, and we believed that wasn't right. Some soldiers got even angrier when we advanced into Germany and started finding out about the camps where the Nazis murdered the Jews. We had a few Jewish guys in our platoon, and no one wanted to beat the Nazis more than those fellows did."

"I get that, Dad. But what does it have to do with your feelings about Vietnam?"

Dad looks at me with raised eyebrows, like I should know the answer to my own question. I shrug because I don't.

"I felt like my war was a just war because nearly every soldier I knew realized that Nazi Germany was evil. That's a big reason why we stood our ground in the Battle of the Bulge and our lines didn't break. The men believed they fought for a cause that was worth seeing their buddies killed and injured over.

"When I see the reports coming from Vietnam and read interviews with men who've served over there, I'm not convinced that's true about Vietnam. That's my criteria for whether a war is a 'good' war. If the rank-and-file soldiers believe they're fighting for an important cause and that their sacrifices are worth it, that's a war I should support. If they don't, then I think people should reconsider what's going on. It's hard to win a war when the common soldier doesn't believe that victory is worth dying for."

I'm not sure the last time I heard my father speak so many words consecutively. Maybe tonight at dinner Mom and I should close our mouths and let Dad talk because what he just said makes so much sense.

Chapter 6

Visiting Ted

On the evening of February 2, 1968, I make my first trip to visit Ted and his family in Inglewood. The city of Los Angeles surrounds Inglewood, so in Vietnam, Ted simply told people he was from L.A. like me.

I'm anxious to speak with Ted. I read the papers sometimes, so I know that just two days ago, the Viet Cong launched a major offensive throughout South Vietnam. The news shocked me as much as anyone. I know better than to believe the people who claim America is winning the war handily, and it's only a matter of time until Charlie waves the white flag. But I sure didn't expect Charlie to attack eight provincial capitals simultaneously. I'd thought we were doing better than that, too.

Following Ted's directions, I park on the street outside his family's house. I'm a little surprised at where they live. Ted told me both his parents are teachers, and that he and his younger sister, Rachel, grew up with a pretty good lifestyle as a result. Their neighborhood, however, strikes me as rather rundown and poor.

The Williamson house appears in good shape, though. It's a one-story bungalow they've painted royal blue. A cement walkway leads from the sidewalk to the short flight of steps ascending to a covered porch and the front door.

Even before I knock, Ted, his father, Eugene, and his mother, Gloria, greet me on the porch.

Visiting Ted

Eugene wears a white shirt and navy blue tie. Although I put on slacks and a white polo shirt with horizontal red stripes, I feel underdressed in comparison.

Gloria also dressed up. She's got on a dark red spring dress with white dots and a large white collar.

Eugene, who is almost as tall as Ted, offers his hand. "I'm glad you could make it, Scott. Ted mentioned you often in his letters home. It's a pleasure to meet you finally."

"You, too, sir."

After shaking Eugene's hand, an awkward moment ensues. To be honest, I don't know enough Black people to know how I should greet Ted's mother. A handshake? A hug? Something else? What would be most polite?

Gloria seems to sense it, too. "Oh, come here," she proclaims with a wide smile while embracing me. "Come in and make yourself at home, Scott," Gloria adds while extending an arm to the living room.

The Williamson home doesn't look very different from mine on the inside—just a little smaller, and one story rather than two. Eugene and Gloria have a number of potted plants placed around the living room, and their brown sofa and padded chairs form a semicircle around their Zenith television-radio-phonograph combo player. It's a large wooden rectangular box with the television in the middle and speakers to the right and left. The left top of the box pulls up to reveal the radio dials while the right top contains the record player. It's a nice model, for sure.

One of the padded chairs has a well-worn ottoman in front of it, and the living room has a large Persian-style rug in the center to cover the brightly polished hardwood floors. The living room is spotless, and a hint of Lysol hangs in the air.

"This is really nice," I say, remembering my manners. Then I spot the checkered quilt over the back of the sofa. "Did you make that quilt yourself?" I ask Gloria.

"I sure did. It's nice of you to notice," she bubbles, warm smile still in place. "I hope you're hungry, Scott. I've got hamburgers on the grill for dinner."

"That sounds great, Mrs. Williamson."

"I'll see to the food while you men talk a bit," she declares while disappearing into the kitchen.

"You've seen the news, I take it?" Ted asks me.

"About Vietnam?"

"Yeah, this morning was a shocker, wasn't it?"

"Something big happened again this morning? I didn't look at the papers yet today."

"Dig this, man," Ted says, extending a folded newspaper to me from the coffee table. The top headline of the *Los Angeles Times* declares, "10,500 Reds Killed, S. Viet Carnage." But the real shock comes from the photograph below the headline. It shows a South Vietnamese officer on the streets of Saigon shooting a Viet Cong captive in the head from only inches away.

"Oh my. That doesn't look good," I remark.

"The caption clearly states that the guy getting killed is an officer in the VC, so he's a bad guy. But Americans aren't going to like a photo of an execution right there in public."

"Do you keep careful track of what's happening in Vietnam, Scott?" Eugene asks.

"I do follow along, yeah. Ted and I still know plenty of guys over there, so I have a lot of interest in how the war is going. I don't dwell on it night and day, though."

"The part that makes things confusing for me is that in Vietnam, there doesn't seem to be a front line to the war. Following progress is difficult," Eugene states.

"That's true, sir. Sometimes Ted and I would help capture a village, but then we'd have to go and capture it again a second or third time. That got frustrating, I'll admit."

Visiting Ted

As I speak, I notice some of the photographs Ted's parents have framed on their wall. I see several of a man who looks like Eugene posing at large gatherings.

"Is that your brother, Mr. Williamson?" I ask, pointing at some of the photos.

"It is. He lives in Bombingham."

"Bombingham?" Who would name their city Bombingham? I have no idea where that is.

Eugene smiles grimly. "That's how many Black folks refer to Birmingham, Alabama."

"I'm not sure I understand, sir."

"Birmingham is where the 16th Street Baptist Church was bombed by the KKK just five years ago. The Klan has been behind several bombings in Birmingham each year for decades."

"Oh my. I guess I never followed that news. I was only sixteen back then. How come the police let the Klan get away with that?"

"Because the police chief, Bull Connor, was one of them. Well, technically he was Commissioner of Public Safety, but he ran both the police department and the fire department. Connor once tried to organize a boycott of businesses in Birmingham that didn't segregate enough against Blacks."

I raise my eyebrows. This is new to me.

"But we don't need to talk about those things today if you'd rather not, Scott. You came over for dinner, after all, not to talk about Birmingham."

"Well, you've got me curious now. Is that why you don't live in Birmingham and moved to California?"

"It's a big reason, yes. Gloria and I wanted to get away from the violence, especially once she became pregnant with Ted, but my brother says Birmingham is his home, and he wants to stay."

"How long have you lived in Inglewood?"

"More than twenty years. I arrived in California when I was just a little older than you and Ted are now. It was right at the end of World War 2, and the shipyard in Long Beach had plenty of jobs building ships to fight the Japanese. I saved money from that to go to college, and then I became a math teacher."

I glance at the photographs once more. In addition to Eugene's brother, I see a photo of Martin Luther King, Jr., flanked by one of Franklin Roosevelt, the former president, and a woman whom I don't recognize.

"I apologize for asking so many questions, Mr. Williamson, but why do you have a photograph of President Roosevelt on your wall?"

"He was a hero to my parents. It's their picture, but since they're dead now, I keep it on the wall as a reminder of someone they cared about."

"That sounds like a good idea to me. My parents just have paintings of birds and orchids and the ocean on their walls."

"That sounds beautiful. Every family is different. What do your parents do, Scott?"

"Dad owns a bakery. Mom's never had a job that I know of."

"Sticks, would you like to see my models?" Ted asks, reentering the conversation.

"Of course."

"Right down here, in my bedroom."

After he closes the door, Ted says, "Sorry about my old man. You get him going on Birmingham, and it can be hard to get him to stop."

"I didn't mind. What he said was new to me."

"Well, I have to hear about it every evening at dinner, you know?" Ted says with a smile. "But here, take a look at these."

The top of Ted's dresser is covered with his models. Others rest on small wooden stands he's nailed into the wall. I see Corvettes and Mercedes as well as a number of fighter planes from World War 1 and 2. "You put all these together? They're smaller than I thought."

"Yeah, you gotta be careful and get the pieces to fit perfect, then use just the right amount of glue, so they'll hold together. I gotta be careful when I move out, so they won't break."

Visiting Ted

"You're getting your own place soon?"

"Yeah. It was nice to live here for a bit after being in the Nam, and Mom's a great cook, but it's time. I'll try to find work repairing cars, so I've got the dough to rent something of my own."

"Wait. You don't have a job as a mechanic yet?"

Ted shakes his head.

"How can that be true? I found one on my second try. The first place I looked didn't want me because the owner believed Vietnam vets were all irresponsible drug addicts. But the second garage where I applied, the owner said sure because he needed mechanics. Everything I know about engines I learned from you, though. You're way more qualified to fix cars than I am. I can't believe no one has hired you yet."

"That's just how it is, man."

Ted's looking at me like I'm missing something obvious.

"A lot of businesses won't hire a colored person to work on cars," Ted says after I look at him dumbly for a few more moments.

Immediately, I feel ashamed for not figuring that out. "Damn, I'm sorry. I should have known."

"It's okay, man," Ted tells me. "That's not your fault."

Still, I feel lousy at the realization that I needed help to understand something that's a part of everyday life for Ted. It's just that in Vietnam, skin color seemed less of a consideration. Ted was superb at fixing helicopters, so his job was fixing helicopters. People respected him because he was talented at something important. Some pilots specifically asked for him to look at things because they knew if Ted fixed something, it stayed fixed.

This brings up a thought. "Say, Ted, I didn't want to say this in front of your father, but something occurred to me when I was looking at your family photos."

"Yeah? What's that?"

"I saw the picture of Dr. King on the wall. I'm a little surprised your dad has that up there."

Ted's posture stiffens a bit. "Why is that a surprise? My dad's a big civil rights advocate. Dr. King is one of his heroes."

"Well, I was more surprised that you're okay with it. I mean, hasn't King given a bunch of speeches against the war?"

I know the answer to my own question thanks to my mother, who never tires of proclaiming that anyone who is against the war in Vietnam must have communist sympathies. She's no racist, but anyone who publicly opposes the war has committed an unforgivable sin in her mind. So, once King began speaking against the Vietnam War, Mom decided he had turned against America.

"Ah, I see what you mean. Dad and I talked about that once when I asked him about it. He explained how Dr. King's importance transcends one issue, and that even if I disagree with King about Vietnam, his work to better the lives of colored people is something no Black person has ever been able to accomplish before in this country."

"Your dad sounds like a smart man. That makes a lot of sense."

Again, I don't say it out loud to Ted, but his comments make me realize something else that's different between his life and mine. Growing up, I knew who Martin Luther King, Jr., was, of course, but my life never required a nuanced view of his actions. To me, King was the minister who wanted Black people to have the vote, and his methods were nonviolent. That was all to the good.

But my parents certainly never hung a photograph of King on their living room wall, and the parents of my other high school friends didn't, either. To me, King was a good person trying to make America a more equal country, but that was all. The idea that families hung on his every action as a source of hope was a foreign one to me.

"Boys, food's ready!" we hear Gloria call out.

"You're gonna like this," Ted tells me. "I told Mom to go easy on the traditional Southern foods she knows how to cook, so no grits or collard greens, but she barbeques a great hamburger, too. Maybe sometime I can get her to fix fried catfish for you."

"Can I ask you one more thing before we eat?" I ask hesitantly.

"Sure, man. What about?"

"Have you had any flashbacks since we came home?"

"No. Have you?"

I nod.

"Like when you tripped on that acid?"

"No, not quite. I keep seeing the Plain of Jars again."

Ted's face turns serious. He was part of that mission, too. "You mean, like, images coming into your head?"

"Yeah, kinda, but more than images. It's like watching a movie I've seen before, except I'm in the movie. The scenes are that clear and vivid. I feel like I'm *there* again, and when I'm there, I'm oblivious to anything going on here in California."

"That sounds serious, Sticks."

"Maybe. I don't know. Do you think it'll pass in time?"

"I can't say. I've never felt anything like that. You ever think about seeing a doctor about it?"

"I'd rather not."

"How come?"

"My dad fought the Germans, remember? He never needed drugs or doctors afterward. I'm scared that if I do, he'll think I'm weak and have less respect for me. I'm already worried that somehow he'll find out about me dropping acid. It'll be even worse than if my mom finds out any of that. And, well, I shouldn't *need* help, right? I mean, I'm home, and the danger is over. Charlie isn't a threat to me in Los Angeles. Shouldn't I be tough enough to move on and live a normal life?"

"Boys, I said food's ready!" Ted's mother shouts with a little more urgency.

"We'd better go eat up," Ted says. "I tell you, you're gonna love Mom's food. Let me think about the flashback thing, okay? Maybe I can ask around discreetly and see if any other guys we served with know anything about it that might be useful."

One Kind Of Hero

I hope that works because although I'm too scared to admit as much, the flashbacks remain as frequent as ever.

Chapter 7

Compassion Becomes Weakness

"Scott, did you know a boy named Alex Thomas in high school?" my mother asks me a few days later over breakfast. It's a Friday, and I've nearly completed my first week as an auto mechanic.

I think for a moment while chewing some Wheaties. "Yeah, but only a little bit. He was one grade older than me, but I remember him because he played drums in the band. He's a good guy, though, from what I remember. Why do you ask?"

"He committed suicide."

"Damn."

My mother gives me a cross look.

"I mean, geez. Did the paper mention why?"

"I didn't learn about his death from the newspaper, although it'll have an obituary soon, I'd imagine. A woman in one of my church groups called and told me. She thought maybe you knew him."

"Did she say why?"

"Alex's note blamed going to Vietnam. It said he didn't deserve to live anymore after the things he'd seen and done there."

I'm not sure why my mother's source gave her such specific information about Alex's death, but she isn't the type to make up stories, so the details probably are correct.

"I don't understand that at all," she continues.

"What do you mean? It sounds like he was really depressed."

"The lady at church said he was totally healthy. Alex was never wounded in Vietnam. He had a regular job as a grocery clerk and a steady girlfriend. What did he have to be depressed about? It doesn't make sense, Scott."

"Maybe only Alex could tell us."

"What does that mean?"

"Just what I said. Maybe he saw some heavy things in Vietnam that got to him. It happens."

My mother pinches her lips and shakes her head. "I don't believe that. He was a hero, going over there to fight the communists. Alex had everything to live for. His whole life was ahead of him. There must be more to his death than that. I'll bet it's those antiwar cowards and traitors who got inside his head. Don't you think?"

"How can I say? I'm not Alex."

"But you were there. You know what it's like."

Even though I realize I'm not getting through to my mother, I decide to give it one more try. "Not everyone who goes to Vietnam sees and experiences the same thing. And even if they did, each person has his own reaction. Some men can handle the stress and strain better than others. A guy doesn't know until it happens to him."

"That's the kind of talk I read about from the so-called experts in psychology who try to explain away why we haven't won the war yet. I still think it's the anti-war crowd that got to him. Or maybe he was just weak. Why else would a kid who had so much going right kill himself?"

I decide to take the last question as a rhetorical one and not answer. Besides the fact that someone who fought the Viet Cong shouldn't be considered a kid, I know that Mom's mind is made up and trying to explain things any further is a waste of breath. So, I guzzle the milk still in my cereal bowl. "I'm going to go get dressed for work," becomes my excuse for ending the conversation.

When I go to my bedroom to shave, though, I sit on my bed a moment and try to imagine what Alex Thomas might have seen or done to make himself end his life. Did he lose a friend in a particularly horrible way? Or maybe he felt he could've saved a friend but failed? Did he make a mistake and kill someone who he knew was innocent of wrongdoing? The possibilities for one or more of those things to happen in Vietnam were nearly endless.

My thoughts about Alex lead me to think about another mission I took part in. This one came shortly after our landing on the Plain of Jars.

Once again, we're supposed to move villagers out of an area infiltrated by Charlie, but we're in Vietnam this time. The Chinooks have landed, the depopulation mission is in progress, and the villagers run around in utter confusion. It's a small village, only a few dozen huts, and I watch their thatched roofs sway in the wind created by our big helicopters. It's scorching hot and beastly humid, like always, so I'm constantly wiping sweat from my eyes while I stand guard. The tree line isn't that far away, and that's where trouble usually lurks. I bat at the insects swarming my face, futile as that is, while scanning repeatedly.

When I glance at my commanding officer, he puts up one hand, five fingers out, to signify we have five minutes to finish boarding the villagers and get airborne. Nearby, an infantryman watches two young girls, maybe ten years old, maybe twelve, lead an old man toward my Chinook, their dark hair blowing out behind them as they walk. Probably they're his grandchildren. The girls each hold one of his hands to lead him forward, but he seems reluctant to follow.

An argument ensues. The girls point the old guy toward us, stamping their feet in the dust on the edge of the village. They also lean in close and shout in his ears, so maybe he doesn't hear so well. Or maybe it's because the noise from our Chinooks makes it hard to hear for everyone. Finally, he complies and shambles in our direction, his back stooped with age and his balding head lowered.

I thought the young girls were going to follow, but then they look back toward the village. Another woman runs in their direction.

Their mother, maybe? When the children run over to meet her, the woman hands them each something. Then she runs back into the village. Meanwhile, the old man slowly boards the helicopter.

The two young girls each have something clutched to their chest. When they get close to my Chinook, the soldier on guard at the boarding ramp yells at them to slow down and put their hands out.

They keep running, of course. They can't speak English. While I glance around for one of the interpreters, the GI opens fire. Instantly, the two little girls are dead.

As their bodies hit the earth, the things they carried fall from their grasp. One is a tiny black puppy. The other is a small, framed family photograph.

At the time, I'm a little ashamed to admit now, I didn't feel that bad about watching two people gunned down. Even two people of that age. They might've had grenades clutched to their chests.

The words of my CO were still fresh in my ears at the time. *"All these gooks are the same. They all hate us. You've gotta assume that all of them are enemies. You forget that, you go home in a body bag."*

So, watching those two kids get killed was tragic, yes, but it was war. The more I think about it now, the more unsure I am how I'd have reacted if it'd been me that those kids ran toward. Would I have pulled the trigger? Maybe so.

That was one of the hardest things about the Nam. Most of the time, a GI had no idea if the Vietnamese he met were friendly or hostile. Charlie seldom wore uniforms, so a guy could never tell for sure. Most of us chose to err on the side of shooting first and finding out the facts later. Harsh? Absolutely.

"I made you a ham sandwich for work today, Scott," I hear Mom call from downstairs. I rub my hands over my eyes, trying to clear my head. Up to this point, loud noises had set off my flashbacks. But this one happened just from thinking about a guy I barely knew and what might've caused him to kill himself. I shake my head and blink my eyes rapidly. This has to stop. Not only do I have a full day of work today, but also I'm supposed to meet Elaine tomorrow morning.

I've got a surprise for her, too. My plan is to pick her up in the new car I bought with the money I saved from my military pay. It's a black Corvette Sting Ray, the 1967 model, and, boy, can it move. Plus, since I live in Southern California where the sun shines three hundred days a year, I bought a convertible.

But first, I have to pull myself together and make it through a full day of work. Clearly, I need to get tougher and figure out how to block these flashbacks I keep getting. I never had them while I was in the Nam—they only began once I returned to California. Perhaps my problem is that I've gotten too soft since I left? Maybe if I get my edge back, things'll be better again.

I hurry to shave and get going, but I nick myself several times in my haste. When I get downstairs, my mother sees it.

"Your face is bleeding, Scott. Everything okay?"

"It's fine, Mom. Just breaking in a new razor blade."

Perhaps I should be a little more honest with my own mother, but I really will be late for work if we talk much longer.

She looks at me, head cocked to the side, a skeptical frown on her face. But Mom finally says, "I'll see you this evening, then."

I truly don't know how my mom would react if she knew how bad my flashbacks were. Better to get rid of them and never find out, I figure.

"Oh my goodness, Scott!" Elaine exclaims when I pick her up in my new Corvette the next morning. "When did you buy this?"

"Two days ago. It's great, right?"

"It looks amazing. Is it fast?" she asks while climbing in, wicker lunch basket in hand.

"Let me show you," I say while pulling out onto the street.

"Where are we going?"

"To the beach, like we planned. But first we're gonna hit the Ventura Freeway. It's not too far." It might only be February, but in L.A. sometimes February is warm enough to enjoy a day at the beach, and today is one of those days. Elaine's wearing a red T-shirt and white shorts.

I don't push the Corvette until we get on the freeway, but once we do, I open it up and watch the speedometer ease past sixty, seventy, and then eighty. The top is down, and Elaine's hair billows out behind her. I look over at her, grin, and depress the accelerator a bit more to make the speed touch ninety.

As I weave through the traffic I look over at my girlfriend again. She's trying to tell me something, but I can't hear her. After flying on a Chinook in Vietnam, I can read lips tolerably, however, and she's telling me to slow down. For a moment I consider it but change my mind and decide to show her what one hundred miles per hour feels like.

The other drivers shrink in the rearview mirror while I bob in and out of the left lane. Truth be told, I've never driven this fast before because I've never had a car that I was sure could do it. My adrenaline surges as I dart around the slower cars.

Elaine's touch startles me. She puts her left hand on my right arm and grips it tight. I glance down and see her knuckles turning white. A quick look at her face, and I realize she's legitimately scared.

When I peek at the speedometer and see I'm now driving at one hundred-seven, I decide I've made my point about how fast the Sting Ray can go. I ease my foot off the gas and slow the car in time to take the Highway 23 exit and head south. From there, we'll catch the Pacific Coast Highway back toward the city and go to the beaches at Malibu or Pacific Palisades.

Even after exiting, however, I realize that Elaine hasn't relinquished her grip on my arm. "What did you do that for?" she shouts at me to be heard over the engine. It's hard to tell if she's excited or still scared, so I look over again. Her eyes are staring straight ahead, her posture is rigid, and she's breathing rapidly. Definitely scared.

"I wanted to show you what a Corvette could do. You asked if it was fast, right?" I yell back to be heard over the road and engine noise.

"You could've just said it was fast. You didn't need to drive one hundred-twenty or whatever we just did."

"Would you have believed me?"

"Of course."

"But that was fun, wasn't it?"

"Not for me. You know you only missed some of the other cars by a few feet, right?"

"Yeah. But I missed them, and that's what counts."

"Let's talk about it on the beach. I don't like shouting at you so that you can hear me."

I nod and turn my full attention back to the road. It's only a few miles to the beaches, but the highway here winds in places, so I need to watch where I'm driving. Still, I had no idea Elaine was scared of driving that fast. I loved it. For a minute, the excitement and energy, the tension of knowing I was driving dangerously, reminded me of manning the M-60 machine gun mounted on a Chinook.

After driving a few more miles, we get to Pacific Palisades and head to Will Rogers State Beach. It's named for the former actor who used to own a ranch in the area. While we walk on the sand and find a spot, I sense that Elaine remains tense. She hasn't said a word since we parked.

"You okay now?" I ask her.

"I'm not sure. You didn't need to show off for me like that."

"I loved every second of it. I thought you would, too."

"Well, I didn't. Why did you go so fast? Even after I told you to slow down, you sped up instead."

"I wanted you to see how fast a Corvette can go."

"Yeah, you said that while we were on the road. But why did you think you had to show off for me?"

Her question gives me pause. I know why she asked it. When we got on the freeway, I certainly did intend to impress Elaine with how fast my new car was. But once I got going, really got going, and decided to experience what one hundred felt like, I was no longer trying to impress her. I might've thought I was, but the excitement I felt triggered something inside of me, too. The reason I kept going at that speed for several minutes was because I felt a rush. A rush I'd never experienced except while in Vietnam and that, to my surprise, felt really good.

"Scott?"

"Well, it's hard to describe. I'll admit that, at first, I was trying to show off. But explaining why I wanted to keep going fast is harder."

"Why? I was frightened that whole time."

"I know. Your fingernails almost punctured the skin on my arm."

"Then why did you do it?"

"Like I said, it's tough to explain."

"I want to know."

When I look up at Elaine from arranging our towels in the sand, I see her fists are pressed to her thighs, and her face remains strained. Apparently, I upset her more than I realized.

"Can't we just enjoy the sunshine? I won't do it again now that I know it upsets you."

"Don't say that, Scott. You never used to dodge my questions before."

She's right. I've always tried to be open with Elaine, and she's done the same with me. That's part of why our relationship has lasted. So, I decide I'd better give in on this one.

"Well, this might sound weird to you, but in a way, it was fun."

"Fun? How about dangerous?"

"Yes, it was a little dangerous. That's part of the fun."

"I don't understand that. Since when did dangerous become the same thing as fun? It certainly wasn't fun for me."

"I realize that now. That's why I won't do it again."

"But why did you enjoy it?"

"That's the part that's hard to explain, but it reminded me of being a gunner on a helicopter in Vietnam."

"You told me that you sprayed chemicals and moved supplies, and that most days you never fired a weapon."

"And that's the truth. But I never knew when I might need to. The fear and anticipation that I *might* have to fire at someone kept me on a nervous edge. Driving one hundred was the closest to that nervous edge I've felt since I came back to California."

"But why would you *want* to feel like that? Isn't it better to be here and feel safe all the time?"

"It should feel better, I suppose. The anticipation that danger could strike at any moment is something that's hard to describe. It might sound like a contradiction, but I've never felt more *alive* than I did when manning an M-60 on a combat mission. Most people would find a situation where they might get shot to be scary, and it is, but it's also a rush at the same time. Racing along the Ventura Freeway is the closest I've had to that feeling since I left Vietnam. I didn't know how much I missed it until now."

I look in Elaine's eyes to see if what I said made any sense to her. She's narrowed her eyes a bit, and I see a hint of a frown, so I'm doubtful. "I'm not making sense, am I?"

She shakes her head. "You never acted like that before you went to Vietnam. Why are you different now? You were only there for one year."

"I'm just telling you how it felt. As to why I feel that way, I wish I knew."

"Scott, I keep telling you that you need to put Vietnam behind you."

Elaine sits down next to me finally and puts an arm around my shoulders. She's smiling now, but it's a nervous smile. "Why can't you do that? I'm not naïve enough to think you can go over there for a year and not have it affect you at all. But that's over. You don't need to be the person who you were in Vietnam because you're here with me now."

"I'm trying. But it's not like turning the lights on and off. I can't flip a switch."

Elaine looks down at our white beach towel while running her hands through her hair.

"What are you thinking now?" I ask, a little nervous myself.

"I'm not sure what to think. You keep telling me you're trying, and I believe you, but it doesn't seem to be working. Have you had any more of those, what do you call them, the flashbacks you told me about?"

"They happen sometimes, yeah."

"Have you figured out what causes them?"

"I know some things that do. Sudden, loud noises, for one, like the fireworks on New Year's Eve. But other times, they're unpredictable. I'm pretty sure that once I figure out all the causes, I'll be ready for the flashbacks before they happen, and I can avoid them better."

"That's the best thing you've said all day. If you tackle the problem head-on, I'm sure you'll beat it."

When I look at Elaine now, I can see the sincerity in her eyes. She loves me, and she wants to help but isn't sure how. But I also notice that her skin seems drawn and tight, and her legs look skinnier than I ever recall seeing them.

"Have you been getting those fevers again?" I ask. "You look like you've lost some weight."

"Sometimes, yes," Elaine admits. "I've had to call in sick from work a few times lately, but I try not to talk about them."

"Do you know what's causing the fevers?"

"I think it's several things. You know that I worry about you, Scott, and that makes me nervous. I also worry about myself sometimes lately, too. It's always been my dream to go to college, you know, but I'm not sure I'll ever be able to afford it. Plus, it seems like my parents argue an awful lot lately. I really need to move out and get away from all that negativity, but if I do, it'll be even harder to save money for school."

"You haven't mentioned your parents before. What are they upset about? Each other? I always thought they had a great relationship."

"No, not that. Mostly they argue about my brother, Glen. He's seventeen now, and his birthday is in October. Glen wants to drop out of high school as soon as he turns eighteen so that he can volunteer to fight in Vietnam. Mom wants him to finish high school first. Dad says they should support him if he wants to volunteer that badly, and that they can't prevent him from enlisting once he's eighteen, anyway."

"I haven't talked to Glen in quite a while. He never told me that's what he wanted to do," I say, taking Elaine by the hand and rubbing it.

"For once, I agree with my mother wholeheartedly. I don't want my little brother to go to Vietnam unless he has to."

"Is worrying about Glen making you feel worse?"

"Probably my fevers come from all these things combining at once, yeah," she states, finally relaxing her shoulders a little as I continue to rub her hands. Then she gives me a wry smile. "It's funny how life goes sometimes, you know? I'm an adult, but sometimes having all these things happen to me and not knowing what to do about them makes me feel like a little kid again."

That gives me an idea. "Wanna build a sand castle?"

"A sand castle? Where did that idea come from?"

"I don't know, but I haven't tried in years. It seemed like a fun idea, something different. Maybe that'll help both of us, doing something we used to do to take our minds off things. And it'll give you an excuse to act like a kid and know that sometimes, that's not a bad thing."

"Okay, a sand castle, then," Elaine responds, her growing smile indicating that she's warming to the idea.

Our sand castle is a castle in name only. Really, it's a pile of sand that we sculpt with our hands. But it keeps us distracted and talking about lighthearted, fun things all day, and that's the point. For a couple hours, Elaine doesn't dwell on the drive here or why she's nervous about going home. Instead, she molds mermaids and whales surrounding our castle. She has a lot more artistic talent than I do.

I'd also forgotten how good my girlfriend looks in a bathing suit. Elaine wears a white one-piece with big red dots. She's a little pale because it's only February, but still, Elaine looks very fashionable with her swimsuit and dark glasses.

It's now late in the afternoon, we've both gotten plenty of sun, and I'm finally feeling relaxed. Despite a bumpy start, we've had an enjoyable day. I'm also feeling tired, maybe because I've just worked a full week, so I doze off while Elaine finishes her mermaids.

I wake up later when Elaine shakes me gently. "Scott, I'm finished. Come look at everything."

Startled, I jump up with a shout and scan for Charlie, pivoting my head while crouching on my right knee. My trigger finger curls around the rifle I don't have. Only after Elaine gasps do I realize that in the process, I'm kneeling on one of her mermaids, and I've already trampled two others.

Elaine sits down in the sand, puts her head in her hands, and cries. I'm too embarrassed and disappointed in myself to ask her if she's crying because I ruined her sand sculptures or because I'm still acting like I'm in Vietnam.

From nearby, I hear some high school kids laughing.

"Look at that weirdo," one says to his friends. "He's three bricks short of a load."

"He must think he's back in the jungle looking for Charlie," another cackles.

"Yeah, except he's in the wrong country. Charlie don't surf," the first jeers.

Compassion Becomes Weakness

Rather than respond, I put my own head down in shame. What the hell is wrong with me?

Chapter 8

On My Own

That night I lie in bed, almost ready to sleep, when I stop and think again about the depopulation mission where we killed the two young girls—the ones with the puppy and the photograph. It's been on my mind all day despite my best efforts to concentrate on other things.

The two bodies lie in the grass, bleeding and not moving. The little puppy licks the face of one of the girls. She doesn't stir.

That's when I hear the howl of grief from the old man who'd just boarded the Chinook. I turn my head. He's trying to force his way back out of the helicopter, but other villagers restrain him.

When I turn my head back to the soldier who'd just shot the little girls, he looks at me and shrugs. He yells, "Don't mean nothin'," and then he boards the Chinook himself. I follow, stumbling up the ramp after him.

Once we're on board, the old man starts wailing at the soldier who shot the girls. He responds by shouting at the villager to shut up, poking him in the stomach with his rifle.

It has no effect on the old guy. He grabs the GI by his uniform shirt and starts shaking him. He's weak because he's old, so the soldier hardly budges. Still, I can sense a few other villagers are agitated, too. I see them muttering to each other.

Next, the soldier beside me prods the old guy in the chest again, pushing him away with some force. You'd think he'd get the message by now, but the old guy keeps wailing. Finally, the GI responds by grabbing the villager and tossing him out the back of the Chinook.

I look down—we're probably thirty or forty feet off the ground and rising. I can't hear the impact of his body over the noise of the rotor blades, but it doesn't look like the old man is moving.

Now the inside of the Chinook is absolutely still.

The whole scene sickens me. I realize I'm having trouble breathing. Not because the old guy got thrown out of our chopper, however. If he'd have kept going on like he was, other villagers might've panicked, and when a Chinook is airborne, that can mean trouble for everyone.

So, cold as it sounds for me to admit it, that's not what makes me ill. I feel horrible because we soldiers are in a spot where such decisions become so instinctive. I look at the GI again. He's a tall guy but looks really young. Maybe eighteen, maybe nineteen. He even has acne on his face. And guys our age have to make decisions about whether to kill people or let them live. A year ago, many GIs were graduating high school, and their biggest worry was getting turned down on a date. If they did the wrong thing, they got embarrassed when the girl said no. In the Nam, if you do the wrong thing, people could die. Hell, sometimes they still died even when a guy did the right thing.

Finally, I remember I'm still in my bed in California. My heart beats wildly, and I feel sweat slide down my face. When dizziness follows, I raise my knees, trying to breathe deeply. Slowly, I feel calmer, but I'm wide awake now.

Throwing back the sheets in frustration, I walk downstairs and pop the top of a Budweiser while taking a seat at the kitchen table. My body still feels too warm to sleep, and my mind is all over the place, trying to figure out what's going on with me. After a few minutes I crack another beer, just staring at the roses on the kitchen wallpaper and trying to make sense of things. I'm not sure how long I sit there staring before I realize I need a third beer.

I'm about halfway through my third can when I hear my mom clear her throat in the door separating the kitchen from the hallway.

"I didn't expect to find you up drinking," she says when I raise my head. She's wearing a heavy white bath robe and has her arms crossed over her chest.

"I'm having a rough night."

"But drinking beer at three in the morning?"

"What else is there to do about it?"

"Go back to bed. Your job starts in five hours, Scott."

"It'll be fine. This will help me crash. I'll sleep a couple more hours, and things'll be okay."

"You can't do good work on four hours of sleep."

"Shit, I did that all the time in Vietnam."

This time I don't bother to correct myself when my mother frowns at my language.

"I don't want to hear about what you did in Vietnam. You aren't in Vietnam now. You're in California, you have a job, and you need to act like a responsible adult who wants to keep his job."

"Oh, how far the mighty hero has fallen," I say while draining the can. Perhaps it's a bad idea to mock my mother after how many times she's called me a hero, but I don't appreciate the advice on how an adult should behave. Anyone who's been a gunner on a helicopter in Vietnam is adult enough to make their own choices.

"Don't take that tone with me in my house, young man. I won't stand for that."

I nod and toss my empty beer cans in the trash. "Good night, Mom. What's left of it, anyway," I say while pushing past her to go upstairs and try to sleep again. I have the feeling she's staring holes in my back as I climb the steps, but I don't turn to verify.

It was due to happen soon anyway, I suppose, but that day at work I decide it's time to leave my parents' house and find my own

On My Own

pad. It was good to have a familiar place to live while I got used to being a civilian again, but after nearly three months, it's time. Maybe even past time. The little argument with my mother early in the morning only had a little to do with the decision. She's a forgiving person and rarely holds a grudge, unless the person under discussion is a Democratic president or one of Lisa's recent boyfriends. I'm confident that by dinner, she'll have gotten over our little spat. Rather than being the motivation for my decision to move out, it's better to say that the argument gave me the nudge I needed to make up my mind.

The apartment isn't big, but I don't have that many things. I guess that's the downside of spending most of my saved-up military pay on a Corvette. The walls are a powder-blue color. I guess the owner must be a UCLA fan.

It's a pleasant surprise when my father suggests I take Pete to live with me. I agree without hesitation, of course, and the more I think about it, having Pete with me is perfect. At ten years old, he's docile enough that he's content to sleep while I work during the days, but a city park is near my apartment, so we can get exercise in the evenings.

Pete is the classic Labrador in many ways. He's always been friendly and outgoing with other people but gentle. Pete loves to fetch things, and he's always up for a swim. In other words, he's got the personality everyone wishes that they had. We've bonded again since my return, and once again he sleeps next to me on the bed, even though he needs a little help getting up because of his age.

Naturally enough, I invite Elaine over for dinner two days after moving in. I've had just enough time to find a pan for cooking some chicken when she arrives. She's got on a heavy white sweater over tan slacks.

"This is for you—a housewarming gift," she announces after I open the door, producing a box from behind her back.

"You've got a wonderful talent for disguising gifts," I tell her with a broad smile. Elaine wrapped a frying pan in the box, but the handle sticks through a hole in the side.

"I know you've probably got one, but my mother suggested that if you're like most people, you'll need two pans—a clean one and a dirty one." We both laugh. Although I've never lived on my own and cooked for myself, I imagine that isn't far from the truth. I leave my new pan on the counter, since tonight I'm baking instead of frying.

Elaine sits at my grand kitchen table, which is actually an old card table I borrowed from my folks until I can get something nicer. I've tried to hide its shabby nature with a double-folded, red-and-white checkered tablecloth.

"Say, we haven't been to your parents' house in quite a while, now that you mention them."

Elaine winces slightly. "Yeah, I know. To be honest, I'm still thinking it's time to do what you did and find my own place."

"Same things wrong between you and them?"

"I don't know if I'd say something is wrong between us, exactly. They aren't angry with me. But still, lately I feel a lot of tension when I'm in the house, and I wonder if I'm the cause of some of it."

I wait for Elaine to elaborate.

She releases a big sigh. "How can I describe it? The arguments are getting more frequent, and I don't know what to do about it. So, even though I haven't done anything big that they disapprove of, I still feel like I share some responsibility."

"They're arguing even more now? Surely, they aren't upset with anything I've done, are they?" I ask while checking the chicken in the oven. I'm pleasantly surprised I remembered to turn it on and let the oven warm up ahead of time.

"No, they still like you as much as ever. But they're upset all the time, it seems like. My brother hasn't changed his mind about wanting to enlist. On top of that, Dad's mad that our country isn't doing more to win the war. He rails about how the commies are duping President Johnson. Mom's upset that a couple of Black families have bought houses in our neighborhood in recent months. She thinks the family should move because of that."

"Why would your parents want to move, Elaine? You've lived on that street since you were a little girl."

"Mom's convinced that property values are going to go down if too many Black families move into the area. You know how penny-pinching my parents can be. Dad had to scrape and save to get that house in the first place. It's by far the most valuable thing my parents own. The thought of working so hard to get a decent, suburban house, only to see it lose value, is more than my mother can stand. And even though she won't say it out loud, I think she's worried because one of the families has teenage boys."

"Why does she care about that?"

"She believes they might be a threat to the young girls of the neighborhood."

"Has she ever met them, Elaine?"

"Of course not."

"Then that's stupid. Why does she assume they're dangerous when she doesn't even know them?"

"I think her sister feeds her fears about Black people. Mom's sister lives in Atlanta, you know."

I shake my head. "That's insane. What if one of those boys was someone like Ted? Ted and I spent fourteen months together in Vietnam, and we watched out for each other the whole time. He's a faithful friend, and his parents are both teachers. Someone like him is no threat to anyone. His greatest joy in life is building model airplanes, for crying out loud."

"You don't have to convince me, Scott. I'm just relaying what she says. A few times I tried to talk her into being more open-minded, but she got upset, and said I was too trusting and naïve."

"And that's why you think you're making things worse at home," I finish for Elaine.

She nods. "That's one reason. I'm not sure my dad is right about Vietnam, either. But maybe he is. I don't know. Maybe I should follow along in the news better than I do. But he gets really angry when I suggest that not everything the president does is a conspiracy to turn America over to the communists, and when he gets angry, he expects people to agree with him. You remember that about him, I'm sure."

I do. All too well. And he gets a lot worse after a tumbler or two of bourbon.

Elaine sighs again and continues. "So, a lot of the time, I feel like an argument is waiting to happen at home. Things feel so tense some days. Usually, I try to stay in my bedroom and read a book or play my trumpet. It's kinda sad, really, that I mostly avoid my parents other than at meals."

While Elaine speaks, I look at her face. The stretched skin and tired eyes I've noticed often lately seem worse than ever, and that makes me feel awful that I can't do more to help her.

Then, a thought strikes me. Maybe I can help her, after all. "You don't have to do that anymore, you know."

"What do you mean?"

"Well, you just said you're thinking about moving out, so why not move in with me? I don't have a roommate, and I could use one."

Elaine's mouth makes a little "o." Apparently, she hasn't had the same thought.

"It's perfect," I tell her. "You need a place to live, and I've got one. We've been dating for nearly two years, or four years, if you count my time in the Army."

"My parents would never allow it. They're way too traditional and conservative when it comes to things like that. Would yours approve?"

"Probably not. With my mother, definitely not. But we're adults, right? Do we have to have the approval of our parents for everything we do together?"

"I don't know, Scott, living together is a big step. I don't know if *I'm* ready for that."

"You don't have to decide today."

I go to the oven to turn the chicken over, remembering to use my sole oven mitt when grasping the pan, but when I turn back around, Elaine's running her hands through her hair while gently chewing her lip.

"You look nervous. Was my suggestion really that out of left field? Hasn't the idea of living together at least crossed your mind before today?"

Elaine frowns and looks down, and when she takes her hands out of her hair, I can see them tremble slightly.

"I just don't know what to do right now, Scott. Everything is changing around me, and it's changing faster than I can handle. My parents never used to fight very much, but now it's getting common.

"You've made a bunch of changes, too. You bought a new car and then got your own apartment. Those are big new things, especially when I didn't see you for so long. And now you're talking about living together. I was also thinking maybe I should try to find a second job. I'll need another one if I do leave my parents' house because I need to save for college. It's just so much, and I don't think I'm ready for it all."

Elaine has a point, I'll admit. I stand behind her, since I only have one kitchen chair at the moment and eat my meals on the couch. Gently, I rub her shoulders. What can I say? I wasn't aware things had gotten so hairy for her at home.

"Forget I asked about moving in with me," I tell her after a moment. "I forgot you were dealing with so much stress."

"We talked about it at the beach a few days ago," Elaine sighs plaintively.

The comment hangs in the air for several moments. Was that an accusation, a statement of regret, or something else? However Elaine meant it, I concede she's probably right. She did describe things at her house to me a little while ago. I've been too worried about my flashbacks and the tension in my own family, and Elaine's worries slipped my mind.

I decide to say the only words that fit. "I'm very sorry. Things haven't been easy for me lately, either, but I should do a better job of asking you about your feelings. Maybe that's another thing about Vietnam I need to let go of."

"What do you mean by that?"

"Over there, if a guy spends too much time asking other guys how they feel, he looks soft. Soldiers are supposed to be tough and suck it up when things aren't perfect. The same is true if a GI complains too much or shows any vulnerability. Other soldiers will think he's weak, and he loses their respect. Same thing with officers. I got used to that attitude after so long in uniform. But I admit it's not a part of military life that translates very well into being a civilian. I'll try to do better from now on."

As I speak, I keep rubbing Elaine's shoulders and back, and she does relax a little. "I promise, I'll try to ask you about your feelings more often. And I'll drop the idea of living together if you don't feel good about it. The idea came to me because I wanted to find a way to help you. That's why I brought it up."

"Thank you, Scott. That means a lot. Somehow, I thought you were ignoring me and my feelings on purpose. That isn't true, but part of me started to fear that it was. I'm very confused sometimes lately, and fears pop into my head when they shouldn't."

I've been so focused on Elaine I've forgotten to check the chicken, so I go to the oven and pull it out. "Almost forgot, but it looks about right."

"You know, ovens have timers so that you won't forget," she says, a tiny smile appearing on her face. This time, I know Elaine isn't criticizing me. She's speaking in the joking tone people use to state the obvious to someone who's forgotten the obvious.

"Another thing that's different from Vietnam—cooking for myself," I respond in the same tone. Elaine's smile grows and she manages a laugh.

On My Own

"What would you ever do without me?"

"Burn the chicken, probably."

"Did you fix anything besides chicken?"

"I've got apples, oranges, and some bread from Dad's bakery."

"That does sound very good. How is your dad?"

I take out two ceramic plates, white with a blue band around the outside, and metal utensils and set the table.

"Real plates? Not paper?" Elaine jokes again.

"Nothing but the best at my house. Until my only two plates get dirty. But, yeah, my dad. He's doing fine, mostly. I think."

"Mostly, you think?"

"Well, you know he isn't one to talk that much. But he always says business is decent at the bakery, and he always has food on the table and gas in the Buick, so I guess business is decent."

"I would've thought that you two would talk all the time."

"Why is that?"

"He fought in Europe, and you went to Vietnam. I assumed you would talk with him about being a soldier and what you did overseas."

I nod while handing Elaine a napkin and pouring her some milk. "We have a little. But he keeps saying that every soldier experiences war differently, and that when I want to talk about it, he'll be there. He's never forced it, though. You know that isn't his style."

"He's never asked you about your flashbacks? Your dad knows, right?"

I slice some bread and give Elaine a piece. Then I hesitate. "I'm not sure how much he knows, and I'm kinda afraid to bring it up."

"How come?"

"I'm scared. I'm scared that he'll think I'm not as strong as he is. My dad fought in the Battle of the Bulge and nearly lost his fingers to frostbite, and he never has flashbacks. He's the same even-keeled guy every day. I want to be like that, and it scares me that I'm not."

"You don't think he'd understand?"

"I don't know. But I'm scared to ask. It's hard for me to talk about, to be honest. Can we just eat for now?"

"Sure. I'm not demanding anything, of course, but I think maybe you should try to talk to your father. You'd know better than me, but I think he would understand why you struggle with the flashbacks and the nightmares at times. But you do what you think is right."

Chapter 9

I Wish It Would Rain

All through the rest of February and March, life is good. My job is going well, and Elaine and I spend many happy, relaxing days together. Things are peaceful at my parents' house as well. Lisa and her boyfriend parted ways, giving her one fewer reason to clash with my mom, and my weekly visits for dinner are a welcome respite from having to cook.

Not only that, but my flashbacks have become more sporadic. Perhaps too much stress is one of the causes, and now that life is more relaxed, my mind is more at ease. I don't know for sure. I'm happy to be free of the nightmares most nights, though.

I've found a roommate as well: Ted. We spoke on the phone a few days after I moved out, and he repeated that he was getting restless living with his parents, too, so we did the obvious thing.

One of the great things about having Ted for a roommate is the music. I hadn't spent much time listening to the Temptations, the Supremes, Otis Redding, James Brown, or Sly & the Family Stone until he moved in. But Ted got me hooked on Motown and soul music. He swears the Temptations' song "My Girl" is the greatest piece of music ever performed, and he's got me half-convinced, too. Whereas I spent most of the money I earned in the Army on my Corvette, he spent a bunch of it on records. We both kid each other by claiming we made the smarter move.

Today is April 4, and we're in Inglewood after work to pay an impromptu visit to Ted's parents.

One Kind Of Hero

I got Ted a job at the garage where I fix cars. The owner was a little reluctant at first, claiming he had enough mechanics, but then a guy quit a few weeks back. He gave Ted a couple repair jobs to show what he could do. Once the owner saw what a whiz Ted was at fixing things, he hired him on the spot.

But today, business was light, so the owner told us to take off work at three in the afternoon instead of the usual five o'clock. That's when we decided to visit Ted's folks.

When we near the Williamsons' house, we stop to get a sandwich at a local deli, so as not to impose on Ted's parents for dinner when we aren't expected. The sun is out, it's warm, and we're both feeling good. Only one day of work left this week.

After eating, Ted and I step into the street to finish the drive. I had to park several blocks away, however, because the area doesn't have much parking.

Something's different than when we went inside to eat, however. I sense a buzz, a murmur from somewhere that wasn't there when we went inside. I can't place it, though.

"What's that noise, do you think?" I ask Ted.

"I dunno, but it seems to be getting louder. You agree?"

"Yeah. Let's get in my car, just in case."

"Good plan, Sticks."

We've only traveled one block when the noise becomes a roar. Rounding the corner a block away, between us and my Corvette, a mob of people storm down the street toward us, shouting angrily as they advance. It's not a huge crowd—maybe fifteen, maybe twenty people—but most of them have guns.

"What's going on?" I shout to Ted.

"Don't know, but let's get the hell out of their way."

Then they open fire.

The mob isn't firing at us—or at anything in particular. Instead, people fire handguns and shotguns into the sky as the shouts grow louder and more frenetic.

I Wish It Would Rain

I dive for the doorway of the nearest business when I hear the gunshots. I sink to a knee even as Ted hurries over to stand beside me.

"I got you, Sticks, I got you," he says. Through the blur of action, I notice the swirling red, white, and blue pattern that signifies a barbershop on the awning above our position.

But then a new cry drowns out Ted's voice even as he helps me back to my feet.

"Get that white boy!" someone calls. Belatedly, I realize that everyone in the mob is Black. Their pace accelerates. They're coming right for us.

"Yeah, kill the killer!" someone else yells.

"What're they talking about?" I stammer.

"I don't know, but they'll have to go through me to get you," Ted declares, straightening up to his full height of six-three.

Next, Ted does the bravest thing I've ever seen. Unarmed, he strides forward to meet the mob, arms in the air, palms out.

"What're you boys doin'?" he shouts as loud as he can.

"We out to get Whitey!" comes the answer from a young man with a semi-automatic rifle at the front of the crowd. He brandishes it toward Ted angrily, and then points it at me, but the mob slows down to gather around Ted.

Ted doesn't blink, and he doesn't retreat. "What in hell for?"

"Don't you know nothin', brother? White man just killed King!"

"What're you talkin' about?"

"It's everywhere, man! Reverend King just got shot in Memphis. He dead. Now stand aside!"

Again, the man who seems to lead the mob lowers his weapon and points it at Ted. A number of others in the crowd shout affirmation as the mob pushes in on Ted. He still doesn't back up.

"This White boy here had nothin' to do with that. Are you people blind? He ain't done nothin'. Now go on home."

While Ted speaks, I scan the street so that I can run, as pointless as that would be under the circumstances. Maybe I can duck inside a doorway to a local business, but I doubt that'll stop the mob.

"But he White! All White people the same, man. They all Whitey. They all killed Dr. King. Every one of 'em hate our people."

"This man fought for America," Ted says, gesturing at me. "Just like I did. He hasn't even been in the country for—"

"What you boys doin?" a new voice booms out.

I turn to see a large, rotund, bald Black man with a white beard lumber out of the barbershop right behind me.

"Who're you yellin' at, Otis Butler?" the heavyset man shouts while gesturing toward the mob's speaker with his barber's scissors.

"We gonna get this White man for killin' the Reverend King."

"Who put rocks in your head, Otis?" the barber declares. Then he points to Ted. "Don't you know who this man is you're threatening? This is Ted Williamson. His mom was your teacher in elementary school, young brother."

I can't believe it, but Otis pauses. The barber presses his advantage.

"And what do you think you doin'? Reverend King preached nonviolence. You think he'd agree with you young folks takin' to the streets like this? I'm mad, just like you boys are. I'm mad as hell. But this is a time for sadness, not for anger. You keep shootin', and them White cops'll be here in no time. And they shoot back."

Now, some members of the crowd are looking to each other, uncertainty in their expressions.

"I seen the woman who owns the beauty parlor across the street on her telephone. Who you think she just called?" the barber claims.

I don't know if that's true or a bluff, but it has the desired effect. First one and then another member of the crowd backs away. Most of the rest stand looking around, uncertain of what to do.

"It's okay, boys, you've every right to be mad. Go on and march, but put the guns away and don't hurt nobody. That's what Dr. King would want. You all know that. Honor him the right way."

I Wish It Would Rain

I stand there, stunned, as the crowd disperses with barely a sound. Then the barber's large, dark hand clasps my shoulder. "It's okay, son. Those ain't all bad kids, despite what you just heard. They's angry, all right, and some of 'em ain't got no job to keep 'em busy, so they sit and watch too much television. I'm sure that's where they heard about Dr. King's murder."

"I don't believe what you just did," I tell the barber breathlessly. "I thought I was a goner, for sure."

"And you mighta been if not for your friend Ted here."

"Thank you, Mr. Hudson," Ted tells the barber while giving him a hug. Only now can I see Ted shaking in fear. Still quivering, he turns to me, his voice ragged. "This is Reggie Hudson. He's run this barbershop for years, and he's also friends with my parents. He's an institution in this neighborhood."

"Eugene and Gloria would never have forgiven me if I'd a let something happen to Ted right outside my shop." Reggie smiles, but it's a weak smile, and now I can see that he's shaking, too.

"And this, Mr. Hudson, is Scott Reynolds. We fought together in Vietnam."

I shake Reggie's hand properly.

"You here to see your folks?" he asks Ted.

"Yes, sir."

"I'd invite you in for a talk, but now isn't the time. I'm closing for the day. Then I'm gonna pray all night that I still have a barber shop tomorrow and someone hasn't burnt it down in rage. Let's hope that this isn't the start of another riot like in Watts three years ago."

"Good luck, Mr. Hudson. If God is a just God, he'll spare your shop."

"I sure hope that's true," Reggie says as he turns to finish closing. As Ted and I get ready to make a run for my car, he turns back and says, "You boys really didn't know King was dead, did you? No, I guess you probably didn't. The news broke less than an hour ago."

"No, sir. We've been at work all day, and then we washed up and drove over here to see my parents. We didn't have time to hear any news."

Reggie nods. "You boys say your prayers tonight, too. For yourselves, for our city, and for our country. We're gonna need all of them."

Chapter 10

The Williamson House

"I'm so glad you men are safe. Reggie is an amazing man. I guess it pays to know everyone in the neighborhood," Eugene Williamson tells Ted and me while we sit quivering on his sofa. Ted just repeated the story of what happened outside the barber shop, and his mother Gloria broke down in tears twice before he could finish.

"Ted saved me, Mr. Williamson. He's a hero, too," I put in.

"I thought it was the end of me, Dad," Ted says, his voice almost failing. "That mob scared me more than Charlie ever did. We had no way to see them coming and no chance to get away. One minute we were eating sandwiches, and the next this crowd wanted to kill Sticks over what happened in Memphis."

"Let me get everyone some food," Gloria declares while giving her son another hug. "Food always helps calm the nerves. I baked some molasses cookies yesterday. You boys just wait for a moment."

It's hard to deny Gloria's logic about cookies.

"Are you okay, Son? And how about you, Scott?"

I put my hands in the air. They're still twitching. "I'm kinda humbled to admit it after fourteen months in Vietnam, but yeah, I'm still scared," I concede. "In Vietnam, we would've at least had weapons to defend ourselves."

Eugene nods. "This neighborhood can be volatile. It's a poor neighborhood, and sometimes people get frustrated by that—the younger people especially. Folks can only stand so much frustration. I'm going to turn on the television and see what's happening in other parts of Los Angeles."

The dial of Eugene's television is set to ABC when he turns it on. He's in time to see the network cut from its usual programming, so it can televise an address from President Johnson at the White House. The President has on a navy blue suit and solid red tie. His hair is combed back like usual. I glance at the clock on the wall. It's 6:07 in the evening.

America is shocked and saddened by the brutal slaying tonight of Dr. Martin Luther King.

I ask every citizen to reject the blind violence that has struck Dr. King, who lived by nonviolence.

I pray that his family can find comfort in the memory of all he tried to do for the land he loved so well.

I have just conveyed the sympathy of Mrs. Johnson and myself to his widow, Mrs. King.

I know that every American of good will joins me in mourning the death of this outstanding leader and in praying for peace and understanding throughout this land.

We can achieve nothing by lawlessness and divisiveness among the American people. It is only by joining together and only by working together that we can continue to move toward equality and fulfillment for all of our people.

I hope that all Americans tonight will search their hearts as they ponder this most tragic incident.

I have canceled my plans for the evening. I am postponing my trip to Hawaii until tomorrow.

Thank you.

In the wake of the president's short speech, Eugene keeps the television on to see if violence has broken out anywhere in Los Angeles. It hasn't. Yet. Once we learn that, he switches it off.

The Williamson House

"You boys okay to drive home?" Eugene asks us when it's clear we have all the information that exists to be had. Ted nods.

"I'll get you both some more cookies," Gloria puts in.

"Thank you, Mrs. Williamson. Your molasses cookies are almost as good as your hamburgers," I tell her.

She smiles before heading for the kitchen, but it's a weary smile. Clearly, the news has drained her emotions, too.

"Can I ask something before we go?" I say to Eugene.

"Of course, Scott."

"How come you and your wife live in this neighborhood? You said the area is poor, and it isn't always safe, but you aren't poor. How come you choose to stay here?" I'm still shaken by what happened to Ted and me, and if it were me, I'd be looking for a reason to move anywhere but here.

Eugene sighs and scratches his chin while his face molds into a frown.

"Did I ask the wrong question? I'm sorry if I did. Maybe that wasn't polite."

"No, Scott, it's a fair question, especially after what happened to you today. It can be hard to explain, but I think you can understand. We didn't buy this house because we loved the neighborhood. Gloria and I have talked about moving someplace better off, maybe even someplace in the suburbs like your family, but that's easier said than done."

"How so? I don't see what you mean."

"Have you ever heard the term 'redlining' before?"

I shake my head.

"I'm not surprised. Redlining is when real estate agents, banks, and insurance companies refuse to allow people of all colors to move into certain neighborhoods. The real estate agents will only show them houses in parts of town where other colored people live. Even if colored people can afford to live elsewhere, banks won't loan them money, or they charge extra-high interest rates that make home loans far more expensive. Insurance companies won't insure houses to people of color, or, like the banks, will only do so at a higher price. That's why in cities like Los Angeles we have entire areas where people of only one color tend to live instead of the people being spread out more evenly."

As Eugene explains redlining, I remember back to what Elaine and I spoke about several weeks ago. She said her parents were considering moving because a few Black families had bought homes in their neighborhood, and they feared property values would plummet as a result. It sounds like this might be part of the reason why.

I'm also a little upset that redlining happens, and I've never even heard of it. "That sounds horrible. It sounds like something that should be illegal," I tell Eugene.

"Yes, it should be. But it isn't. Gloria and I probably would move somewhere else if all things were equal, but they aren't equal. Not when it comes to housing, at any rate."

This goes against what I'd learned about America. I remember learning about Dr. King in civics classes at school, of course. I graduated high school in the spring of 1965, a year after the Civil Rights Act had passed Congress. The Voting Rights Act became a law in the summer of '65. Because of those two things, I'd believed that America now treated all its people equally. Discrimination was over, and everyone could vote. What more could people ask for?

But it appears that isn't the whole story. Some forms of discrimination live on. How many others are there that I don't even realize exist?

"I never knew about that, Mr. Williamson," I say after thinking his words over for a moment. "Now I know why you frowned at my question. I thought I might've asked something too personal. Everything today has me pretty shook up, I guess."

"That's not your fault. Sometimes, a person can only learn about something when they experience it for themselves. I'm glad you won't have to worry about redlining when you decide to buy your

The Williamson House

own home. It's a practice that needs to end, and I hope that someday it will."

While driving home with Ted, we're both quiet. As I drive, I wonder how many other forms of discrimination continue that I've never heard of or experienced because of my color.

I also reconsider what I have believed about Dr. King. Like most people I hung around in high school, I supported his efforts to end segregation and get the vote for Black people. Not only because fair is fair, and I hated to see people treated badly who'd done nothing to deserve it, but also because of the dignified way in which King lived his life. I mean, when I turned on the television and watched Black people getting swept down the street by fire hoses or attacked by police dogs in Birmingham, that was too much. No one deserves that, especially when all they want to do is vote in elections, which they should've been allowed to do all along.

Once King and his supporters had secured the vote in 1965, however, many of the people I knew changed their views on King. The Civil Rights Movement had done what it sought to do, right? Why did he continue to demonstrate and give speeches? While I was in Vietnam, I heard that King had spoken against the war several times. He wasn't attacking me personally, granted, but still, I believed in the war and resented it when he called the reasons for the war into question.

Likewise when I learned about his campaign for poor people in Chicago. That went well beyond voting and putting an end to segregation, and I wasn't sure why King wanted to get involved with the poverty issue, either.

But after talking with Eugene earlier this evening, what King was doing makes more sense to me. If one reason so many Black people lived in poor neighborhoods was because no one would sell them homes anyplace else, that wasn't their fault. And, like keeping people from voting, it wasn't fair, either. And I hadn't realized that redlining even existed.

When we reach our apartment complex and step inside, Ted asks, "You thinkin' what I'm thinkin', Sticks?"

"What's that?"

"We should probably stay home tomorrow and watch television to see what happens around the country. I have a feeling it's gonna be dramatic. Maybe tragic, too."

I nod. "Yeah, that's probably true. Say, I think I'm gonna turn in early tonight, see if I can get a little extra rest."

"I dig that, Scott. Dig that," Ted says quietly.

"I owe you, buddy."

"You don't owe me. You'd a done the same for me. Hell, you already have done the same for me."

I walk toward my bedroom but then turn around. "Ted, can I ask you about something?"

"Of course, man."

"You didn't say much tonight. Are you mad about King's murder, too?"

"Yeah. Absolutely. Reverend King is probably the most important Black person to ever live in the United States. More famous than Frederick Douglass or W.E.B. DuBois, even. He was dignified, brave, and nonviolent, too. But that was too much for America, and White America killed him. He was the most peaceful leader Black people have ever had, and White America killed him."

"What do you mean by 'White America?' The police haven't caught the killer yet, have they?"

"Maybe they haven't caught the guy who pulled the trigger, no, but White America did it. White America killed Dr. King when it started to ignore his message. When he linked discrimination and racism to war, poverty, and militarism, White America stopped listening and got angry. You ever hear Reverend King's speech at Riverside Church last year?"

I shake my head.

"My dad saved it for me to read. King spoke about how the resources used to fight the war for the landlords of Vietnam was stealing the resources that we could use to fight poverty here in America. That's when I started to think he was going to die soon. I knew that White folks wouldn't stand for anyone questioning their wars or pointing out how war makes poverty worse here at home."

Ted and I have never spoken about this side of his life before. I didn't know he was a strong civil rights supporter, although now that I've met his father, it surprises me less.

"I had no idea, Ted. I'm sorry."

"I'm not blamin' you, Sticks. Neither Dad or I blame people like you. I know you want to do right. But some things are different for you and me, you know? You said you'd never heard of redlining before, but I grew up with it in my face. Even before I knew that redlining was the word for what I saw, I lived it every day. And when I drive a car, I *never* go over the speed limit. Dad once got a ticket for going two miles per hour over the limit. Two miles per hour."

I think back to the drive to Inglewood this afternoon and how I consistently did five or ten over the limit, never worrying I might be going too fast.

Ted sighs and shakes his head. "I'm not even a very religious person. I go to church because it keeps my parents happy, and lots of friends from the old neighborhood still go. But Reverend King was the most Christian person this country has, and White people wouldn't allow that."

Instead of going to bed like I'd planned, I now grab two beers from the fridge and sit down by Ted on our couch. Popping the top on mine, I say, "How did your dad feel about you going to Vietnam, then? From what you've said, it seems like you must've been conflicted while we were over there. Your dad, too."

"More than once Dad told me I was foolish and should've enrolled in college so that I couldn't get drafted. But he also told me I was grown up enough to make my own decision. I told him I believed in America, and that having Black people prove ourselves against the communists was another way to help the movement."

"Do you still feel that way?"

"I used to, even after some of the things we saw over there, but after this, man, I don't know anymore."

Ted takes a long drink of beer and shakes his head before continuing. "Now I know why one guy from my old neighborhood decided to move to Oakland and join those Black Panthers they've got up there. I don't think I'd ever do that myself, but now I understand better why he did it. Maybe he wasn't as crazy as I thought at first."

I've heard of the Black Panthers, of course, mostly because of my mother's negative remarks about them as vigilantes who take the law into their own hands. After tonight, I'm starting to suspect that might not be the whole story of who they are.

"I'm not sure what to say, Ted. I mean, when the mob came after me today, I thought I was dead. Even after your barber friend helped us, and I got done being scared, I was furious because I never did anything to any of those people. It looked to me like a bunch of out-of-control, angry Black people who hated me for being White."

"That might be true. I know a few young guys who hate all White people. Even though I don't agree with that, I understand it."

"But that's a problem, isn't it? I didn't do anything to those people. If they're angry, shouldn't they take out their anger on the people who make their lives miserable rather than the first White person they come across?"

"In a perfect world, I suppose they would, yeah, but they can't touch the people who own the system, can they? Besides, you remember Nam. How many guys did we meet who shot at people without knowing if they were VC? They wanted payback because they'd taken fire in that area, so they suspected anyone they met was with Charlie."

"That makes sense," I admit with a sigh. "Damn, this country is messed up sometimes, Ted. I almost died because of that today. My hands still shake when I think about it. We were in the wrong place at the wrong time, and it almost got me killed. Which ain't much different than in Nam, like you said."

"Do you ever wonder if the villagers we met looked at us like that?" Ted asks me earnestly. "Over there, we were the ones with the guns and the power. If they were in the wrong place at the wrong time, sometimes they got killed, and some soldiers didn't care. Maybe they were VC, maybe not, but some Americans didn't draw any distinction. How many times did we hear somebody say—"

"They all look the same to me," I finish Ted's sentence. "Damn. What else can you say? Just, damn." I run my hands through my hair and slouch back on the couch.

"Yeah, that about says it," Ted concurs. "I'm not sure what we can do about it, but I still think stayin' home tomorrow is a good move. You dig?"

"Agreed."

I stand, finish my beer, and start for bed. "Thanks again, Ted."

"You don't have to say anything, Sticks. Even though we're different on the outside, you're kinda like the brother I never had."

I nod. "Oh, try not to mention what happened today to Elaine or my parents, okay? Especially my mother. I don't want her to worry about me any more than she already does. Besides," I finish with a weak laugh, "if she hears about today, she won't want me to visit your folks again, and then I'll miss out on more of your mom's molasses cookies."

"Dig that."

Instead of sleeping, I lie in bed and hover on the edge of consciousness. I can't get over what Ted and I concluded about the people in Vietnam. *They all look the same to me.*

That's what my CO told me. They're all the same, and they all want to kill you. It also makes me recall the conversation I overhead after the old guy got thrown out of our Chinook in Nam.

We were offloading after the mission when a new GI who'd only joined us a couple weeks before pushed his way over.

"What the hell was that, man?" he asked the guy who did it.

"Damn gook was gettin' on my nerves."

"You shot his granddaughters, you bastard. Of course he's upset."

"So what? He was old. Dude was probably gonna die soon, anyway."

"What the hell's wrong with you?"

"Shut up. No one cares but you."

"That ain't true."

Now the two men stand chin to chin.

"Listen up, Cherry. All these gooks are the same. They'll all kill you. The sooner you learn that, the better off we'll all be."

I thought the guy who tossed the grandfather out of the Chinook was gonna take a swing at the other guy, but finally, our CO intervened and separated the two.

I sit up in bed with a start, shaking everywhere until I realize I'm still in the darkened bedroom of my apartment. Turning on my bedside lamp, I look at my alarm clock. Two twenty-seven, and now I'm wide awake. I go to the kitchen, in search of coffee instead of beer this time. Drinking coffee means I won't sleep much tonight, I realize, but I don't care. Even though I was in bed for about three hours, my body and my brain feel like it was three minutes. But I'm so on edge, I give up on sleep for now. At least drinking coffee in the kitchen doesn't lead to nightmares and flashbacks.

Chapter 11

The Days After

All day on Friday, April 5, Ted and I sit in front of our television watching ABC, CBS, and NBC in rotation to follow what's happening in the wake of Martin Luther King, Jr.'s murder. We do the same for most of Saturday, too. My dog Pete sits beside us the entire time. In fact, the only breaks I take on Friday are to give Pete short walks.

By the late afternoon of April 6, rioting begins. Washington, D.C., and Chicago are the worst, but places like Baltimore, Cincinnati, Pittsburgh, and Trenton are also on fire in spots. Even medium-sized cities like Raleigh and Greensboro in North Carolina have reported disturbances and damage. Many other places seem on the verge of erupting.

To our surprise and relief, Los Angeles is not among them. Our city gained infamy for the riot in Watts in 1965, but nothing serious has happened so far. A few other places where one might expect disturbances have avoided them, and help has come from unlikely sources. The singer James Brown spoke to the crowd during his concert in Boston last night, urging people to remain calm. New York City's mayor, John Lindsay, walked the streets of Harlem personally, trying to meet with people and reassure them.

But anger remains palpable, if what we read and see is any indication of the national mood, and the places where rioting has begun show no signs of letting up. Ted and I have finally turned the television off Saturday afternoon when Elaine comes over to check in with us.

The first thing she says after walking through the door is, "Ugh. I had to get out of the house. My parents are driving me crazy today."

Pete hops down from the couch to give Elaine a welcoming lick. "Hi there, old Pete," she says while giving him a hearty ear scratch.

"You been watching about King on TV, too?" I ask her.

"Yes. My parents are furious, and I needed to get away from them."

"They're furious about Reverend King's death?" Ted asks hopefully.

Elaine looks down and shakes her head. "No. I'm sorry, Ted, but my parents don't like Dr. King. They're furious about seeing disturbances on television, and they keep saying how police should shoot all the rioters. Even before he spoke publicly against the war, my parents hated King. They believe the nonsense about him being a communist agent and all that. Sometimes they call him Martin Luther Coon."

"I'm surprised they'll allow you to come over here," Ted replies.

"Besides that I'm old enough to go where I want, they don't know you're Black," Elaine says, breaking an ironic smile. "I told them you were Scott's roommate and let them draw their own conclusions."

"Still, it's a little disappointing to hear that they're so angry," Ted says, even though Elaine's clever ruse draws a bit of a smile from him, too.

"I thought they'd finally calmed down this evening, but then the news reported that the Black Panthers engaged in a shootout with police in Oakland."

"We finally turned off the news this afternoon," I admit. "It got to be too much, and we had to do something else for a while, so we missed hearing about that."

The Days After

"I know it's hard to hear that my parents hate one of your heroes," Elaine says, addressing Ted in a sympathetic voice. "My parents are both the children of Arkies, you know, and some of the prejudices of my grandparents rubbed off on them."

"What's an Arkie?" Ted wonders. "I've never heard that term."

"Arkies are people from Arkansas. They moved to California during the drought and dust of the 1930s. Enough of them moved all at once that the group got a nickname. It wasn't considered a compliment, either, but some Arkies accepted the name, and a few still wear it like a badge of stubborn pride."

"I've heard worse nicknames, both here and in Vietnam," Ted grunts. Neither of us need to ask him to clarify.

"Will you be okay, Ted, while Scott and I go to dinner with his parents tonight?" Elaine asks.

"I don't see why not. My plan was to lie low this weekend, but I've had about all the news I can take. I'll probably go for a walk after eating my own dinner. Our neighborhood is quiet."

"How is Ted doing, Scott?" my mother asks once we're seated at dinner. She's cooked everyone a steak to go with salad and some bread from Dad's bakery. "And don't forget to eat up. We've got apple pie for dessert."

"He's okay, I guess. I mean, he's sad that Dr. King died, but we're happy nothing violent has taken place in Los Angeles."

I've decided not to mention to my parents or Elaine what almost happened to me on Thursday evening. That stays between Ted and me for now. Besides, Elaine seems preoccupied now that we've sat down for dinner. She's eating very slowly and picking at her green salad, like she isn't hungry.

Mom continues, saying, "Yeah, I guess he probably has to feel sad, even after King turned against America and came out in opposition to the war. I don't blame Ted that he wants to stick with his people right now, though, even after King betrayed brave soldiers like him."

"That's not what he told me today—" I start to say, but Mom cuts me off.

"I just hope that people don't lump Ted in with the rioters, hooligans, and thugs I've been watching on the television these past two days. I'd hate to see that happen. Ted's a good young man, always so polite when he answers the phone, and I'd hate to see anyone blame him by association for what's happening right now."

"Have you considered people might have a reason for being angry—" I try to say, but again I'm cut off. I notice my father has stopped chewing his food.

Mom continues, oblivious to the looks around the table. "I mean, I hated to see King murdered and all, but I think America is better off without him. His statements about the war in Vietnam were so badly off target and ignorant, he was doing more harm than good."

Even my father is looking askance at my mother now.

"Just stop," I growl. "Just stop talking for once when you have no clue, all right?"

Mother pauses with a dinner roll halfway to her mouth and turns and stares. "What did you say to me?"

"You want to know why Ted went to Vietnam instead of going to college?" I ask her. "It's because he believes in America but felt he needed to prove that Black people love their country as much as anyone else. To prove that, he risked being shot by the VC ten thousand miles from home. For that alone, he deserves your respect no matter what he chooses to believe.

"But you know what else? He shouldn't have to prove his patriotism. Neither you, or me, nor anyone else has the right to pass judgment on Black people. Why should anyone get to decide when they're acting properly or acting fully American? Being American isn't a club that has the right to admit groups of people when they meet the qualifications of groups who are already members."

Now my mother is looking at me like she can't believe I'd be so brazen as to question her. I'm a little surprised I said that myself, but my blood is up, and I go on.

The Days After

"And you know one more thing? When Ted and I talked about Reverend King's murder, we realized something. The way we soldiers treated the Vietnamese people has similarities to how Black people have been treated in this country. We set all the rules over there because we claimed the authority to do it, and most of us judged the Vietnamese by our standards."

"I can't believe I'm hearing this from you. That man, King, he betrayed America when he started speaking against the war. The same country you were brave enough to fight to save. How can you side with him?"

My mother's angry tone and deep scowl is warning me that I've crossed a line, but for once, I disregard that. I'm not going to shout at her like Lisa would, but I'm not backing down, either. Part of me wishes Lisa were here to help right now. She'd understand. When I glance at my father, I see a pained look on his face.

"I'm not 'siding with him,' as you put it, Mom. What I was trying to get you to see is that not everything that happens is simple. It's not always day and night. Ted loves America, too. He believes in America, but he wants to see the country treat all its people like full citizens. That's how he could fight in the war but still love Dr. King at the same time. The same is true of me. It's possible to love the United States but still want to see it do better at solving its problems. Don't you see that?"

Mom's withering glare tells me she doesn't see that. I try again. "You know how many times King was put in jail for peaceful protests, right? You remember when his home was bombed? When people in Chicago tried to stone him last year? He never fought back, and he wouldn't let his supporters fight back, either. That's brave in a way that I'll never be brave. Anyone who can put up with all the abuse that King did and stay a Christian and keep turning the other cheek, well, he deserves the chance to say what he wants."

Mother shakes her head. "Not when it comes to war, he doesn't. If you're a patriot, you support the war. People who don't aren't patriots. It's that simple."

Mom's now speaking in what I call her "final tone." It's the angry, insistent voice she uses when she won't hear any more argument and needs to have the final word. Well, this time she won't get it.

Even though my stomach is churning, I'm about to say something I'll regret later when my father speaks. "I don't believe it's that simple, Susan. I have trouble supporting this war, too, and I hope my patriotism is not in question."

Although my father speaks softly, without anger, his words cut the tension. Mom and I pause. I've never heard Dad use his war experience as a way of claiming respect before.

"When I fought the Germans over in Europe, one of the reasons I fought was because Germany was a fascist dictatorship where everyone had to believe certain things or else be judged traitors to the Fatherland. If the Germans had won the war, the whole world might've ended up like that. Yes, I enlisted in the Army because of Pearl Harbor, but as I learned more about Nazi Germany, I realized how disastrous it would be if Germany won. For me, and for some of the men I fought with, that was a good reason to fight. We didn't want to live in a country where only one point of view is allowed."

I don't think I've ever heard my father contradict my mother in front of anyone else. She's not used to it, either, if her open-mouthed stare is any indication. Mom mutters something under her breath and leaves the table, throwing her cloth napkin on the floor as she departs.

Elaine and I look to my dad to see what he'll do next. After a moment, he puts down his knife and fork. "I'll speak to your mother," he tells me quietly. "You and Elaine go ahead and finish your food."

Even though he's calm like always, I know it hurt Dad to have to say that to Mom. He's put on the thoughtful face he uses when thinking about something he'd rather not think about, his lips pressed together and his eyes down.

The Days After

"Go on, finish," he repeats. "This topic was bound to come up at some point, anyway. We might as well have everyone's thoughts out in the open," he states while he picks up Mom's napkin and carries his plate to the kitchen.

While Elaine and I drive home after dinner, she's quiet for a long time. Eventually she says, "I think I understand something better about you now, Scott."

This surprises me. I thought Elaine would ask about the argument at dinner. "What's that?" I ask nervously, not knowing if her next words will be a compliment or a concern.

"I misjudged how much you changed and grew up during your time in the Army. Back when we were in high school, you had a few arguments like that with your mom. But today you did it without shouting at her or getting out of control like you used to. You were disagreeing while she was arguing."

"I haven't shouted at her yet. I almost did. Several times."

"Yes. I could see your face twitch, and I knew you were angry on the inside. But you didn't lose control and shout. You almost did, but you didn't. I'm proud of you for that."

"Still, I wish the conversation hadn't turned out that way. I noticed you didn't eat all your food. I'm sorry I messed that up for you, but it seemed like I should stick up for Ted—and for Dr. King."

"That wasn't your fault at all, Scott."

"What do you mean?"

"I didn't have much appetite tonight. Even if dinner had been normal, I'm not sure I would've finished."

"Really? You've always had a good appetite."

"I know. Probably it's the stress of all the things at home that's bothering me."

I think about this for a while, and what I've observed about Elaine's weight loss since I got back from Vietnam. Perhaps things at her house are even worse than she's letting on. Still, I trust her. If she wants my help with that, she'll say so.

"I've realized something else, too," Elaine says quietly.

"What's that?"

Elaine's tone trips an alarm in my head. Usually, when she has something important to say, she says it with confidence.

"I've been thinking about some of the other ways you've changed from being in Vietnam and why they make me uncomfortable sometimes."

My heartbeat speeds up. I haven't had a girlfriend break up with me since my sophomore year of high school, but Elaine's quiet and serious tone makes me scared she's going in that direction.

"Do you want to talk about it now?" I ask nervously. Part of me is glad it's dark so that Elaine won't see my hands shaking on the steering wheel.

"Probably it's for the best, yeah."

I wait for her to begin.

"I realize now that you're a very different person than the guy I knew in high school. You've grown up much faster than I have, and sometimes when I'm around you, I don't know what to do because I feel inadequate."

That was not what I expected Elaine to say.

She takes a deep breath and goes on. "Like when you were speeding on the freeway a while back, and you told me you liked the rush of driving fast. Not only did you scare me that we might crash, but you also made me afraid that I can't make you happy anymore because I'll never be comfortable with doing things like that. If that's what you need to be happy, then I'm not good enough for you." Elaine's voice cracks at the end.

Her words speeding up, she continues. "I think that's one way that the war changed you—you like risky things now. That's partly why I said no when you suggested that I move into your apartment. It didn't seem to bother you that other people might disapprove of us living together, but it scared me.

"And here's the last thing that frightens me. I know that besides your flashbacks, you have nightmares sometimes when you sleep.

Ted mentioned that to me once because he worries about you, too. Because of that time at the beach when you stomped on my mermaids, I know he's telling me the truth, and that he's right to be worried about you.

"I guess I'm saying that I don't know how to help you with your flashbacks and your nightmares. If I can't do that, and I can't make you happy as your girlfriend because I'm not adventuresome enough, then I'm no good to you. I love you, Scott, but I'm scared that pretty soon you'll decide to leave me for another woman who's older and can relate to you better than I can."

That was *really* not what I expected Elaine to say. Even though we're almost back to my apartment, I pull over to the side of the street and park, so I can turn and face her.

I take her hands in mine and look Elaine in the face. "Elaine, have I ever said that I'm not happy spending time with you?"

"No."

"Have I ever told you that I blame you for my nightmares?"

"No."

"Did I accidentally imply to you that you need to be more adventuresome because the things we usually do are boring?"

"You've never said that, no."

I grip her hands tighter. "What if I told you that the three people who give me the greatest joy to spend time with are you, Pete, and my father, in that order?"

That brings a weak smile to Elaine's face, along with a little laugh.

"I must be doing something wrong, though," I say next, sitting back and staring through the windshield into the night.

"Why do you say that?" Elaine asks, not releasing my hands.

"If you were having all those doubts about me and how much I love you, that means I haven't been a very good boyfriend. If I were a better boyfriend, you'd know what I just told you beyond any question. I guess I need to keep working on being more open about how I feel. It seems like your fears are mostly because I'm so poor at that."

"I guess that's one more way that going to Vietnam has changed you. Maybe I need to help you talk about yourself instead of getting scared that you don't love me anymore just because you haven't said so lately."

"Here's how much I love you," I say while taking Elaine's head in my hands and leaning in to kiss her. I keep it up for several seconds before letting go. When I open my eyes and look at her, I see Elaine's shoulders relax and her warm smile replace the tentative one that she'd had a moment ago. Then I kiss her again.

"Please forgive me," she says.

"Forgive you for what?"

"For letting my doubts get the better of me. I shouldn't have let that happen. Sometimes lately I'm not sure what to think, and I get scared."

"Do you need another kiss to chase away any more doubts?"

"It couldn't hurt, just in case," she says warmly while leaning in.

When our kiss ends, I say. "I love you, Elaine. I've never stopped loving you, even if I struggle to show it sometimes. A lot of things are worrying you right now, I realize, but please, don't let that be one of them."

After one more kiss, I resume driving home. Elaine has her arm around my shoulder, which I realize she hasn't done in quite some time.

"Can I ask you one more question?" I say when we pull into a parking spot.

"What's that?"

"Why did you laugh when I said that you, Pete, and Dad were the people I enjoy seeing the most?"

"Because Pete is a dog. You might treat him like a person, and spend more time with him than with anyone but Ted, but he's still a dog."

The Days After

"Roger, copy that," I say with a grin. Then I notice the light in our apartment isn't on. Ted must've gone for a really long walk. I consider asking Elaine if she wants to come in and erase some more doubts, but she's already opened the door of my Corvette and is digging in her pocket for her car keys to drive home.

"You're sure you feel better?" I ask while getting out and locking my car door.

Elaine nods. "Hopefully, my folks will have finished arguing by now. Maybe that's part of the reason I was so nervous tonight, too. My parents have been together for nearly twenty-five years, but this is the worst I can ever remember them fighting."

"You know you can come over any time you need to, right? Call if you can, but if you can't call, just come over. The apartment will look cleaner if you call first, though."

That brings a wide smile. Neither Ted or I are likely to win awards for housekeeping, and we both know it. The main reason we ever clean anything is so that we won't be embarrassed when Elaine drops by.

"Good night, Scott. I love you."

"I love you, too."

When I go inside the apartment, I feel relieved. It's possible I've finally helped Elaine realize why parts of me have changed since being in Vietnam, and I think we just cleared up an issue that was clouding our relationship more than I realized.

I feel relieved, that is, until I get in the door, hit the lights, and see that Ted is home after all. He's on the couch with his head in his hands. When he looks up, I see his face is wet, and he's shaking.

"What happened?"

"Some White boys chased me in a truck when I went out after dinner."

"What? Why?"

"Don't know. All I heard was them White boys shouting about shooting looters, and then I heard a shotgun click. That's when I ran.

They chased me in their truck. I only got away because I hopped the fence into a schoolyard and hid there."

"Then what happened?"

"I hid for, I don't know how long, probably thirty minutes until things looked clear. When I was about to leave, a police car showed up, and two officers got out. I could overhear them from where I was hiding, and the one cop told his partner that several people in the neighborhood had reported a suspicious colored person on the school grounds. I didn't move because I was terrified what'd happen if they found me. After they left, I waited another thirty minutes before sneaking back here. I only got home four or five minutes ago."

"Damn. That's hard to believe. You're the one who got chased, and people thought *you* were the suspicious one?"

Ted puts his hands in his lap and bows his head, shoulders slumped. "It's hard for you to believe, maybe," he says quietly.

"What's that mean?"

Ted gives me another somber look.

Finally, I see his point. "This isn't the first time that's happened to you, is it?"

"It's the third time. The other two were in high school. Both other times the police picked me up off the streets because they claimed they had reports of suspicious people in the area, and I fit the description—tall and colored."

I stare, open-mouthed. Ted is among the kindest people I know and about the least likely to do anything suspicious or commit a crime.

Recovering and walking to the fridge, I ask him, "You want a beer? Maybe it'll help you calm down some."

"Nah. I don't think I'm gonna sleep tonight no matter what I do."

Popping the top on mine, I sit down beside him on our couch. "I'm sorry that happened to you. I don't know what else to say except you don't deserve that. This country is screwed up sometimes."

The Days After

"Nothing we do is gonna change that, either, from what I can tell."

When Ted speaks, he sighs and sags down even deeper on the couch.

"Let's talk about something else. How did your dinner go?" he says after a moment.

"Not so good. Mom and I got in an argument, so we didn't make it all the way through dinner."

"What about?"

"She still holds a grudge against Dr. King because he spoke against the war. To her, anyone who does that is being disloyal, no matter what other good things they've done."

Ted puts his head back in his hands.

"I know it makes her sound worse than she really is. When White people speak against the war, she gets upset with them, too. I tried to explain that sometimes things are complicated, and that someone can like America without agreeing with everything that the country does. But she thinks that war overrules any other considerations."

"What did your dad do?"

"I couldn't believe it, but he took my side. I don't think he's ever straight-up told my mother she was wrong before. Not in front of anyone else, at least. So, he must've felt strongly about it."

Ted straightens up after a moment. "I'm gonna try and get some rest, even though it's probably pointless. Maybe I'll feel less scared tomorrow. I'm glad of one thing, though."

"What's that?"

"That I work at the same place as you do so that you can drive us to work. I'd be too scared to walk or take the bus right now."

Chapter 12

Elaine's House

In the weeks after the death of Martin Luther King, Jr., things in Los Angeles return to something like normal. The city never experienced rioting, thank goodness, although I later read that violence broke out in more than one hundred cities after King was murdered. Why Los Angeles wasn't among them, I'll never know.

Tonight I'm going to Elaine's house for dinner, which I haven't done for quite some time. She tells me her parents still argue frequently, but they've promised not to tonight. I've finished shaving and cleaning up after work when Ted walks into the kitchen.

"Sticks, how do you do that?"

"Do what?"

"If I shaved twice in one day, my whole face would bleed, no matter how gentle I was with the razor."

I laugh. "One more way I'm kinda lucky, I guess."

"Are you square with your mom again, Sticks? You mentioned you got into it with her pretty good a few weeks ago."

"She's never brought up our argument since we had it. I doubt she's changed her mind about King, or her belief that a person can think a war is a bad idea and still love their country, but she rarely holds grudges. Not against family members, anyway," I finish with a little laugh. "If I were President Johnson, her attitude might be different."

"Yeah, I suppose so."

"Maybe this isn't the best time to ask, but I notice you've been spending a lot of time on your models and with your music lately. You doin' okay?"

"Mostly. Sometimes."

"That doesn't sound okay."

"I'm not scared of anyone in particular. But I'm nervous about going out still. If I didn't have to work, I'm not sure I'd wanna leave the apartment."

Although I'm sad that Ted still feels scared, I get it, so I nod. "That's a shame. I don't know what else to say."

"You think I'm okay with the boss still? I've been kinda quiet in the garage, too, and he doesn't say too much to me. Business hasn't been so good lately, either, and we're the two newest people. I'm afraid he's gonna let me go."

"Are you kidding? The boss loves you. You're the best mechanic he's got. He'd let me go before he'd get rid of you, and he'd be right to do it."

"You sure about that?"

"Everyone knows you're better at fixing things than I am."

"Is that the most important thing when it comes to letting people go?"

I pause before answering. Ted's got the morose look on his face he sometimes gets when talking about people and their motives.

Finally, I say, "You think he'd let you go instead of me because of your color?"

"I can't say for sure, but the thought has crossed my mind. What do you think?"

Once again, Ted has reminded me of why we sometimes view life differently because of our backgrounds. The first thing to come to my mind was that the man who owns the garage would make his decisions based on talent. He has money at stake, after all.

For Ted, however, the first thing he thought of is that skin color would be the deciding factor. A few months ago, I wouldn't have put much stock in that. But after the last few weeks, I'm starting to see why Ted defaults to this point of view.

"Boy, I hope that isn't true," I say. "I mean, why would the boss have hired you to start with if he was prejudiced?"

"I don't know, but I'm the only colored person in the garage, and not everyone at work likes me. Maybe some of the other guys are talking to him about me behind my back. That happens, you know, like some guys tried to do to the officers over in Nam."

"You've got a point. I'll keep my ears open and see if I can find anything out. The guys at work know we're friends, but maybe they'll let something slip when you aren't around."

Ted nods. "Hopefully, it's all my imagination. But damn, Sticks, these days I'm getting suspicious of almost everybody. A lot of days, I don't know what to think."

I'm still replaying my conversation with Ted when I pull into the driveway of Elaine's house. Her house is similar to the one my parents own except it's a one-floor rambler with garage attached. But the tiny front yard is the same, the palm trees in the driveway are the same, and the street with cookie-cutter houses on either side looks the same as where my parents live.

What little lawn exists is perfect, however. Elaine's father mows his grass every Sunday, no matter what, and waters it religiously from March until October. The inside of the house is always spotless, too. In the minds of Elaine's parents, even the battle against communists takes a back seat to the battle against germs. It doesn't surprise me at all when I go to the front door and see a new coat of dark green paint on the siding.

I expect Elaine to greet me when I ring the doorbell, but instead it's her mother. Mildred Collier is as typical a suburban housewife as one can ever meet. Her husband, Ed, refuses to allow her to work, so she spends her days minding the house, cooking, and reading magazines and newspapers. Elaine sometimes jokes that Mildred has modeled her life on the women she finds on the cover of

Elaine's House

Reader's Digest, *McCall's*, and the *Ladies Home Journal*. At times, I think her apron is part of her daily outfit, like other people wear a shirt or pants, but the upshot is that her pies and roasts are second to none.

Another surprising thing about Mildred is that she's taller than her husband by several inches, standing just over six feet. That makes her the same height as me. It's not often I look eye to eye with a woman.

"Come in, Scott, come in," she says, gesturing me inside. "I'm afraid I've got bad news, though. Elaine is very sick again today. I'm not sure if she'll join us for dinner. But you're welcome to stay, of course, even if she doesn't."

"Is it the fevers?"

Mildred nods. "They seem to be worse lately. Ed finally scheduled an appointment with a doctor for her. Elaine is going in next week whether she feels better or not. For a girl her age to get sick as often as she does isn't normal."

"How has her appetite been?"

"Weak. I was hoping having you over tonight would help, and I fixed plenty of food, but it looks like we'll be eating leftovers for a while."

I wince and shake my head. That means Elaine has probably lost more weight. "Can I go talk to her for a while?"

"Of course, you can, although she might not be awake."

I nod and start toward Elaine's bedroom.

"Oh, and Scott?"

"Yes, Mildred?"

"Could you do one thing for me while you're here?"

"Probably. What do you have in mind?"

Mildred leans in close to speak softly. "Has Elaine told you about Glen and what he wants to do?"

"You mean about dropping out of high school to go to Vietnam?"

She nods. "Would you mind speaking to him about Vietnam?"

"I can speak to him, sure. What do you want me to say?"

"I don't want you to talk about anything in particular. I feel like Glen doesn't have a good picture of what being a soldier is like, that's all. Ed fought in the Pacific against Japan, but Glen says that was so long ago that it's different than Vietnam. You've been to Vietnam, and I want you to tell him about what you did, so he'll have a clearer idea of what he's getting into if he joins the Army. Maybe he'll listen to you more than he does Ed or me. You know how that is for teenage boys sometimes."

"That sounds easy enough. I can tell him what the Army is like."

"I'm worried that he has a romanticized idea about Army life and war. Glen likes to watch war movies on television. He admires you, though, so I hope you can get through to him."

"Sure, no problem. Is he in his bedroom, too?"

"Yeah, finishing his homework, I hope. Don't get me wrong, Scott. Ed and I support the war unconditionally. You know that. We're proud that Elaine picked a boyfriend who does, too. But I think Glen at least needs his high school diploma. If he wants to enlist after that, then God bless him, and we'll both back his decision. I want him to make his choice in an informed way, though, and maybe you can help him with that."

"I'll give it a shot," I tell Mildred while walking toward Elaine's bedroom. At the last second, though, I decide to detour and talk with Glen first.

I pass *it* on my way. The skull. Even though I've seen it dozens of times, I'm still taken aback every time I walk by.

As Ed tells the story, he saw a lot of difficult combat in the Pacific Theater of World War 2. Capturing islands after the Japanese had dug in was no easy task. After one particularly tough fight, his platoon came across a number of Japanese soldiers whose bodies had been destroyed by artillery. Ed took the skull as a souvenir and sent it to Mildred, whom he'd started dating before going off to war. The skull has occupied a place of pride on their bookshelf ever since.

Elaine's House

Even though I shouldn't by now, I still shiver when I see it. I've never gotten used to the idea of taking body parts as war souvenirs. Knives or guns, absolutely. But things like skulls, scalps, teeth, or trigger fingers? I wince at the thought.

What makes the skull even stranger is that someone passing Ed on the street would never guess he'd do something like that. I mean, he's a manager at a local drug store. Ed wears a suit and tie to work. He fills out papers and keeps track of inventory for a living. It's not as though he lives off in the woods by himself, laying boobytraps for the Soviets for when they invade. How could someone who seems so normal collect human body parts and proudly keep them on display for twenty-five years?

Realizing I have no answer for that question, I stop outside Glen's bedroom door. I give a soft knock.

"Come in," Glen calls. "Oh, hey, it's you, Scott. It's been a while."

"Yeah, it sure has. How've you been?"

Glen is neither tall like his mother or short like his father, but right in between, about five-nine or -ten. Immediately, I notice he's shaved most of his hair away, as if he's already in boot camp. A math book is open, and I see paper on Glen's desk, but he's looking out the window and drumming with his pencil when I enter.

"I'm doin' okay. Just bored of living in Los Angeles, is all. This algebra is pointless, too."

"You're almost a senior in high school. I thought that age was supposed to be fun."

"Well, I just want to get out of here. I'm tired of this place, you know?"

Since I'm not sure how to begin the conversation, but it's headed in that direction anyway, I say "Elaine and your mom tell me you want to join the Army."

"Yeah, I plan to do what you did. I wanna go to Vietnam and waste some commies." While Glen says it, he pulls his pencil to his eye and looks over it like he's aiming a gun.

"I see."

"I'm gonna drop out of school as soon as I turn eighteen."

"You can take your time, I think."

"What do you mean, Scott?"

"Your birthday is in October, right?"

Glen nods.

"You'd graduate next June. That's about eight months from your birthday. Call it a hunch, but I have a feeling the war will still be going on by next June."

"Why do you say that? Aren't we whupping the red bastards? Didn't you hear how high the body count was in March?"

American military commanders have started a practice called the "body count" to measure progress in Vietnam. Their idea is that if Americans kill enough VC soldiers, Charlie will give up eventually, so a high body count is the path to victory.

I can't say if the body count is a good strategy. One thing I know is that it's been going on for a while and hasn't produced victory yet. Another thing I know is that whatever numbers Glen sees on the news, the numbers are too high. "If it's dead and Vietnamese, it's VC," is a phrase I heard often from my CO.

"No, I don't always follow the body count anymore," I admit after a moment.

"Why not? Don't you want to know how well we're doing?"

"I've been focusing on learning how to be a civilian again. It's not quite as easy as most people think."

"What do you think? Should I try to fly in helicopters like you, or should I drive a tank instead?"

Obviously, the hint I just dropped made no impression, so I try again. "We don't use a whole lot of armor in Vietnam. And flying in a chopper can be dangerous. If you take fire while in the air, it's a long way down."

"Or maybe I can fly a fighter jet. Those things are so fast, Charlie would never see me coming."

Elaine's House

Now Glen has his hands on an imaginary control wheel, veering this way and that. Strike two for me. I resolve to take one more swing, since Elaine told me she agreed with Mildred and wants Glen to finish high school.

Since my subtle remarks have been ineffective, I decide on bluntness this time. "Glen, have you thought about what you'll do after your tour?"

He looks at me as if I'd suggested he read a book about cats. "I'll enlist again, of course. I plan to keep fighting until America's got Charlie whupped. We can't let the Reds get the best of us, and they won't if I have anything to say about it."

"What I'm trying to say is that the war will end someday. When it does, you'll need to do something. And you'll have a lot more choices if you've finished high school, that's all."

"What's the matter, Scott? Don't you want me to serve my country like you did?"

"I don't presume to tell you what to do. All I'm saying is that if you join the Army, that'll be a few years of your life. What you do after the Army will be several decades of your life. That's worth keeping in mind."

"Oh, all right, then."

I leave and close the door behind me. Damn. Was I that thick-headed and single-minded just thirty months ago? I sure hope not.

Turning around, I knock gently at Elaine's door. "I'm awake," comes the answer. I turn the knob and step inside.

My girlfriend has her blankets pulled up to her chin even though it's a warm April evening. A plaid quilt covers her, too.

"Oh, it's you, Scott. I'm so sorry, but I don't think I'll be at dinner tonight. I feel terrible."

I stand by Elaine's dresser with the big, full-length mirror beside it. She's strewn T-shirts and blue jeans here and there, and the tiny wooden jewelry box on top of the dresser has a small silver necklace hanging out of one drawer. The drapes are open, letting in the evening sun so that it falls across Elaine's body. I'm sure the light isn't helping, but she looks exceptionally pale.

"What's the matter?"

"I've got this fever again, and no matter what I do, I can't get warm enough." Elaine coughs and grimaces.

"It started this morning?"

"Yesterday."

"You've been in bed since then?"

"Pretty much, yeah. Except I can't sleep very well because lying down kinda hurts. Breathing isn't too comfortable when I'm on my back. So, mostly I've sat in the rocking chair in the living room and tried watching television."

"Lying down hurts, too?"

"It didn't used to, but now it does. It hurts a little bit right here."

Elaine slowly extracts her hand from the covers and waves it over her breastbone.

"Damn. That sounds really bad. I'm glad your parents are finally taking you to the doctor. Do you think you might have malaria? That's what your symptoms sound like to me."

"I don't even know what that is."

"A couple guys I knew in Vietnam suffered from it. They got these awful chills. The chills were so bad, some guys could barely get out of bed. I mean, I'm talking healthy guys in the prime of life who could barely walk around their barracks on their own. And the chills come and go, like what you're fighting. Mosquitos spread malaria around, I think."

"How bad is it?"

"Well, it can kill people if they don't treat it, but I think that treating malaria is easy. You take quinine. It might take a while, but people nearly always get better."

"I don't care how long it takes, I just want to feel myself again. My heart is still set on finding more work, so that I can move to my own place, but how can I work if I can't even get out of bed?"

"I'm sure the doctors will know what to do. Once they've made a diagnosis, it shouldn't take long."

"Scott! Dinner!" I hear Mildred call out from the other side of the house.

"You want me to bring you something?" I ask Elaine.

She shakes her head. "I don't know if I could keep it down, anyway."

I squeeze my eyes closed for a moment. It hurts to see the woman I love so sick that she can't even get out of bed or eat food.

"You want me to come with you when you go see the doctor?"

"I don't think you need to take off work for that. You don't need to be there. I already know how much you care."

I nod and turn to go. "Oh, by the way, I tried to talk to your brother about finishing high school. I know how important that is to you."

"Did it work?"

I shake my head this time. "I think his heart is set. Maybe I can try again if you want—approach the conversation from another angle. But what I said tonight sure didn't have much effect on him."

"Thanks for trying," Elaine says, but her eyelids are drooping.

"I love you."

"I love you back."

Chapter 13

My Latest Mission

I don't see my sister as often as I'd like, but today we're meeting at the same coffee shop where we met on New Year's Day. She called yesterday and asked if I could get together. It's a Saturday in the middle of May, so I said sure. I even pick the same seat as last time—near the large, plate-glass windows that give a view of the street.

Lisa didn't say anything unusual on the phone, so I'm shocked when she walks in. She's wearing a bright yellow cage dress and has her hair pulled back, which is normal enough, but the black eye and bruises on the left side of her face certainly aren't. Lisa wears lots of makeup and keeps her dark sunglasses on until she sits down across from me, but when she takes the glasses off, it's obvious what's happened to her.

"Jesus Christ, Lisa, who hit you?"

"My latest ex-boyfriend."

"That sonofabitch."

"Yeah, that describes him pretty well."

"Do you want me to pummel the bastard for you?"

"Ease up there, Scott. He outweighs you by forty pounds, minimum. Your nickname is Sticks, remember?"

"I don't care. He didn't spend fourteen months in the jungle looking for Charlie."

My statement has plenty of bluster and bravado, it's true, but Lisa and I were close growing up, and my blood surges at the thought that a man got rough with her.

Despite her injuries, Lisa grins. "Thanks, little brother, but leave him be. I probably deserve a slice of the blame, considering how much we both had to drink two nights ago. My face will get better. Nothing's broken. And besides, he's probably still icing his balls after the kick I gave him on my way out the door."

"Damn," I say, both at my sister's actions and because she told me about what she'd done to another man's genitalia. Close or not, I don't recall ever talking with her about *that* while growing up.

She smiles again. "I was going to call you and ask to get together today, anyway, even had our fight never taken place."

"You're sure you don't want me to make him sorry?"

"It's over, Scott. Let it go. We have something more important to talk about than that chump. You remember what's happening soon, right?"

I bite my lip gently while thinking for a few moments. Whatever it is, it isn't coming to me.

I'm about to give up when a woman brings us the coffees we ordered. I thank her off-handedly, ready to resume my futile musings, when the woman says, "It's good to see you again. Scott, right?"

Her comment forces me to look up and pay attention. The waitress looks familiar—she's short with long blond hair, a button nose, a few extra pounds, and sea green nail polish. But I can't place her. "Have we met before?" I finally ask.

The woman's smile dims a touch. "You were here on New Year's Day. We talked for a little while. I'm Sandra."

It all comes back to me as soon as she says it. I helped a woman who forgot her money by paying for her coffee. Sandra was at her second day of work and didn't know what to do when a customer couldn't pay. She was nervous, and we talked for five or ten minutes while I helped her calm down.

"Right, right, I do remember that now." I recite her the details that just ran through my mind to prove it. "You've got your feet under you now, it looks like," I tell her in conclusion. It's an awkward statement, I know, but Sandra took me by surprise. I'd forgotten her completely.

"My goodness, what happened to your sister's face?" she gasps after taking a look at Lisa. Then, "I'm so sorry. Maybe it's not my business to ask."

"It's fine," Lisa tells her. "I got in a slugging match with my jerk of an ex-boyfriend. But I gave as good as I took."

"I'm so sorry. I still remember the first day you came in," Sandra says. "I thought that you were Scott's girlfriend."

"That's some memory you must have, Sandra," I tell her. "We were just two people who had coffee five months ago, and you still remember us."

"I remember everything because you were so kind to me, Scott. It was my second day, and I was horribly nervous. But you took the time to have such a nice conversation with me and make me feel good, even though you didn't have a reason to. I've never forgotten that because I didn't believe I was cut out for holding a job at the time. I didn't think I'd ever see you again so that I could tell you thanks, but now I can. So, thank you."

This wasn't what I expected when Lisa said she wanted to get coffee, but the second surprise of today is much better than the first.

"You're welcome," I tell her. "I'm happy that I helped. You looked like you were having a rough day, so I did what anyone should have done."

"I want you to know how much you helped me, and I've never forgotten it. But maybe I should let you get back to whatever you were talking about."

"Actually, maybe you could stick around for a moment," Lisa says out of the blue.

I look at my sister. The last time we were here, she got upset at me for talking to Sandra for too long.

My Latest Mission

"Scott may need your help with something," Lisa tells Sandra with a smile. "Before you came over, he was about to admit he didn't know what important thing is happening in a couple weeks."

"It's true," I say, conceding the obvious.

"Mom and Dad's twenty-fifth wedding anniversary," Lisa says in answer to my puzzled look. "We should do something special for them."

"That's a great idea. What did you have in mind?" I've always been lousy at remembering things like that.

"Their anniversary is in three weeks. Even you ought to be able to think of something fun to do in three weeks. Write it on your calendar when you get home, so you don't forget again."

"Thanks for the vote of confidence."

"The twenty-fifth anniversary is called the silver anniversary, so I'm thinking we should get them both something silver—a pocket watch, a bracelet, a necklace, maybe a picture frame, something like that. I'll take care of the gifts, you plan the party. Can you handle that, Scott?"

I nod.

"You're sure?"

"Yeah. As long as you don't find another hippy boyfriend in the meantime, I'm sure Mother will be happy with whatever we do," I say with a laugh. Lisa replies with a sardonic smile.

"Why are you telling me about this?" Sandra ventures nervously.

Lisa smiles a genuine smile at Sandra. "I was hoping you could give my brother and me an idea on where to get food. I'm not much of a cook, and I know that he isn't, either, so I wanted to ask you for a suggestion of where to get catering."

Sandra smiles and relaxes her shoulders. "Oh, that. I wondered why you needed me for anything. Let me think . . . um . . . well . . . oh yeah, I know a great place. Right down the street we have this bakery, and it sells *the best* pastries. The owner is such a nice man. I go in there two or three times a month just for the doughnuts."

We both laugh.

"Why is that funny?" Sandra asks, and I notice she blushes a little and looks at herself self-consciously. Maybe she thinks we're laughing because she's a little overweight?

I don't know if Lisa noticed Sandra's look, but she says, "Our dad owns that bakery. That's what's funny. We'll be sure to tell him you like the doughnuts, though."

"Oh, I get it now. For a minute I thought you were laughing because my suggestion was silly or dumb."

"Not at all," I say to Sandra gently. "Any other time, it'd be a great idea. But it would seem weird to ask my dad to cater his own party."

At that moment, some customers come through the front door of the coffee shop. I watch Sandra look in their direction and greet them.

"Well, thank you for trying to help," Lisa tells Sandra. "Like my brother said, if it were any other circumstance, we'd go with your suggestion."

"Okay, that was a little awkward," I say to Lisa while Sandra moves off to see to the new arrivals.

"Didn't hurt anything, did it? She seemed really grateful to you, so I was trying to give her an easy way to think she'd returned the favor."

"Fair enough. Do you think we embarrassed her, though?"

"Embarrassed her? How?"

"After we laughed, she looked at herself like she was worried about something. I thought that she maybe thought we were teasing her for eating too many doughnuts."

Lisa sits back and folds her hands. "I never even thought of that. Sandra doesn't seem too overweight to me. But you might be right. Hopefully she doesn't still think so, after we had a chance to explain ourselves. Now, if there's someone who's had a few too many doughnuts, that'd be my ex-boyfriend. I'm still trying to figure out what I ever saw in him to begin with, other than he seemed like he had a good sense of humor when we met."

"It's those damn hippies. You really ought to stay away from those commie-lovers," I say in a poor imitation of my mother's voice. That earns another sardonic smile from my sister.

"Oh, speaking of hippy boyfriends, a friend wanted me to ask you something," she says.

"Go on."

"He wants you to speak at a war protest meeting he's planned for next month. I told him you'd never do it, but he seems to think if he can talk to you long enough, you'll come around."

"That's not going to happen."

"I know. I told him that, but he insisted I ask, so I did. He's rather stubborn about such things, and sometimes it's easier to tell him okay, even when you know what he wants is pointless."

Looking down, I see my coffee cup is empty. "Well, I guess I'd better go get working on that party."

"Don't swing and miss on this one, Scott. I don't think we need to keep it secret, but we should do something fun and memorable."

Chapter 14

Disaster

The day after my parents celebrate their silver wedding anniversary, I spend the day on my couch crying.

Elaine called me in the morning. Her doctor finally had a diagnosis of what was causing her fevers: Hodgkin lymphoma. The lymphoma had spread into her lungs. Neither me or anyone else ever thought Elaine might have a type of cancer. Who ever heard of someone in their twenties who got cancer?

Through her tears, she explained to me that it's a rare cancer, but people her age sometimes have it. Then she added that her lymphoma seemed to be very aggressive from how far it had already spread. When I asked her what the chances were for people in her situation, she broke down and didn't have the heart to tell me. All I could get out of her from between her tears was that she was going on chemotherapy immediately and probably radiation therapy after that.

That was at the end of May. It's now November, and I'm sitting next to Elaine in her house with my arms around her. We're the only ones there. She's swaddled in blankets to cover the fact she's still got on the same clothes she wore two days ago when I came to visit.

My girlfriend scarcely resembles the person I knew when the year began. About half of her hair fell out after her radiation treatments, so she now keeps it very short, like mine, to hide how thin it's become. The laughter I used to see in her face is long gone, replaced by drawn skin and deep, dark bags under her eyes. Elaine told me she doesn't sleep much because the lymphoma in her lungs makes it tough to breathe comfortably when on her back. I don't know how much weight she's lost, but her clothes hang from her bony frame now. A bowl of untouched chicken noodle soup rests on the coffee table nearby.

"How did the results of your CT scan look today?" I ask her, my voice shaking.

Elaine looks at me and then puts her head back down. I hug her again but say nothing.

"The lymphoma remains progressive," she croaks after a moment. "It's still getting worse, not better."

I feel a tear drop onto my arm. "What else is there to try?" I ask, even though I know the answer.

"Nothing. My body hasn't responded to any of the treatments," Elaine says as more tears begin.

Neither of us has cried often over the past few months. To the end, we both held out hope that the next treatment would show progress and that Elaine would eventually recover. What else could we do? But this really is the end. No next treatment exists.

"I'm going to die, Scott, and I don't want to die. I had so many dreams of what I could do in life. I . . ." she starts to go on, but can't finish.

I pull Elaine's head to my chest and squeeze her shoulders. "You've been very brave all the way, Elaine." I can't bring myself to add the words "all the way to the end," even though we both know it's the end. "Maybe, sometimes, that's all a person can do," I finish lamely.

It's true that Elaine has been brave. Just now was the first time I've ever heard her admit the inevitable and feel sorry for herself. She's tried to go on with her life even though the chemotherapy and radiation left her feeling drained of energy and ill more days than not.

"Thank you for staying with me, Scott."

"Of course I stayed with you," I reply, rubbing her shoulders. "I never thought of leaving, and I'm not going to now, either."

"Some guys would've left a girlfriend who was sick and who wasn't getting better. Who isn't going to get better. But you've never left my side."

"That's because I love you. I always have. For six years I've been in love with you."

"Six years?"

"You're the whole reason I practiced to get better at the trumpet. The only reason I practiced when I was a freshman and sophomore was so that I could sit next to you every day."

Elaine gives a weak smile. "I thought that might've been the case, but I was never sure."

"It took me almost three years of high school to get the courage to ask you out. I still consider it the best thing I've ever done."

"And I almost didn't say yes. Luckily, I didn't listen to my friends who thought you were too awkward and skinny to be handsome," Elaine replies. She tries to smile at the fond memories, but I know my efforts to take her mind off her cancer diagnosis aren't working. For long intervals, her red eyes stare vacantly at the walls.

"Life is so strange sometimes," she tells me after a pause. "When you went to Vietnam, I lost so many nights of sleep worrying that you wouldn't come back. Sometimes, I would get these feelings that something bad had happened to you. They were so strong, I was convinced you'd been hurt or killed. Then, it seemed like it took months for your next letter to arrive. I'd go to the mailbox every day and look for one. But you did come back. Now, I'm the one who won't be coming back."

"I wish you wouldn't say it like that."

"The point I want to make is that I don't want you to do the same over me when I'm gone. Don't be afraid to move on when the time is right." The statement ends with a sob.

"I haven't even thought about that. The only thing I've thought about is you getting better," I reply while squeezing Elaine's shoulders again.

"And that's one more reason that I love you. But it doesn't look like I'm going to get better, and someday, you'll need to move forward without me."

I want to reply, but I'm rendered speechless by Elaine's courage.

"There's only one thing I regret I didn't do sooner," Elaine goes on.

"What is it?"

"When you came back from Vietnam, it took me too long to realize what Vietnam did to you. I know I put too much pressure on you to be the person you were before you left. It's just that I wanted so badly for things to be perfect for us. We stayed faithful to each other while apart for most of two years. Not many people can do that. But we did. I thought that meant we'd spend forever together, and I wanted forever to be like it was before you left.

"That wasn't right of me. It wasn't fair to you. I took too long to understand that some things about Vietnam can't be undone just by wishing for it or by trying harder. If I could do something over again, that would be it. My heart was set on spending my life with the high school Scott Reynolds. Even though I love you today as much as I did in high school, I needed time to understand why you were different and why you couldn't go all the way back to who you used to be—too much time. I loved you so much that I held on to that hope for too long. Do you forgive me for that?"

"You don't need to apologize for that now. It's in the past. You've always had my forgiveness, even before you asked for it."

Elaine rests her head on my shoulder and gives a sigh, but it's a content sigh. As content as someone in her position can be, anyway.

"Are you tired?" I ask her.

"Yes. I'm tired all the time anymore. How about you? Have you been sleeping okay lately?"

"Most of the time, yes. The flashbacks seem to be coming less often."

This is a lie. In fact, the flashbacks and nightmares have been my constant companions for weeks. But Elaine doesn't need that on her mind right now, so I hope it's okay to lie to her this once.

"I'd always hoped you'd get better over time. Too bad I won't be around to see it when you're finally free of the nightmares."

I put my arms around Elaine and hug her again. We talk for a considerable time that day and in the days to come. I can't help Elaine fight the cancer that's killing her, but I can spend all the free time I've got with her. Sometimes, maybe, that's all a person can do.

Chapter 15

My First Anniversary

"Sticks, you know what today is, right?" Ted asks me one Sunday morning over Corn Flakes. We've managed to save the money for a kitchen table, so we've replaced the old card table with the real thing for meals.

I rub my four-day scruff while I think. It can't be Thanksgiving. That was a week ago.

"I dunno." I truly am awful at remembering why certain days are important.

"It's December 1, the first anniversary of our DEROS. Our enlistment in the Army ended one year ago today."

"Oh yeah, that's right," I say dully. Since I've been out of the Army, I've forgotten how much military people love acronyms. DEROS stands for Date Eligible for Return from Overseas.

"You think we should do something to celebrate?"

"To be honest, I don't feel like doing anything today."

Ted pats me on the shoulder. "You were thinking about Elaine again, right?"

I nod. "I never expected things would end like this for us."

"How are her spirits?"

"Up and down, but they're starting to be more down than up. She's in considerable pain most of the time."

"It's awful, Sticks. I feel awful for her."

Then I say, "I made another big mistake yesterday, Ted. I dropped acid."

"In Nam you told me you would never do that again."

"When I said it, I didn't anticipate that my girlfriend would be dying of cancer and that I'd be powerless to do anything to help her."

"Was it another bad trip?"

"No, not especially. I kept the dosage moderate, and it's been more than a year since my last trip. But I feel horrible now. Not from the drugs, but from knowing I gave in and did it again. I promised myself I'd be stronger than that, and I wasn't."

"You're going through a rough stretch, Sticks. I can't imagine what it'd feel like to spend so long in the Army missing a girlfriend, only to have her get cancer. It ain't right."

"There it is."

Ted shakes his head. "You expect 'there it is' to happen in war. You don't expect it when you get home. At least, not like this."

I have no reply. When a military guy says "there it is," they're admitting that no reasonable explanation exists. When you're in a firefight and the guys on both sides of you get hit but you end up without a scratch, there's no explanation for why they got wounded and you didn't. There it is. Some guys even shrug when they say it to emphasize the point.

When I haven't responded after several moments, Ted says, "I take it you want to pass on celebrating."

I pause for a while longer, thinking back on several conversations I've had with Elaine lately, but one thing she told me sticks out. "No," I finally say. "I would like to celebrate with you. After weeks and weeks of being miserable, maybe it'll help to do something fun. Elaine told me not to be afraid to move on when the time is right. This isn't exactly what she meant, but it's in the spirit of what she meant."

"Dig that, Sticks. What should we do? I don't wanna get raging drunk, and I don't think that you do, either, so how do we celebrate?"

Ted asks a good question. In the military, celebrations often involve enough alcohol that everyone who partakes would like to sleep until noon the next day. But that doesn't seem appropriate right now.

"Actually, I already kinda planned an idea," Ted admits after a few moments. "It involves my mother's talents with frying catfish."

"Dig that," I reply with a smile.

We attend a modest party at the home of Ted's parents in Inglewood that evening. Gloria has prepared fried catfish, cornbread, greens, and two plates of her molasses cookies. Gloria also insisted that I bring Elaine if she felt up to leaving her house.

Gloria and Eugene have a Christmas tree up already, decked with tinsel and lights. When we arrive, I see that Ted's sister, Rachel, and a couple of his neighborhood friends are present.

Eugene and Gloria show Elaine and me true hospitality. Their manners toward Elaine are the embodiment of the word gracious. They help her to a seat, pull out her chair for her at the table, keep a plate of cookies and a glass of sweet tea at her elbow at all times, and hardly fifteen minutes go by without Gloria remarking on how adorable Elaine's white bonnet, orange blouse, or blue skirt looks. Clearly, she's trying to lift Elaine's spirits, yet she does so without sounding insincere or contrived.

I've never known Eugene to be much of a talker, but he displays a wonderful knack for including Elaine in our conversations without nagging her with questions and making her uncomfortable. Apparently, Gloria and Eugene learned a few things about choosing the right tone for the occasion during their careers as teachers.

It's been months since I've seen as many smiles from Elaine as I see this evening. She doesn't eat very much, but she forces down a little catfish in gratitude for Gloria's effort to cook an amazing meal. I eat Elaine's share and then some. Maybe it's because I've been so depressed about Elaine lately, but my appetite has been weak, too. Tonight I make up for that.

When the evening is over, I thank Eugene and Gloria.

"Your girlfriend is a real jewel, Scott," Gloria tells me.

"We're so happy you convinced her to come," Eugene adds.

"You've treated Elaine like a princess all night. I can't thank you enough," I tell them, nearly choking up.

"Ted's told us all about her illness. It's the least we could do. And would you look at that," Eugene says, pointing to his living room.

Elaine sits speaking and smiling with Ted's younger sister Rachel. Perhaps it was because they were the only women present tonight besides Gloria, but they struck up a friendship before dinner, and they're still talking with each other now.

"I overheard them talking about books at one point," I say. "It sounds like they've read some of the same ones."

"Ted also told us about the nice things you've done for Elaine."

"I'm trying to do everything I can think of that she likes. We eat dinner with each other all the time, even though she doesn't have much appetite these days. A few times we've rented horses for a ride on the beach, and we've become regulars at the movie theaters. I've got a secret plan, too. The week before Christmas, I've arranged to take days off from work and rent a cabin for us in the Sierras. It's one of those places that normally rents to couples on their honeymoon, but when I told them about our situation, they agreed to rent me a cabin. It isn't going to save her, I know, but I'm going to spend all the time I can with her until our time is up."

"Bless you for being her friend," Gloria tells me before one of her hugs.

I glance over while Elaine walks slowly toward us, beige overcoat in hand, and turns to Eugene and Gloria. "I was speaking with Rachel about what books we've read. She's offered to let me borrow *The Black Pearl*, and I promised to give her my copy of *Across Five Aprils* when I return it. Your daughter seems like a very smart young lady, but I guess I should expect that from the daughter of two teachers."

My First Anniversary

"Eugene and I are so pleased you came to the party tonight," Gloria replies. "We've been waiting to meet you for so long, and I'm happy we finally got the chance to see Scott's angel."

On the way home Elaine remains upbeat, which encourages me. "You seemed like you had a great time tonight," I tell her.

"I did. The Williamsons were so kind to me. I almost didn't go, you know. Part of me was afraid to go because I didn't want to drag down a party that was in honor of you and Ted. But his parents managed to include me in everything without distracting from the party."

"Yeah, they were amazing. If they're as good at being teachers as they are at hosting a gathering, their students are some lucky kids. Say, I've got something else to tell you about that I think is amazing."

"What's that? Another party as good as this one was?"

"Better, I hope."

"What is it?"

"In two weeks, I want you to go on a little trip with me. I've rented a cabin in the Sierra Nevadas for three days. We can have our own little Christmas there, you and me, and then come back to L.A. in time to celebrate the real thing with our families, too. What do you think?"

"That does sound amazing. I love it." For once, I can almost see the old smile on Elaine's face and hear it in her voice.

On a whim, I decide to visit my parents after seeing Elaine home. It's been a while since I stopped by. I suppose my father may gloat that the Southern Cal Trojans are playing in the Rose Bowl once again this year. Only a tie against Notre Dame prevented them from an undefeated regular season. I need to tell them about the upcoming vacation Elaine and I are taking, though.

When Dad opens the door, however, his face is pale and his hair disheveled. He's got a dustpan in his left hand.

One Kind Of Hero

"Something's happened, hasn't it, Dad? What's going on?"

"Come in, Son, come in."

"Has something happened to Mom? Is she okay?"

"Yes and no."

"What's that mean?"

When I follow Dad to the kitchen, I see what it means. Shards of plates and glass cover the linoleum floor, and Dad has the mop next to a deep purple pool.

"What on earth happened?"

"Your mother and sister got in another fight. Bad. Your Mom became so incensed that she threw her plate at Lisa, and Lisa threw her wine glass back. They screamed at each other, and I thought they might come to blows after they got done throwing what was at hand. I think Susan is in bed upstairs now. She has no voice left, she screamed so loudly at Lisa."

"Let me guess. They argued about the war again."

"Well, that started it, yes. It always seems to set them off. But things went further this time."

"What escalated it? Do I even want to know?"

"You probably don't, but you should in case either of them wants to talk to you about it later. Susan blamed the Democratic Party and all the anti-war protests for the violence we saw happen this year."

"I'd believe she said that, even though I don't believe those things are connected."

"Of course, she was looking right at Lisa at the time, taunting her with it. Then she told Lisa she was glad she'd voted for George Wallace in the last election because he would authorize the National Guard to shoot protestors dead in the street."

I give the whistle that indicates "wow." George Wallace is the racist former governor of Alabama who ran for president as an independent candidate in the recent elections. He didn't have much of a platform other than racism, appealing to White peoples' fears about Black people, and pledging to wipe the streets clean of anyone who dared to protest about either Vietnam or conditions in America's cities. Wallace even held a couple rallies in California that mostly involved whipping the crowd into a fury over how real Americans were losing their country to the communists, and that only a superpatriot like Wallace could save America.

As the presidential campaign went on, Wallace never ceased spitting out conspiracy theories about Jews, liberals, foreigners, and anyone else he thought might get people angrier. At first, the newspapers in California laughed at him, giving him no chance outside the South. The papers pointed to his campaign's shoestring budget, his incoherent positions on national and international issues, and the ridiculous things he kept saying to reporters.

But in his own way, Wallace had the last laugh. One out of seven American voters marked their ballot for Wallace, and he won the electoral vote of five states in the South. Very few of the national experts had realized that he could tap into the anger of people the way he did, and that that would be enough to gain the votes of nearly ten million Americans despite his weak grasp of issues and lack of policies.

Growing up, I was never a person who cared particularly about politics. The only reason I know so much about George Wallace is that I studied this election carefully because it was the first one in which I was old enough to vote. I just turned twenty-one in December of last year, so I never had much need to examine the candidates until now.

While I think this over, my dad continues with his explanation of the fight. "Lisa screamed that Susan had lost her mind, that Wallace is an odious pig and an idiot, and on and on."

"I think I agree with Lisa on that one," I say quietly.

Dad nods sadly. "Me, too. You know I disagree with how Wallace always tried to stoke people's anger as a substitute for command of important issues. I was happy voting for Eisenhower and the Republicans during the 1950s, but since they started nominating people like Nixon and Goldwater for the presidency, well, I don't agree with leaders who feed fear and anger in order to earn support. If they get elected, they feel compelled to lash out against the people they just spent their campaign condemning, and people suffer who shouldn't have to."

"But what does that have to do with the argument?"

Dad hangs his head. "I tried to say these things to both your mother and your sister to put out the fuse I saw burning. My point was supposed to be that getting angry only leads to more problems, and that everyone would be better off if they calmed down some. It didn't come out right, though. Instead of letting the argument die and agreeing to disagree, Lisa started gloating and crowing about me taking her side, and you know how your mother responds when she feels backed into a corner."

"She got mad at you, too? That doesn't happen often."

"We disagree sometimes, yes, but we've been married long enough that we know we aren't attacking each other. That's a point your sister has yet to take to heart. She's young, and at times she worries more about being right than about what damage being right can cause.

"Things went downhill from there, and eventually dishes and wine glasses started flying in between the curses. Even though I tried again to get them both to calm down, things had gone too far."

"How long will they stay furious at each other this time, would you say?"

"Well, Scott, that's hard to know. Before I could stop her, your mother told Lisa she didn't want to see her in the house again."

"Oh my."

Not a profound remark on my part, perhaps, but this goes well beyond anything my mother has ever done before, and it takes me by surprise.

"I have no idea if Susan will reconsider and relent in time, but I fear it won't be soon."

My First Anniversary

My dad's shoulders slump again, and a deep sigh escapes him. He shakes his head and slaps one palm on the counter in frustration. "Things never should have gone so far, and I couldn't stop them."

I put my arm around my dad's shoulders and give him a hug. "I'm sorry, Dad. Maybe Mom will have calmed down some by tomorrow. If you need me to mediate or be a go-between to get them talking again, I'll do what I can."

"I know you will, Son. Maybe things will blow over in time, but I can't say for sure. Did you at least have a good time at your party?"

"Elaine and I had a great time. Ted's parents are amazing hosts. Speaking of Elaine, I made plans to take her on a vacation in a couple weeks. I rented a cabin for us in the Sierras. Can I bring Pete over while we go? He'll need someone to feed him and take care of him."

"Of course. I miss the old fella. And for what it's worth, I think you're doing a good thing with taking Elaine to the mountains. If she feels up to traveling, I'm sure you'll have a great time together."

"Thanks, Dad. Well, I think I'm gonna go home and crash for the night. Let me know what I can do to help between Lisa and Mom, okay?"

While I lie in bed, I try to understand why my family is tearing apart. Mostly, it's Lisa and Mom, but once things start to unravel, well, who knows where they'll stop? What if they both insist that I take their side? Or what if they both get angry at me because I won't take a side?

After the fun evening with Ted and Elaine, I'd hoped the memories would stay away tonight, but no. Instead, I'm back in Vietnam once more.

We'd just captured a village and were taking off. Or, at least, I thought we'd captured the village—right until the VC opened fire.

Maybe they'd been hiding in the trees on the far side of the village all along, or maybe they'd just arrived. Either way, our intelligence had given us no warning of their presence in the vicinity. Instantly, I hear the sound all helicopter crewmen fear most: we're taking hits. Lots of them.

Even as our gunners take aim to return Charlie's fire, our craft lurches and begins losing altitude. We're going down.

The Chinook isn't in freefall, but it's going to be a hard landing.

I brace myself as best I can, but the impact throws open the loading ramp of the Chinook and bodies spill out, mine among them.

It takes a moment to reorient and get my bearings, but regaining focus takes less time than one might think when bullets are flying. Miraculously, I kept hold of my rifle when I was thrown from the Chinook. My first thought is to find cover.

We crashed in the middle of the village, so I'm surrounded by thatched houses. They aren't much protection, however. Without a better option, I roll behind the stonework of the village well.

From there I take stock of the situation. Not five feet away a young girl spasms in the mud and dust, blood leaking out around her. I can't tell if the blood is from the crash or because she's been shot.

A look back at my Chinook shows that the craft is a smoldering pile of scrap. A few people struggle from the wreckage, climbing over and around the bodies of those who aren't moving.

The scene is pure chaos. Between the bodies, the noise of guns firing, the wind from the other Chinooks, injured people crying for help, screaming villagers, and my own Chinook crashed on its side, it's hard to know what to do first. Return fire? Run for better cover? Help the people wounded in the crash?

That's when I realize that nothing hurts. Somehow, I avoided breaking any bones or anything else when the crash threw me from the Chinook. I sigh in relief, but it's short-lived. The survivors are taking fire from Charlie. I decide I need to get into the fight right away.

I locate a target and open up with my M-16 rifle. Or, maybe better to say I locate where the VC fire is coming from and return fire to the general area, since Charlie lies concealed in the vegetation.

Behind me, I see a few Chinooks trying to give us cover fire. Chinooks primarily are for moving cargo and people, but they mount 7.62-mm machine guns, too, for times like this.

Momentarily, another soldier emerges from the wreckage and dives beside me. I realize it's my CO. He's a tolerable pilot, despite that his Chinook just got shot down. Dirt and blood smear his face, and his eyes look concerned. Not panicky, but definitely concerned.

"You hit, Reynolds?" he shouts to me.

"No, sir. How many of our guys survived the crash?"

"Don't know. Not enough, though."

I'm trying to aim and fire again when he says, "Save it, Reynolds. We gotta get out of here."

"While taking fire?"

"Charlie's advancing into the village. We stay here, we'll be surrounded. If we aren't shot first."

"Where is everyone else?"

"Standard procedure is to call in an air strike on Charlie's position when we're this close to an airfield. Presumably someone on one of the other Chinooks already has. I don't know if we're in the blast range, but I'd rather not chance it. We need to fall back for evacuation."

"Right."

"I'll lay down some cover fire first. You run."

I'm crouching to do exactly that when a mortar round explodes nearby, the force knocking me on my back.

Chapter 16

The Sierras

Before Elaine and I leave for the mountains, I stop at Dad's bakery because he promised us doughnuts for the trip. It's a pleasant surprise when I pick them up and see Sandra, the waitress from the coffee shop, come through the front door.

"Hi there, Scott. I've never seen you in here before," she tells me with a cheerful smile when I emerge from the back, paper sack with maple bars and jelly doughnuts in hand.

"Normally, I'm at work on Thursday morning, but not today."

"I'm here to get some croissants for the coffee shop. I told the owner about your dad's bakery, and now he sends someone here to get something a couple times a week. That's how much he likes your dad's food."

"Well, I grew up on the stuff, and I'm still eating it, so I'd have to say I agree with him."

She laughs and then waves when my father emerges from the back of the bakery. "Hello, Darryl, good to see you. I'm here to pick up the usual."

"Good day to you, Sandra Larson. Do you and Scott know each other?"

"Yeah, a little. He and Lisa have come to the coffee shop a few times this year. Your son was a gentleman one day and helped out a woman who was having a tough time. It was only my second day of work, and he helped me calm down when I didn't know what to do."

The Sierras

"At least the boy learned one thing, then," Dad says with a joking laugh. Sandra joins him.

I always marvel at what a different person Dad seems to be when at the bakery. It's not often I visit him at work, but when I do, he seems more at ease and less reserved than he is at home. At work is the only time he consistently makes small talk with people for the sake of saying something. He's standing tall, his shoulders look relaxed, and his smile is easy and unforced. I don't know why he acts so differently. Maybe he figures a guy shouldn't be serious *all* the time. Or maybe it's because he doesn't need to keep the peace between my mother and Lisa while at work.

"Well, my shift starts soon. I should probably get moving," Sandra tells us. "But it was nice to see you again, Scott. And thank you for having everything ready, Darryl. Here's your money."

My dad keeps smiling while Sandra walks out. "A nice young woman."

"I agree. You should have seen her that day in January when Lisa and I went to get coffee the first time. Sandra was almost shaking, she felt so nervous. But look at her now—relaxed, comfortable, friendly, and polite."

"I'm heartened to hear that you had something to do with that."

"It wasn't that much. Like I told her, I was doing what anyone should've done."

"Yet, you did something that not everyone does. I'm proud of you for that, if it's still okay for me to say so."

"Why wouldn't it be okay for you to say you're proud of me?"

"I've always thought those words sounded a little condescending when adults say them to other adults. But if you don't mind, I'll keep saying it—because I am proud of you."

It's hard to put into words how much it means to hear that from my father, the man I look up to above anyone else. I don't know if I should hug him in his bakery, though, so instead I ask, "Has anything changed between Mom and Lisa?"

He shakes his head sadly. "Neither of them has budged from the ground they took after their argument."

"Are you getting worried about this? I think that I am."

A slow nod. "I don't think I can force the issue, though. They'll come around when they come around."

"I'm not sure how much I can help on this one. Both Mom and Lisa called me about a week ago. Just like I feared, they both want me to take their side against the other. Lisa seems to feel that if she, you, and I all take her side, maybe Mom will relent. Mom feels like she's been abandoned by the child she put so much effort into raising."

"That about sums it up. Like I said, they'll come around when they come around. Well, you and Elaine should probably get going. Do you still want to go through with your whole plan once you get there?"

"Yes."

On the second night of our vacation, Elaine and I look out the huge front window of our cabin while a gentle rain falls outside. I hope to see another radiant orange and yellow sunset like last night, but the rainclouds are spoiling it. When I first saw the angry clouds roll in, gray and low, my hopes changed to the possibility that we'd see snow. What could be more romantic than spending a night with my girlfriend in a mountain cabin with snow gently drifting down?

But then I remembered I don't want to drive my Corvette home in the snow. I've never driven in snow before, and I doubt my tires are up to the task. So, Elaine and I sit wrapped in thick blankets while we watch nature's tears drip from the pines, junipers, and mountain hemlocks spread throughout the valley below.

Our cabin is perfect. The wood-frame furniture matches the log cabin walls on the inside. It feels very rustic. But the electric heater works, and the cabin has a fireplace, too, so warmth is no problem. It also offers a kitchen, a bedroom, and a living room that overlooks the woods on the mountainside.

The Sierras

"This was such a good idea, Scott," Elaine tells me. "Your early Christmas present was perfect, too."

I got Elaine a thick flannel shirt, which she's now wearing. It looks comically loose on her thin body, but neither of us care.

"What should we do this evening?" she asks.

"Well, these cabins are supposed to be for people on their honeymoons. I think they work on the assumption that people will spend their evenings in bed and not need a lot of other entertainment," I say with a teasing tone. Although Elaine and I have had sex a few times, we stopped when she got ill this spring. After her cancer diagnosis, neither of us felt right trying it again.

I continue while sipping hot chocolate. "Since that isn't what we're gonna do, I think we have the same options as last night."

That means cards or the board games we brought. Since neither of us had played board games in several years, we could only come up with a couple of the old standbys to play—Clue and Sorry! Somehow, I didn't think Elaine would enjoy the tabletop game I played most as a teenager: Strat-o-Matic baseball, the classic 1962 season. I left that one in my closet.

"Let's do Clue again," Elaine suggests. "That was so much fun last night. Although, truth be told, I don't care what we play. Spending the time with you is what matters to me."

"You want some hot chocolate, too? Or maybe a coffee?" I ask while rising to retrieve the game.

"A little hot chocolate sounds good, sure."

After returning with Elaine's drink, I start to set up the board, but then pause. For several seconds, I just look at my girlfriend.

"What's the matter, Scott?"

I start to answer, but stop when the words don't want to come out.

"Scott?"

After a deep breath, I try again. "I have something I want to ask you."

"Go on. You don't need to be nervous."

"How do you do it, Elaine? If I were you, I'd be so angry about the bum hand life dealt me. And here we are, just playing kids' games, and you act like it's all okay."

She puts down her mug while I sit patiently beside her.

"This summer, when the exams revealed that the treatments weren't helping, I realized I might not ever get better. I kept hoping, but I could see the odds turning against me. When that happened, I knew I had two choices. One was to do what you just said. I could be miserable, be angry, hate the world, hate God or whatever caused my sickness, and spend my last few months being bitter and bringing everyone else down with me.

"My other choice was to embrace the time I had left and make the most of it—see things I've always wanted to see, do things I've always wanted to do, and spend time with the people who mean the most to me. That way, when my time comes, I can go knowing that I used my days the best I could. It won't give me any extra, I realize, but it'll seem like it has because I've squeezed the most out of the days I've got."

"You're so beautiful," I tell her.

Although Elaine is smiling, she says "Stop. If you didn't know me, you wouldn't say that." She runs a hand over her head, the sparse hairs brushing her fingers lightly.

"I meant your personality and attitude are beautiful. And I'll always remember how you looked before you got sick. That Elaine was beautiful on the outside, too. I don't know how to describe it, but you're almost glowing from the inside. That's how incredible and heroic you are."

"Heroic? I don't think of myself as a hero."

"Absolutely, you're a hero. A person can be more than one kind of hero, you know. I knew fellows in Vietnam who weren't scared of anything. They stayed calm under fire, never panicked, and could stand almost any amount of pain. That's what we usually think of as brave or heroic, and it's one kind of hero, for sure.

The Sierras

But I also met guys who were another kind of hero. These were guys who got tough missions. Really tough missions. The type where they stood a good chance of earning a medal—and having that medal sent to their family. Guys who would take those missions anyway were a different kind of hero because they knew the odds of not coming back. That's the kind of hero you are. It's a kind of bravery I don't think I'll ever have."

She throws her arms around me. "Oh, Scott, that's such a wonderful thing to say. I never thought of being a hero that way before."

"It's only one of the ways that you're amazing," I say to her softly. "I'm not sure even I realized how amazing until the last few months. You've acted with dignity when most people would've given up and stopped trying. You still encourage the people around you and want to see them succeed. Above all, you still show love. If that isn't what a hero does, then what is? I think I would've turned into a burned-out, angry husk of a man if I were in your shoes."

I hadn't planned to say all that and make it so flowery. The words tumbled out once I got going. But I mean them. They aren't fake or intended solely to puff up Elaine's spirits.

But now Elaine is crying into my shoulder even while I hold her close. It beings with a few sniffs, and then they turn into sobs.

"What's wrong? What did I say that hurt you?" I ask her once she's gotten the tears out.

"You didn't say anything wrong. Everything you said was kind and wonderful. But it made me think about the fact that soon, we'll see each other for the last time. That feeling broke my heart. I don't know when that day will be, but knowing it's bound to happen soon was more than I could take. It won't matter to me when I'm gone, but it'll matter to you."

That stuns me. Elaine is the one with the terminal illness, and she's worrying about how I'll react to life without her.

"Believe me, Scott, I've had so many nights filled with dark and bitter thoughts. Since I often struggle to sleep because of the pain,

I've seen the sun come up in the morning more times than I'd like to admit. You can't imagine how many black thoughts I've had, how many times I've offered bargains to God to get my life back, how many times I've wished to have the energy to do normal things like take Pete for a walk on a sunny day. But I finally stopped doing that because it was pointless."

Now I'm crying, too. Elaine mentioned Pete, and Pete loves her almost as much as I do.

She goes on, half-talking and half-sobbing again. "I even considered putting myself out of my misery once. My parents have guns, you know, and I've overheard where they keep them. It's hard to do anything during the day when you hurt too much to sleep at night. These days, night and day blend together because I spend most of both trying to rest. But you know why I don't go and get one of their guns? Because of you. I don't want to miss the days I have left with you."

I just hold my girlfriend and whisper, "I love you." What else is there to say when she tells you something like that?

"But that's why I never thought of myself as brave or heroic. I don't think that someone brave would consider killing herself."

"Elaine, remember a conversation we had back in April? It was the night we drove home from eating dinner with my parents, and Mom and I got into it a little bit. You told me you were nervous that being in Vietnam had changed me, and you got scared that I'd grown up too much for you because of it. You were worried I'd leave you."

"Yes, I remember. I felt so nervous that night, and my fears ran away with me. But then you pulled over and said a bunch of wonderful things that reassured me."

"You were wrong about something."

"I know. Like I said, I got scared."

"No, not that. You were wrong about the part when you said that I'd grown up faster than you had because of going to Vietnam. That's not true. I don't know if I'll ever be grown up enough to handle myself with the courage you have these past months."

154

This puts Elaine on the verge of tears again. "I never thought of it that way."

"Maybe being a grownup is different than what we think sometimes. As a kid, I always thought of it as having my own house, a car, a family, and all that. That's what being a grownup looks like on television, anyway. But maybe that's not it at all. I'm starting to think that being a grownup is about learning to deal with setbacks without letting them get the best of you. We only think it's the other way because we want to make judgments about people, and the houses, cars, and children are the things we see on the outside."

"Is it possible we were both right, Scott? Maybe both of us have grown up a lot but in different ways?"

"I'd say that's a good way to put it."

We both pause for a moment. Then Elaine laughs and says, "You never got around to setting up our game."

"That's because I have one more thing I'd like to ask you."

"Go ahead."

I've thought about this for a long time, unsure if I should do it or not. I guess I'm still nervous because I fidget while trying to get my courage up.

"Was getting married important to you? You never mentioned it that I can remember."

She leans back a little. "That wasn't what I thought you'd say."

Elaine pauses to consider her words. "But, yes, I guess I do regret that I'll never be married. I mean, I always assumed that we would be someday. But after I got sick, I put that thought out of my mind."

"Would you like to be?"

"Are you proposing, Scott?"

"Yes. But only if it's what you want. I know it may only last for a few months. But if you're scared of dying without ever being married, then let's get married. What do you say?"

Chapter 17

Changes

Elaine died on Sunday, July 20, 1969. It's the same day that Neil Armstrong and Buzz Aldrin make the first moon landing. The funeral is the following Saturday.

We never did get married. Elaine thought about it for a long time. Finally, she told me that she wanted to say yes but didn't want to get married for the sake of saying she got married. I thought that was what she would decide, but I'm still glad I proposed. Although I would've been happy taking care of her as her husband for the last seven months, we parted as best friends instead.

I wish I could say that the length of Elaine's illness prepared me for losing her so that it hurt less, but that would be false. Some people fear sudden losses more than anything. It's the shock that gets them, and they have a hard time recovering from the shock and bouncing back. But I'm the other way. Maybe it's because fighting in Vietnam desensitized me to sudden loss. For me, the fear of knowing something bad and unavoidable is going to happen, but not knowing when, is worse because the fear drags you down every day, sapping your emotions and your energy.

After the funeral, I join Lisa for beers. I regret to admit that my drinking has increased substantially in 1969. Sometimes the buzz helped me forget the pain of watching Elaine decline. I wonder if I'll still want it now that she's gone?

We're sitting in my apartment, six empty bottles on the coffee table in front of us. We both have a fourth in hand.

"Where's Ted tonight?" Lisa asks me. "I saw him at the funeral, so I assumed he'd come here afterward."

"He took Tanya to meet his parents for dinner."

Lisa smiles. "It worked, then?"

"Seems like it."

Lisa and I couldn't figure out why Ted had a hard time finding dates. So, she set him up with a young Black lady from her office. I didn't know if he'd accept, but he did, and it seems like they've hit it off.

"At least I can do one thing right when it comes to relationships. Maybe I'm only good at finding matches for other people, though. I can't seem to do it for myself."

"You and Shawn are done already, then?"

My sister runs her hands through her blond hair and leans back. These days, she wears her hair in a side-swept bob. "Yeah. Turns out he was kinda nuts. Not mean or a jerk, but just nuts."

"How did you meet him again?"

"Same thing we're doing now," Lisa replies with a weary smile, raising her beer bottle. "He seemed different after four or five drinks at the party where I met him, but he was crazy. Shawn actually went through my apartment looking for bugs one time. Even I'm not that paranoid."

"Bugs? He's a neat freak?"

"No. I mean wires and listening devices. Shawn thought that COINTELPRO was after him because he spoke at an anti-war rally one time in college."

"Oh, got it."

"At least I got a couple surfing lessons from him before I realized he was cracked in the head," Lisa says with a smile. "I can do a bottom turn now."

I didn't know that Lisa liked surfing, but I give her a salute with my beer. We clink our bottles.

Maybe I shouldn't, but I decide to ask Lisa the question that's most on my mind. "Are you and Mom ever going to make up and get back on good terms? I don't think I saw you speak at the funeral today."

Lisa sighs. "You aren't supposed to ask me about that. I've tried a couple times, actually. But she won't apologize for screaming at me or let me come back to the house. As long as she holds to that line, well, I'm not sure what I can do."

Although I want to say she can apologize herself for the sake of not staying angry anymore, I don't. I'm too depressed to argue the point. Instead, I say, "You're an adult. You'll figure it out. Just say the word if I can help you patch things up."

"You've said that several times, but thanks again for the offer."

"You know that your argument hurts Dad, too, right?"

"He'd probably like to see me at home, yeah. I go talk to him at the bakery sometimes, though. Even he can't get Mom to change her tune."

"Dad doesn't show it much on the outside, and he's never said it in so many words, but I think he sees your argument as his failure as well."

"Why would he think that?"

"He's always been the peacemaker, the guy who gets everyone to calm down and put their weapons away, right? If you and Mom keep arguing, he feels like he's failed."

"The argument has nothing to do with him, though."

"No, it doesn't. But he still feels responsible in his own way. I'm telling you how it is, that's all, and suggesting you might think about him a little."

Lisa nods and stands up. "Will you be okay if I head home soon?"

"Yeah. I'm not going anywhere tonight, if that's what you mean. The pain will get less in time, I know, but damn, my heart hurts right now."

Lisa smiles sympathetically and gives me a hug. "It will get better. You'll miss Elaine, probably you'll always miss Elaine, but you've still got your whole life ahead of you. That's something to feel good about, even if it's hard to see it right now."

I keep my word to my sister and stay home. Eventually, Ted comes back, and we drink a couple more beers together.

"How'd things go with Tanya? Did she like your mom's molasses cookies?"

"Yeah," Ted says with a big smile, "although I felt a little conflicted tonight, you know?"

"Why is that?"

"Well, I spent a lot of the evening thinking about you. You found this great girlfriend, and she even waited for you to get back from Vietnam. Not many women would do that. But then she got sick, and it wasn't her fault at all. I felt weird having a good time with Tanya and my parents, laughing and eating together, knowing that I'd been to Elaine's funeral earlier the same day."

"Well, I'm glad you and Tanya had a fun evening. No reason for both of us to be miserable all day, you know?"

"You gonna be okay, Sticks?" Ted asks after going bottoms up on his second beer. "I mean, everyone expects you to be sad today and all, but are you gonna be okay tomorrow and the next day and so on?"

"I think so. Why wouldn't I be?"

"I've been thinking. When we lost guys in Vietnam, everyone knew that would happen. Guys got down, but everyone knew why. Other soldiers understood the feeling because they'd been through it themselves. But this is different. No one expected Elaine to get cancer and not recover. It's a different kind of grief than either of us is used to, is what I'm sayin'."

I nod. "I see your point. But I think I'll live."

"All right, then. I thought I should ask."

"Thanks. And thank you for one other thing today, Ted."

"What's that?"

"I realized you were the only Black person at Elaine's funeral. That was awkward for you, I'll bet, but you went anyway. A man couldn't ask for a better friend. Thanks."

Maybe it's because Elaine's death has me thinking about it, but while I try to sleep, I think back on the time in Vietnam when I came closest to death myself.

I'm crouched behind the village well, getting ready to fall back and hopefully board one of the other Chinooks to get me out of the village. Our CO crouches beside me, preparing to lay down cover fire. Everything is so loud. Between the firing, the Chinooks in the air, their machine guns, and the fire of the VC, I can barely hear anything. Although I know it's only luck whether I make it to safety, I need to get up and run. The F-100 fighters with their bombs will be here any second now, and if I'm in the blast zone when that happens, I'm dead.

The noise is why I can't hear the incoming mortar round that hits nearby and throws me from my feet.

I lay on the ground for several moments, stunned. How long I lie there is anyone's guess. I can feel a couple of bullets whizzing around my body, though, and that brings me back to my senses.

By all rights, the mortar explosion should've injured some part of me. But when I flop onto my stomach, nothing hurts any worse than a bruised tailbone.

I'll think about how lucky I was later. Right now, I need to get out of here.

Just as I shift my weight to push up and run for it, I see a dark arm waving feebly from the pile of bodies outside the Chinook. The arm has a uniform jacket rolled at the sleeve, and the roll look just like Ted does it.

For a moment, I hesitate. By the time I see or hear the F-100s, it'll be too late. They're so fast that I won't have time to do anything once they arrive.

But I don't run for safety. Instead, I hustle over, doing a leaping roll to stay low and avoid enemy fire. After pulling away the body that lies on top of him, I realize I was right. It's Ted.

"Sticks!" he shouts, then points to his leg.

I can see Ted's uniform soaked in blood.

"How bad?" I shout.

"Can't walk!"

"I'll get you out!" I yell, helping Ted to stand on his good leg and draping his arm over my shoulder. More bullets speed past.

"Leave me, Sticks, I ain't gonna make it," Ted shouts when I get him to his feet. I can see pain etched in every feature of his face and sweat pouring off his forehead.

"No way! We're going together."

We start off as fast as we can, angling for a Chinook that's still on the ground. In my fear and haste, however, I try to go too fast, and soon we tumble to the earth, Ted screaming in pain from the fall.

When I look up, I see them. The F-100s are here.

Lying there in bed in Los Angeles, I can still remember how it felt when the planes arrived. The sweat stinging my eyes. The bloodstains on my pants from helping Ted. The smell of burning aviation fuel. Other people injured in the crash trying to crawl or limp to safety. And so much noise. I couldn't hear people ten feet away. All that, mixed with the heat and the bullets flying everywhere, and momentarily I thought I was dead and in Hell already.

I probably should've died that day. Between my Chinook going down, the mortar blast, and the bullets, I had ample chances to check out. But I made it somehow.

Elaine faced none of the risks that I did. Yet, somehow, I'm still here and she's not.

For the most part, I kept my self-control during the funeral service today, but now I feel the wetness on my cheeks. Elaine didn't deserve to die. She was kind, loyal, pretty, and smart—better than me in almost every way.

But she's gone. What do I do now?

I'm still thinking about that when the sun peeks through my window the next morning.

The boss gave me Monday and Tuesday off from work, knowing I'd be too distracted to do good work on anyone's car. I'd like to say that I used my time off to find ways to distract myself from my grief, but that's not the case.

On Monday morning, I've got quite a headache. I haven't had that many hangovers in my life, and this feeling is the reason why I used to avoid drinking to excess.

I have dinner with my parents on Monday evening. I almost tell them about my conversation with Lisa the night before but decide it won't help.

"How are you today, Scott?" Mom asks while we sit down to eat. "You look really tired."

"I didn't sleep last night."

"Getting more rest will help you feel better, you know."

I nod. Of course I know that. It isn't that easy.

"I haven't had much to eat today, either. I've lost my appetite."

"Well, we can certainly fix that," Mom says, passing the potatoes and garlic bread my way after piling her own plate with both. I take a subdued portion of each.

"Come now, Scott, you need to eat more than that."

"I'm just not very hungry," I repeat in a dull voice.

Mom's face softens a little. "We all know that you miss Elaine, Son. You probably will for a good while to come. But starving yourself won't change anything."

I'd rather not argue the point, but I don't want to take food I won't eat. Why can't Mom let it go?

The rest of dinner is like the beginning. Mom talks a lot, I guess to try to take my mind off losing Elaine, while Dad says little and I pick at my food. While I'm walking out to my Corvette to drive home, Dad follows me.

"That was a little awkward, I suppose," he tells me.

I nod.

"You know your mother means well," Dad continues. "She feels like since she copes with things best through food and conversation that everyone else must be the same."

I'm too tired to be angry about that, so I mutter, "Yeah, I tried not to argue things with her. But I really wasn't hungry, so I told her I'd take home some leftovers. Pete'll be happy, I suppose, when he gets to eat them."

Dad smiles at the ruse. "How is Pete?"

"Same as ever. Just a little slower."

"Do I need to be worried about you?" he asks me.

"What for?"

"I know it's not quite the same, but during the Battle of the Bulge over in Europe, my best friend in the Army died. He got unlucky, and an artillery shell struck right by his foxhole and killed him on the spot. I watched it happen. My own foxhole wasn't more than forty feet from his. It took me years before I stopped seeing or thinking about it. For a long while I didn't cope well, even after the war was over. I'd go on drinking sprees sometimes, and a couple times, I woke up at home in my bed with no memory of how I got there."

"I can't believe that."

"Like I said, it took a few years to put that behind me. I mention it because you look today like I sometimes felt in those days. Listless movement, weak appetite, monotone voice—I had all of that while dealing with my grief. Or, maybe I should say that I struggled to deal with it. And I didn't always win that struggle. At least, not at first."

"You've never mentioned this to me before, Dad. I had no idea."

"The point is, part of the reason why it took me so long to get my life back in order was that I didn't have much help. You remember your grandfather. Although he was a good man in most ways, he tolerated no excuses and no signs of weakness. Whenever I didn't feel well growing up, he'd tell me to be a man and get over it. That was the only answer he had for life's difficulties—be a man and get over it. Maybe after working all those years in a steel mill, he didn't have time or energy to learn any other answers."

"But it worked, didn't it? You turned out fine. I can't ever remember a time growing up when you weren't in control and at peace with yourself."

My father lays a hand on my shoulder gently. "Perhaps it looked that way to you when you were a boy, but that wasn't always true. And it's my belief that I would have dealt with my struggles much better if I'd had a little support from someone who shared my experiences."

None of this is what I expected my father to say. When I was growing up, I looked to him as someone who had the answer to everything. He was always dependable, always there with a calming word when needed, and he never complained. The thought that he had gone through his own struggles and had made his share of mistakes never crossed my mind. To hear him admit he hadn't always been the way I envisioned him takes me aback, and for several moments, I have no response.

I mean, I know my father wasn't always perfect. No one is. But to hear my idol admit to struggling in such a matter-of-fact way staggers me.

My surprise must show on my face because Dad gives a gentle smile while he waits for me to digest everything. "It's not a sign of weakness to ask someone for help. Maybe to my own father it was, but I think he was wrong about that. So, if you really do bounce back over the next couple weeks, then that's great. But if you still feel sad after some time passes, don't feel like you're letting me down, or anyone else, to admit it."

I nod. "I hear you, Dad, I hear you. That's good advice."

Chapter 18

I Try to Bounce Back

"I miss you."

No answer.

"I miss you so much, and I'm miserable without you. What do I do now?"

Still no answer.

I'm kneeling at Elaine's grave, looking at the headstone.

Elaine Rose Collier

1947 – 1969

Beloved daughter & friend

I put my head down and wipe my eyes. It's my first time to Elaine's grave since her funeral.

"I don't know what to do without you," I say to the air around me. A few other people are in the cemetery, but they stand a good way off. No one else can hear me or see the tears fall.

"Whatever I do, I think of you. I tried to cook chicken for dinner, but that only reminded me of the pan you gave me on your first visit to my apartment. Lisa got me a guitar to replace the one I left in Vietnam, but that made me think of us playing trumpet together. Even walking Pete doesn't help. I know he misses you, too, and I think about us walking him together in the park. Gloria sent me molasses cookies, but even they reminded me of the night we had dinner at her house. I gave some of your books to Ted's sister, Rachel, though, like you asked me to. I didn't forget."

I pull a handkerchief from my pocket to blot some more tears.

"Remember the night we graduated high school? We stayed out all night, just to see if we could, and then we slept until noon the next day. Or our first camping trip together when we forgot the ice and some of our food spoiled? What about the time in band our freshman year when William called me the worst trumpet player in the band, and you stuck up for me? I'll never forget how good that made me feel, even though I probably was the worst trumpet player in the band. But you made me want to practice and get better, so I could prove you right."

My rambling conversation is pointless, I know. Elaine can't hear me. And these are only random memories of us together that come to mind while I kneel looking down. But I can still see Elaine smiling at me, her brown hair brushing her shoulders while wonderful music came out of her trumpet, and me wishing I could play that well.

A thought hits me. In my mind, Elaine will always be the beautiful person I met in high school. No matter how old I get, that's always how I'll remember her—young, attractive, fun, kind, and talented. Is that a good thing? I don't know. All I know is that the thought of going on without her terrifies me. I have to find a way, but I don't know how.

"You are so beautiful. On the inside and the outside. I'll never find another person who compares. They'll never be what you are to me."

I shake my head and dry my eyes with the handkerchief a second time.

When I decided to visit Elaine's grave by myself, I thought I was ready. I've cried plenty in the two weeks since she died, but I had hoped I'd hold myself together once I arrived. That isn't happening. Maybe this is one more way that I'm not as strong as I thought, not as strong as my father is. It seems like I ought to have control of my emotions by now, two weeks later. How pathetic have I become?

Finally, I walk away, my heart in pain and my disgust at my weakness growing with each step.

Why did I come here, anyway? Some people told me talking is supposed to help a person feel better. Maybe that only helps if the other person can say something back.

"How did things go, Ted?"

He shakes his head. "Bad, Sticks, bad."

"So, you're done, then?"

"Yeah, I think so. I don't care to talk with those old guys no more."

It's now a little over a month after Elaine's death, and Ted just returned from his second meeting at the VFW hall. He wanted to see what it was like to spend time with other veterans, and to see if any other Vietnam vets were in the group. We're sitting on our couch talking about the meeting.

"They looked down their noses at you again?"

"Yep, pretty much. They gave me flak because America hasn't finished off the VC yet. Some of those guys kept talkin' about how they had to fight six million Germans, or some number like that, and we can't beat some rice growers and chicken farmers who don't even have tanks or planes to fight back with."

"As if that's your fault."

"I know, I know, but that's how military guys are, I guess. If you aren't a winner, you're nothing. At least, that's how these guys are."

It strikes me that my father is the opposite of that. Maybe that's why I can never remember him going to a VFW meeting.

That thought leads me to ask, "You didn't see any other Vietnam guys there either, then?"

"Only a couple, but they mostly sat there and didn't say much."

"What you said probably also explains why only a couple of young guys bother to go."

"That, maybe, and maybe because those old guys decided to show a pornographic movie at their next meeting."

"You're kidding."

"No lie, Sticks. Those guys are our parents' age, and they want to watch porno movies together."

Maybe *that* is why I can't remember my father joining any veterans' organization.

"That's crazy. But I can't believe they look down on you. You've got a right to hold your head up like they do. We all bleed red. Besides, it's not like any of them fought all those Germans single-handedly."

"Yeah, I had that same thought myself, Sticks. I stuck out my neck for America the way that those older guys did, but because our war isn't won yet, and because my tour was only fourteen months, I'm less of a man in their eyes."

"There it is."

"There it is."

"But you and Tanya are still good, Ted?"

"Yeah, real good. I took her to a Dodgers game recently. She'd never been to a baseball game before."

"I thought you weren't into sports."

"Not as much as you. But Tanya had never been, and I'd only been to Dodger Stadium twice before, so we decided to watch a ballgame."

"Women can do that to you, I guess."

"Do what?"

"Get you to do things you wouldn't normally do."

Ted smiles and nods for a moment, then his face turns serious. "Speaking of, Sticks, I've got something to ask you."

"Go on."

"You've been hanging around the apartment a lot lately. I mean, you get up, you go to the garage for work, you come home, and you sleep."

"You suggesting we go to a Dodgers game together? The season is nearly over."

"No. I'm suggesting you meet this girl I found for you."

It's a good thing I'm already sitting down. That took me by surprise, and I shiver nervously. "I don't know, Ted."

"It's a woman Tanya went to college with. They're friends. Tanya tells me she's a real nice girl, a little shy, but cute. I told her I didn't know what you'd say, though."

"Damn. I don't know what to say, either."

"You know you're gonna need to date other women at some point, and Olivia sounds like she'd understand where you're at right now. You want me to tell Tanya yes or no? Oh, and Olivia is White, if you care about that."

Olivia's color hadn't even crossed my mind, which whirs with emotion at the thought of a date with someone other than Elaine. Ted's right—at some point, I'll need to meet new women. But I lost Elaine only ten weeks ago. Is that enough time? What if it's not, and I embarrass Ted by screwing things up? What if I embarrass myself by bumbling around like an idiot? I haven't been on a first date in over four years, after all.

Finally, I stammer, "I don't know, Ted. I just don't know what to say."

"Well, I guess I don't need an answer today, but Tanya already asked Olivia, and she says Olivia is willing to meet you."

"Did Tanya mention Elaine?"

"Not exactly. She did tell Olivia that you've been having a rough time lately with things that aren't your fault. Olivia said she didn't mind that if you were as nice a guy as Tanya said you were."

"Let me think about it for a day or two."

Despite my doubts, I agree to meet Olivia. She's everything Ted said she was—quiet and softspoken, but kind, sympathetic, and attractive, especially her long red hair and bright green eyes. We meet for dinner at a restaurant, talk, laugh a bit, and share a few things about ourselves. I thought things were going decently, right up until the point when I decide to risk telling her about Elaine.

I thought I could do it without falling apart. I hoped I could mention Elaine's death as a way to explain why I'd dodged some of Olivia's questions about myself and been a little quiet at times. She had treated me very nicely, and I was worried I wasn't being talkative enough in return. I thought I owed her an explanation of why.

But once I say it, I spend the rest of the date thinking about Elaine no matter how hard I try not to. I can't help it. Even though Olivia is quick to offer her condolences, by the time the evening is over, I know it's the only date we'll have. I'm too discouraged with myself to even ask Olivia if she wants to meet again. She doesn't say anything about a second date, either.

When I try to sleep that night, Elaine is still all I can think about. I remember back to our first date at the Santa Monica Pier's amusement park. We rode the roller coaster and snacked on popcorn as the sun went down. Then we walked the beach together for hours. It was both the most exciting and the most frightening time in my life to that point.

Part of the reason I walked so long and was so frightened was that I needed time to summon my courage to give Elaine a kiss. I finally did, and then I spent the rest of the evening wondering if I'd even done it right.

Did she feel the same? Was Elaine as nervous as I was that first night? I never asked her. It's one more thing I meant to find out someday but will never have the chance to do now. I guess I figured that was the type of thing that you looked back on after years together rather than something you asked before you even got married. Now, I'll never know.

Unable to sleep, I do something I haven't done since I was in Vietnam. I pull out the letters from Elaine that I saved while overseas and read some of them. A lot of what she wrote is

I Try To Bounce Back

mundane—about her friends, getting her job as a waitress, and so forth.

But one thing she wrote to me over and over was how happy she felt when she thought about our future together. Nearly every letter I read says something about how much Elaine looked forward to doing something with me once I was home.

When I check the clock and see that three in the morning isn't far away, I know this has to stop. Dwelling on Elaine won't help me have a better day tomorrow any more than it's helping me get a decent night's sleep tonight. But what else do I have?

Chapter 19

Three Strikes

More first dates follow, one in September, another in November, but they go no better. Both are one-and-done, and I bear the responsibility for that. Whatever I do turns out wrong. In September, I vowed not to say anything about Elaine in the hope that avoiding her wouldn't trigger my memories. But because I spent most of the date reminding myself not to say anything about Elaine, I spent most of my time thinking about her. My conversation was dull and shallow as a result. I don't blame Sheila for her politely-worded decision not to meet again.

Today's date didn't even end politely. Carrie walked out before it was over, and I don't blame her, either. I ordered a beer with dinner to try and relax myself. I also tried to avoid my mistake of being too dull by talking about anything that came to mind. She asked about Vietnam, so I described flying in helicopters, spraying Agent Orange, and some of the other things I did. I also mentioned how I repair cars for a living. But I rambled on too long, and eventually Carrie stood up and left after telling me I was too full of myself, just another conceited, macho military guy who thought the world revolved around him.

So, now I'm drinking at home by myself, like I did last night and the night before. Soon enough I'm out of beer, so I grab my keys to get more.

Without knowing why, I find myself driving through my old neighborhood on my way to the liquor store. I've decided I'm in the mood for something stronger than beer. Because it's November, I have the top on my Corvette, so I lock up and go in for some Scotch.

After several sips from the bottle, I realize my head doesn't feel quite right. I don't remember how many beers I had before leaving the apartment, but maybe it was too many. So, I sit down for a minute, my back to the stone facing of the wall of the liquor store.

I don't stay there long, though. After a few minutes, I stand and walk down the street. On my way, I come across a man sleeping on a park bench. He's covered in newspapers, and the guy looks like he hasn't shaved or bathed in several days. The man sits up when I walk near the bench.

"Sorry to wake you up," I say, ready to continue on my way.

Although his eyes look bleary, he replies, "It's okay, man. I thought you might be the cops coming around to hassle me."

Although I really want to drink by myself, this catches my attention. "The cops do that often?"

"Depends on the cop. Some of 'em just tell you to move along, but the mean ones will whack the soles of your boots with their baton to wake you up. That fuckin' hurts. It's one reason I'm a light sleeper and could hear you coming."

That's when I notice he's wearing a fatigue jacket.

"You serve in Vietnam?" I ask. Although the scruff on his face makes it hard to tell, it looks like the guy isn't much older than I am.

He sits up straighter. "Yeah. Marines, I Corps. I fought at Khe Sanh. You?"

I remember Khe Sanh well, of course, even though I was out of Vietnam by the time that battle was fought. The VC besieged it immediately preceding the Tet Offensive in 1968 and bombarded the hell out of it. The military brass decided to hold the base at any cost, only to evacuate it after the Tet Offensive was over and the spotlight had moved somewhere else.

"Yeah, I flew in helicopters. First Cav."

Although his arm shakes a bit, the man salutes me. Not knowing what else to do, I extend the bottle of Scotch to him.

He declines with a wave of the hand. "Nah, I've got a little of my own saved here," he says while patting his jacket. "When did you come home?"

"About two years ago. December 1 of 1967. You?"

"March 15 of 1969."

Barely six months ago, and the guy is sleeping on the streets. Damn. "Sorry again to wake you up," I say.

"Don't be. Sometimes the dreams are as bad as being awake, you know?"

I had already started to move off, but I stop when he says that. "You have those, too?" I ask, turning back.

"Ever since Khe Sanh. Charlie shelled us for six straight days, and I've never had a good night's sleep since then. Between the explosions and those damn monsoon rains, I didn't sleep for three days."

"I see them, too. The nightmares. Not every night, but I see them."

"What's your name, soldier?"

"Scott Reynolds."

"Edward Davis."

This time we shake hands. Edward's hand feels cold.

I draw out my wallet and hand him a few dollars. When he tries to push the money away, I tell Edward, "Use it to get yourself some gloves and new socks. You deserve them."

"God bless you, Scott," he replies after tentatively taking the cash.

After a second mutual salute, I go on my way. Maybe he'll just drink away the money. Who cares? It's not like I'm doing anything different right now.

Soon I reach a familiar street. It's the one Dad's bakery is on. Stopping a few buildings away, I sit down and put my back against a wall to resume drinking. It seems an appropriate spot when I think about it—the lesser son of a better father drinking himself into oblivion within sight of his father's success.

Three Strikes

At that moment, it starts raining. Any normal person would've run for their car, but mine's far away now, so I sit and let it rain. Why not? Who am I trying to impress? Besides, my head hurts, and I feel exhausted.

I take another sip of Scotch and close my eyes. Pictures come to me. Not the flashbacks or the nightmares, but just pictures. I see myself playing catch with Dad in the backyard, followed by the band room where I first met Elaine. Sneaking my first beer with some friends in high school. Pete when he was a puppy and Dad brought him home. My drill sergeant in boot camp. The tarmac at Tan Son Nhut Airfield receding as my Freedom Bird left Vietnam. The apple tree that used to stand in the backyard. Finally, Elaine's casket and my last look at her face. For several minutes, I stop concentrating while more random images flow in and out of my mind.

All the while, the raindrops strike my face and bare arms. I shiver.

Momentarily, the rain stops hitting me, and I hear a new sound, a series of gentle plops. Opening my eyes, someone's standing over me, and they have an umbrella.

"Is that you, Scott?"

I try to focus through the haze fogging my brain and the water dripping into my eyes. The place I'm sitting isn't well-lit, so I'm not sure who's shielding me. Slowly, I wobble to my feet and take a look.

"Sandra?"

"What are you doing out here in the rain?"

I hold up the bottle of Scotch in reply.

"Well, yes, I can see you've been drinking. But why here?"

"Why not? This place seemed as good as any other."

She frowns and puts her free hand on her hip as if to ask, "Really?" Instead of saying that, however, Sandra says, "Come inside with me."

"Inside where?"

"The coffee shop, of course."

Squinting my eyes into better focus, I find I'm sitting near the coffee shop where Sandra works. I hadn't realized the fact until now. Presumably, that's how she found me.

Sandra holds out her hand. "Come on, silly. Let's go inside. The coffee shop is supposed to be closed for the night, but you need someplace dry to sit for a minute."

"My car is right over there," I state, waving my arm in the vague direction of my Corvette even though it's several blocks away.

"Oh no you don't, Scott. You aren't driving anywhere. We may not know each other that well, but I like you enough that I won't let you drive in the state you're in. I wouldn't let a complete stranger drive anywhere in the state you're in. Come on," she says, pulling me toward the front door of the café. "I'll get you a coffee." Before I can protest, she grabs my bottle of Scotch, too.

"Hey!"

"I'll give it back to you—tomorrow, after you've sobered up some. Now, come on," she says, taking down her umbrella and pulling me through the door.

A moment later I'm seated, massaging my temples and trying to clear my head. Sandra brings over a steaming mug of coffee and sets it in front of me. "Here you are. Drink some of this after it cools a bit. Now, what were you doing drinking outside the café?"

"I was doing nothing."

"What do you mean, nothing?"

"Nothing. I'm nothing. My life's going nowhere, doing nothing. It's the only word that fits."

Softly, Sandra reaches over and slides some hair out of my face. I've stopped paying attention to how long it's gotten and let it go. Then she rests her elbows on the table and puts her chin on top of her hands, looking at me. "I almost didn't recognize you out there, you look so different from who I remember. What's happened to you, Scott?"

"Where should I begin?"

Three Strikes

"Begin wherever you need to. At the beginning, if that's what it takes."

"If I do that, I'm going to be sober again before I finish." I mean it as a joke, but my voice is too monotone and quiet to make it funny, so it sounds like I'm being rude and dismissing Sandra's concern.

She frowns a touch and sighs. "Are you saying you don't want to talk to me? If not, it's okay. I'll call a cab to take you home."

Sandra gets up, and even in my stupor, I realize I'm about to leave another woman disappointed in me. That brings on the shameful feelings of inadequacy that've been my constant companions ever since Elaine's death. I put my head down, resigned to another failure.

I raise my eyes when I hear Sandra lift the telephone from its cradle and start dialing the numbers. Suddenly, I don't know from where, anger surges up, taking the place of my shame. I'm not mad at Sandra; my anger is toward myself for being so pitiful.

"Stop, please," I manage to say.

She looks over, pausing in mid-dial.

"That was a bad thing to say to you. I'm sorry. It was supposed to be a joke, but it came out all wrong. Will you sit down for a minute?"

Warily, Sandra deposits the telephone receiver back in its spot and returns to the table.

I know how red my face must look—I can't recall the last time I felt so embarrassed with myself.

"I'm sorry," I say again. "I've had a lousy day, and I'm handling it badly. Please don't think I meant to take it out on you."

Sandra's frown is gone, but her lips are pursed and she's looking me directly in the eyes. "Tell me what's happened to you," she asks quietly.

"What can I say? I'm heading down. Tonight I might have hit bottom." I'm about to spread my arms, palms up, to indicate there's nothing more to say, but I owe Sandra more than that, so I pause and take a deep breath before going on.

"I don't know where to start. I've spent most of this year watching my girlfriend die. Nothing could save her. That's my main problem, I'd say."

Sandra's mouth forms an "o" and her eyebrows shoot upward. "My goodness, Scott. That's tragic. It's horrible. How long had you dated?"

"Almost five years. We started in high school. When I went to Vietnam, she waited for me to come back. I thought we'd spend our lives together. But now she's dead."

"Can I ask what killed her?"

"A form of cancer that gets young people sometimes. Nothing I could do was any help. Nothing anyone could do helped. No one expected someone so young to get cancer. So, by the time anyone looked for cancer, it was too late."

Before I can stop her, Sandra walks around the little café table and gives me a hug.

"How come you did that?"

"How long has it been since someone gave you a hug just to remind you that you deserve better than that?"

"I have no idea. A while, I guess."

"That's why I did it. You look like you needed a hug."

I manage a smile, but it doesn't last once I continue with my story. "Things have fallen apart ever since. I barely leave my apartment except for work. You can see how long it's been since I had my hair cut. I probably would've lost weight, since I don't eat much, but I drink too often," I say with a gesture toward the bottle of Scotch Sandra's placed just out of my reach.

"It's no wonder that my last three dates have been failures— including the one I went on earlier this evening. What woman would want to date someone as fucked up as I am?"

Although I almost never use that word, it's the only one strong enough to fit how pathetic I've become, so I don't apologize or take it back. I expect Sandra to recoil when it comes out, but she continues looking me in the face steadily. Raising the cup of coffee to my lips, I wipe a tear from my eye with my left palm while I wait for what she'll say.

She replies softly, "Maybe it won't help much, but I can think of one woman who would love to spend time with you."

"Who's that?" I respond, unable to hide my bitterness. "You know someone who needs a good laugh at my expense?"

Sandra closes her eyes for a moment, shakes her head slowly, and bites down softly on her lip. I realize my second attempt at a joke has gone awry as badly as my first.

"I'm sorry again. Maybe I should shut up and let you talk," I say while rubbing my eyes. "I didn't realize you were being serious, and I stuck my foot in my mouth. It's another thing I excel at recently."

Sandra gently places a hand on my shoulder. "The woman I was talking about is me."

Startled, I nearly knock over the coffee cup.

"Do you want to know why?"

"I don't know what anyone would see in me, but if I talk, I'll probably say something stupid. So, yeah, go ahead."

"Do you remember the first day you came to the coffee shop?"

I nod.

"I was so nervous that day. It was only the second day in my life that I'd worked, and my first day without someone watching me and helping me. In my heart I didn't think I was ready to keep a job. But you were so nice to me when we talked, it really built up my confidence. I've never forgotten that."

"You've said that to me a few times now."

"I've said so more than once because I mean it. That gave me the faith in myself to not quit at the end of the day. And here's something I know I haven't told you before because I've never said it to anyone. For the next week, every time someone came through the door, my heart fluttered, hoping it'd be you. I really wanted to see you again because I thought you were very kind and handsome. I still do, Scott."

"You do?"

"Yes. And here's something else you need to hear. You also complimented me on my memory one time when we met. That helped give me some confidence to try college. I'm taking a business class at Pierce College this fall, and I'm thinking about maybe opening my own café someday. I've got a plan in life now, and partly it's because you helped my confidence when I needed it."

"I can't believe I meant that much to you. It was just a few conversations."

"Maybe to you that's all they were, but they mattered so much to me at the time. A person's timing can make all the difference. Sometimes, a person doesn't realize how much of a difference until later."

"Perhaps you're right about that. Talking with you tonight has me feeling a little less worthless than I did before."

Sandra smiles. "I'm not going to do anything silly like ask you on a date tonight, but if it's not too crazy, I'd like to meet you again when you're feeling normal, Scott. You look like you could use a friend right now."

"I'd like that." To my surprise, I find myself meaning it, too.

"Believe me, I feel terrible that you lost your girlfriend in such a tragic way. I'm not trying to replace her. But I've always thought I'd like to get to know you better. This is a strange way to do it, I admit, but I hope it'll turn out for the best. Now, I need to drive you home."

"What about my car? And didn't you tell me once that you couldn't drive?"

"I've learned how."

"Are you gonna say that somehow I deserve credit for that, too?"

"Nah, I just got tired of walking to work," Sandra says with a grin. "And don't worry about your car. It'll be there in the morning."

Chapter 20

A New Hope

"That was *so* much fun. Let's go again!" Sandra tells me, her smile beaming.

"Come on, it wasn't even scary."

"I got scared a little bit in the graveyard."

"You did not. You laughed most of the time."

"Okay, so it wasn't scary at all. But I still want to go again."

Sandra and I stand outside the newest attraction at Disneyland, the Haunted Mansion. We're there on the Tuesday after Thanksgiving, and a modest crowd fans out around us as people exit. The sun is out for now, so all we need are light jackets. Mine is a dark gray while Sandra's is navy blue.

"I'd rather do Pirates of the Caribbean or the Jungle Cruise again," I tell her. "We still haven't tried the Davy Crockett canoes or the Matterhorn bobsled, either."

"Don't you have to paddle for yourself on the canoe cruise?"

"Yeah," I answer with a smile. "Are you scared of rowing?"

"Yes. I'm scared I'm gonna strain my inner quadradimus if I have to row."

"Your inner quadradimus? There's no such muscle as a quadradimus."

"I know. I made that up because I don't want to row," Sandra admits with a laugh.

Now I'm laughing, too. I had no idea Sandra had such a good sense of humor, but it's proven exactly what I need to loosen up.

Out of the blue, she asked me last week if I wanted to go to Disneyland with her. When I replied that I hadn't been in six or seven years, she admitted that she hadn't, either, but wanted to know if it would be as much fun as an adult as it was for a teenager. From Sandra's big smile and the mouse ears on her head, it seems the answer for her is yes.

"I'll give you credit for one thing, Sandra. Going to Disneyland on a Tuesday in early December was a good idea. The crowds are less than I thought. We've got time to do several more rides."

"Okay, let's go for the Matterhorn, then. But only if you yodel with me when we get to the top."

"I'm not yodeling."

"If you don't yodel, the yeti will get you," Sandra giggles. "That's the rule my friends and I had last time we were here."

Normally, a woman who giggles would annoy me, but somehow it fits when Sandra does it. She's not scatterbrained or flighty; rather, she has a knack for not taking life too seriously. That means she can get away with an occasional girlish thing like giggling without seeming immature.

"Can you even ride the Matterhorn?" I ask her.

"Why wouldn't I be able to ride?"

"You have to be this tall to ride this ride," I tease, holding my hand waist-high in the air.

She responds with a playful shove and another giggle before pointing toward the Matterhorn. "I'm at least two inches taller than that, and you know it."

"The Jungle Cruise is on our way to the Matterhorn. How about we do both and then get lunch?"

"Sounds great."

We both order hamburgers and fries for lunch. I can't stop smiling. Even though the attractions at Disneyland aren't terribly scary or dramatic, I'm not sure of the last time I felt this easy and carefree.

A New Hope

Sandra takes her time with her food, however, even as I dig in immediately. She keeps squirming, looking down at her plate, and then stopping to examine her fingernails, which she's painted sky blue today.

"Something wrong?"

She starts to reply, hesitates, thinks some more, and sighs.

"What's wrong?"

"Well, nothing, exactly. I was remembering something that happened a while ago."

I wait for her to go on. After another pause, she looks up and asks, "Remember the time you came to the coffee shop with your sister, and she asked me where to get catering for your parents' anniversary?"

"Yeah, I remember." The precision of Sandra's memory consistently takes me by surprise. Perhaps I should be used to it by now, but she's impressive in that regard.

"Maybe I should forget it," she says while taking a small bite.

"Come on. Something's bothering you all of a sudden. Tell me."

"Well, then, you remember when I suggested getting food from your father's bakery because I enjoy it so much? I didn't know you were related to him at the time, and you and your sister laughed before you told me the owner was your father."

"I sure do."

"For a moment, I was sure you were making fun of me."

"Why?"

"Because I'm overweight," Sandra admits, looking down at her plate again. She stirs her catsup with a French fry and says, "When you first laughed, I was sure it was because you thought I went to the bakery too often and ate too many pastries. Even after you explained yourself, I kept doubting. All of which made me feel like crying because even then I knew I liked you. I convinced myself you thought I was too fat, and it took a long time to unconvince myself of that."

"Oh my. I never thought you were too heavy. I think you're very cute just how you are."

"Really?"

The strain in Sandra's voice says she's hesitant to believe me.

"Really."

"You aren't just saying that?"

I put down my burger and take her by the hands. "Sandra, I'm having a wonderful time with you today. Better than I dared to hope for when you suggested coming here. I'll say it as many times as you need to hear it: I like you the way you are. If we were dating, I wouldn't want you to change a thing about yourself."

Sandra manages a weak smile. "I'm so self-conscious about my weight," she admits in a very quiet voice. "At times I try to lose some, but I like food, and when I get nervous, I tend to eat. After I eat, I get embarrassed for letting myself go, and then I get angry for not having more discipline."

I try my best smile to reassure her. "I know better than to think a person can just wish away the things that bother them, but if my word means anything, you don't need to stress over your weight as much as you do. Skinnier isn't always the same as prettier."

Sandra pats my hands, which still rest on hers. "Thank you, Scott. You're a sweet man. I hope I didn't spoil your fun with my insecurity."

"Not at all. I didn't know what to expect coming to Disneyland, but I'm having a great day with you. My insecurity was that you'd decide I was a loser who drank too much after getting to know me better, so I almost was too afraid to spend more time with you. I'm glad I ignored those fears and decided to come today. It can be tough, really tough, to face your fears sometimes. I don't always succeed. No one gets things right all the time. I think the real test is whether you can bounce back when you don't get things right."

"I guess that's one thing that's different between this trip to Disneyland and my last one, Scott."

"How do you mean?"

A New Hope

"I can't speak for you, but when I was a young girl, it seemed like everything was in front of me, and I didn't feel insecure about myself. You'd think a person would gain confidence as they get older, but I haven't. Maybe it's because I'm still learning how to deal with responsibility. Or maybe it's because a few people said very harsh things to me about my weight while I was in school, and I felt vulnerable at the time and believed them. But I struggle with confidence, and maybe that has something to do with why I felt attracted to you when we first met. You seemed so relaxed and comfortable with yourself, and I wanted to be more like that."

"It sounds like you need more people in your life who realize how amazing you are. You need some people who like you for who you are and don't care about the things you aren't. Maybe that's too forward of me to say, but that's how it looks to me, Sandra. I don't mean to criticize your other friends or your family, since I've never met them, but everyone needs those people in their lives who never judge them."

"Things seemed so much easier and less complex when I was young. At fourteen or fifteen, I still imagined the glamorous life I'd have someday with a handsome husband, a big house with a three-car garage, fun parties all the time, and a pearl necklace. I was only dreaming, of course, but when you're a teenager, that kind of dream life still feels possible. Maybe guys don't have the same kind of fantasies at age fifteen, though. What did you wish to be when you were that age?"

"Wow. I'll admit I haven't thought about that for a while." Now it's my turn to stir my catsup while I think of something to say. "I loved baseball when I was fifteen, but I wasn't much of a player, so I never dreamed of being Mickey Mantle or Willie Mays and playing in the major leagues. To be honest, I'm not sure what I dreamed I'd do as an adult. Not fix cars, for sure. All I remember is that life seemed to have a lot less pressure back then. I went to school, stayed up late in the summer, hung around my dad's bakery sometimes, and saw my friends on the weekends."

"That's exactly what I'm talking about, Scott. It was only six or seven years ago, but our lives have changed so much since then. Even when I was in high school, I still hoped that someday I'd get to travel around the world and visit some of the places I read about in books. But once school is over, you find out so quickly that life isn't like that anymore. Before long I had to find work to pay my bills. You ended up going to Vietnam. It's such a big jump from where we were only a few years ago, and sometimes, I get overwhelmed."

"You aren't the only one. Remember, you found me on the street drinking Scotch in the rain a little while ago. I sure didn't see myself falling that low when I was in high school. Back then, I believed only bums and lowlifes did that, which is part of why I wasn't very nice to you at first when you found me that night. I figured I must've become a lowlife since that's what I was doing, and that you would see me in the same light."

"That's why it feels good to be here together, Scott. I know that the Haunted Mansion isn't scary—especially not to you after going overseas to fight in a war. But when we were relaxed, enjoying the moment, and cracking jokes, it made me feel like a young girl again for a little while. And that got me thinking about how much I miss that feeling and how long it's been since I felt that way. So, thanks for helping me find some joy that I didn't even realize I was missing."

While Sandra speaks, a thought hits me. In the past, the sound effects of a place like the Haunted Mansion might've set off one of my flashbacks. But today they didn't. Maybe what Sandra is talking about helps to explain why. Or maybe not, but it's worth considering.

After pondering this, I tell her, "Maybe you've hit on something. At times, I feel so busy with life that I don't have any time to think about what I used to do that was fun. I spend so much time at work or tuning up my own car that time just disappears. After work, dinner, and a little television, I go to bed, all so I can do the same

A New Hope

the next day. I mean, a guy's gotta work to pay the bills and all, but today reminded me that life should be more than only that."

"Do you think going to Vietnam changed your outlook that much?"

"Absolutely it did. When I got drafted into the Army, I'd seen a few war movies, but those didn't prepare me for what it's like. I got to boot camp and got a rifle, and it sank in that I could die, and that when the time came, I might have to kill other people. Nothing in my life prepared me for that feeling, and once I realized that, nothing else has ever felt quite the same."

"Do you have a hard time relating to people because of it, Scott?"

"Sometimes I do. Here's an example. Shortly after I got home, which was about two years ago, Elaine and I went to a New Year's Eve party. I drank a little, we danced some, and I talked with other people at the party. But the entire evening, I never shook the feeling that it was all frivolous nonsense and that the people there weren't serious enough. That's dumb, I know, because that's why someone goes to parties—to relax and forget about why they have to be serious the rest of the time. But Vietnam was too recent for me, and I couldn't get over that the other people weren't more concerned with what might happen the next day."

"Do you still feel the same now?"

"I think I'm getting a little better. If we had come here to Disneyland two years ago, I wouldn't have had much fun. This place is meant for children above all, and I wasn't a child anymore. That's the attitude I would have taken. I wouldn't have been able to let go and live in the moment. To be honest, I'm surprised today has gone so well. When we walked through the gates, I still didn't know if I'd allow myself to act carefree and enjoy the day. I think you're a big part of the reason why I have."

Sandra blushes a bit, and I realize neither of us has finished our food yet.

"I don't get it," she says after a bite.

"Get what?"

"The night I found you outside the coffee shop, you told me several women had turned you down after dates. What were they thinking?"

"Eh, that was mostly my fault. The problem was I thought about Elaine too much. Either I was actively thinking about her, or I was actively trying not to think about her, but either way, I kept thinking about her. I came off looking pathetic and distracted because of it. Those women did what I would've done in their shoes."

"But isn't it partly their fault, too? I mean, you've been to Vietnam, and you watched your girlfriend die of cancer. Why did they expect you to be perfect? For that matter, why did you expect yourself to be perfect?"

What does a guy say to that?

Sandra continues. "If those women really cared, they would've taken some time to understand you and get to know you. Maybe the problem was more with them than you think. Isn't it selfish to only want to date people who fit your mold to perfection?"

Now I'm smiling. I'd been so convinced that my own flaws were to blame for my failed dates that I hadn't even considered the possibility Sandra raises. Finally, I say, "Couldn't I make a similar point about you, Sandra?"

"What do you mean?"

"A little while ago you told me you felt self-conscious about your weight. I don't think it's a problem. Maybe you convinced yourself that it was, and then it became a self-fulfilling prophecy, just like I blamed myself for bad relationships because I had so much self-doubt."

"I'd never thought of that."

"It's crazy, isn't it? We're both so good at seeing positive things in each other, but we can't always see them in ourselves."

"That's why everyone needs friends, I suppose."

"I'd like to ask you something else I've been wondering," I say to Sandra after a moment.

A New Hope

She nods.

"You told me you were a great student in high school, right?"

"Yeah. I was close to getting straight A's."

"Why not go to college full time, then? Why are you working in a café?"

She scratches her head and looks to the side. "To be honest, Scott, my family doesn't have much money. If I'm ever gonna get a college degree, I have to pay for everything myself. Sometimes I babysit for my two younger sisters so that my parents can work second jobs at night. It's also why I'm taking only one class in college right now. I can't afford more than one class, and I don't have the time between work and babysitting. It's a miracle we were both able to get today off to come here."

I consider this before my reply. The stock thing to say would be something like "that's too bad" or "I'm sorry things are tough," but my experiences with Ted and his family have me thinking more deeply. Ted's family lives in a poorer neighborhood because of racism and things outside of their control. Maybe something similar has happened to Sandra's parents?

So, instead of a banality, I ask Sandra, "Is it something you want to talk about today?"

"I'm not ashamed of my parents, if that's what you're inferring. The trouble is that my mother has health issues. Her vision is poor, and she can't hear very well."

"Has she always been that way?"

"Yes. The doctors she's seen think it's probably because her own mother drank when she was pregnant. No one knows for sure, but that's what they told us is most likely. One doctor said that researchers suspect drinking during pregnancy can cause birth defects in children, but they don't have definitive proof yet. My grandmother did drink often when she was alive, though, so it may well be true."

"I'll bet that makes it tough to hold a job."

"It does. The U.S. doesn't have many laws that protect people with handicaps like hers. So, the jobs she can get tend to pay the minimum wage, and employers will often replace her when they get applications from someone who can do the work faster. Mom takes what work she can find, but it's intermittent. Sometimes she has no job at all, and other times she does two at once. It's those times when I do a lot of babysitting."

After a moment's reflection, I tell Sandra, "Some soldiers returning from Vietnam are in a similar situation. Some of them were wounded in the head, and their eyesight, hearing, and memory have been affected as a result. I wonder if they have the same experiences when it comes to holding onto a job? Either way, it seems like your mother is getting penalized for something she can't control. It'd be nice if that didn't happen to people." It's a lame ending, but I'm not sure what else to tell her.

"It's how things are. But when I open my own coffee shop someday, I plan to do everything I can to make it friendly to people with physical difficulties, both the employees and the customers."

"I think that's great, Sandra. More people should do that."

"Maybe other people don't think about it because it doesn't affect them personally. I don't know if I would."

"But you do think about it, and that's what's great. If no one ever thought about problems, life would never get better."

Sandra smiles sweetly. "Our conversation has gotten pretty serious, but I'm glad that it did. I know you a little better than before."

"The question is, do you still like me now that you know those things?" I ask with a grin, for once feeling sure of the answer. It seems we're both ready to move back to more lighthearted things.

"I like you enough to go on at least one more ride with you. After that, we'll see," she replies with her own grin.

"I'm still not gonna yodel. If that breaks up our friendship, then so be it," I tease.

"How about we race in Autopia, then?"

A New Hope

"Can the cars in Autopia even pass each other?"

"I doubt it. I think they go six miles per hour, tops."

"Then how will we race?"

"By beating you to be first in line," Sandra calls over her shoulder while starting toward the Tomorrowland section of the park. I follow, already resigned to a second-place finish but not caring in the least.

Chapter 21

Sabotage

As Christmas of 1969 approaches, Sandra and I see each other frequently. Although we don't refer to our meetings as dates, that's more or less what they are. In the process, I discover she's the same person she appeared to be that day at Disneyland—kind, compassionate, fun, and very bright. It seems like her self-confidence grows each time we meet, too. Still, I'm a little surprised when I meet her at the café for lunch one Saturday, and she asks me if I'd like to visit her parents' house for dinner.

"I don't know about that, Sandra. The thought makes me nervous."

"Sorry, Scott, but I told my parents I'd met a new friend and that we went to Disneyland together. When I admitted that my new friend is a man, they immediately decided we must be dating, and that they had to meet you if we were dating."

"Are we dating? We never call it that, but maybe we should."

"Are you ready to call it dating?"

"I think so, but I'm not sure. It doesn't seem like that should be a hard question to answer, but I've had awful luck on dates this year. The time we spend together is fun. I had no idea what a wonderful, understanding person you are until the past few weeks. But sometimes I think leaving things as they are is the right decision because I feel less pressure to act like a boyfriend. What do you think?"

Sandra laughs and wraps her arm around my shoulders. "I think you're overanalyzing. Do what your heart tells you."

I pause for a brief moment and then kiss Sandra on the cheek.

"Is that your decision?"

"It's what my heart tells me. Call it a date. I'm still nervous, though."

"Why? You look great. You've cut your hair, you shave every day again, and my dad will love your car when you show it to him. Besides that, you haven't had a drink in a couple weeks. Why are you worried?"

"Well, two reasons, really. A year ago something very important happened to me, and I'm not sure how well I'll handle the memory."

"What's that? Are you comfortable talking about it?"

"About this time last year, Elaine and I rented a cabin up in the Sierras. It was after we learned she didn't have a chance to recover. Even though I knew it might only last for a few months, I asked her to marry me. I didn't want her to die without being married if that was important to her."

"But she said no?"

"Correct. It's what I thought she'd say, but proposing was the most powerful way for me to tell her how much she meant to me."

"I think that's romantic. What a beautiful thing to do."

"Like I said, that was exactly a year ago. I don't know how well I'm going to handle the holiday season this year, remembering how heart-wrenching things turned out last December."

"What can I do to help you?"

"Nothing. I mean, you don't need to do anything special. The last few weeks seeing you are the most relaxed I've felt in a long time. A long time. I worry that any change in our routine might ruin the magic."

Sandra hugs me again and leans her head on my shoulder. "I understand. But if we're going to keep seeing each other, my parents will want to meet you at some point. We can't put it off forever. I guess the question is how soon will you feel ready for that?"

"Well, that has to do with my other reason for being worried. You told me once that your parents despised the war. That makes me real nervous. Have you told them I spent fourteen months in Vietnam?"

Sandra sucks in her breath quietly. "It did come up. I think they're okay with me seeing you, but I don't know for sure. We were speaking on the phone, so I couldn't see their reaction in person. I hope they'll be nice to you once they learn what a great guy you are and how happy we are together."

When I look at Sandra, she's looking me in the eye, but her posture is stiff, and she's biting her lip gently.

"You sound more hopeful than certain."

"Well, here's the thing that worries me. Sometimes my dad gets angry and bitter about life. It's not that he's a bad man, but life has chewed him up and spat him out. He spends so much time and energy caring for Mom, trying to keep the family above water financially, and working that it's driven most of the joy out of him. I know he'll be pleased to see us happy together, but he might not show it. I thought you should know that before we visit."

"Sounds kinda like my drill instructors in boot camp. I suppose I can handle that."

"You sure?"

"No, but I'll do my best."

By the time Sandra and I take our seats at the dinner table, I know I need a backup plan. Without telling either of us, her parents invited a second guest to dinner.

"Cory happened to stop by earlier today, and since you claim Scott here is only a friend, we figured you wouldn't mind if he joined us for dinner," Sandra's father, Gus, tells her, cigarette dangling from his lips.

"Wait. What? What do you mean?" Sandra protests.

Sabotage

"Come on, the table's already set. The food's ready," Gus responds, turning and walking into the dining room, his back a sign that the discussion is over already.

Sandra stares hard at her father, eyebrows knit together and a deep scowl etched into her face, but Cory has already taken a seat at the table by the time we arrive. Sandra's two younger sisters share one side of the table with him.

Seven people barely fit around the table. Sandra and I are crammed elbow to elbow even with only two of us on our side. The paint in the dining room is a light green that probably was attractive when new but is now dirty and flaking. The dining room also has a clammy feel despite the number of people in it, perhaps because it was a cool day outside today and no one turned on any heat inside the house.

I see Sandra gave me an accurate description of her father. Gus Larson isn't a towering man, but his broad shoulders and natural half-frown make him appear bigger than he really is. His beard is gray rather than peppered, and he's mostly bald on top. But the most noticeable thing about Gus is that he hunches over slightly when he walks, and he moves with a limp, as if carrying a heavy load. Sandra hadn't been lying when she said life had chewed him up. Gus stabs out his cigarette in an ash tray on the kitchen counter before seating himself.

It's also clear that Sandra had no idea this would happen. She sits next to me at the table blinking rapidly and unable to say anything, but I notice her muscles are tense, and her breathing borders on seething.

What should I do? I elect to start with diplomacy and courtesy. What other choice do I have?

"So, Scott, what is it you do for a living?" Cory asks me once the food, ham and mashed potatoes, is in motion around the table.

"I work in a garage fixing cars."

"A grease monkey?"

Do I see the hint of a smirk?

"Some people call it that, but I prefer mechanic." Even though I know I'm being set up, out of politeness I reply, "And how about you?"

"I'm an assistant manager at a bank. It's a decent job."

Glancing over at Cory, he seems a little older than me, making him probably two or three years older than Sandra. I figure he can't be over twenty-five, though. With his boyish face and medium-length blond hair, he looks like he only needs to shave twice a week.

"And what did you do before that? Or has that been your job since high school?" Cory continues while adjusting the very nice watch on his left wrist.

"I spent two years in the Army," I say with confidence. Cory's game is transparent as hell, but I'm not going to hide something I feel proud of doing.

"You were an officer, then?"

"No. A private. I flew in helicopters."

"Scott is a terrific musician," Sandra puts in, trying to derail where things are headed. "He can play both the trumpet and the guitar."

"Did you learn to play guitar before or after going overseas?" Gus asks gruffly.

"A little of both."

"I'd have thought you'd be too busy looking for villages to burn to learn to play an instrument."

Great. I've barely lifted my fork, and already it's two against one.

"Not actually," I tell them, trying to copy my dad's easygoing tone meant to defuse tension. "Mostly, my helicopter flew around moving supplies. Occasionally, we sprayed stuff called Agent Orange. It kills foliage, so that the VC would have less cover, but it doesn't hurt people. I barely fired a weapon the whole time I was in-country."

The last part isn't all that close to the truth, but I don't feel bad about saying it, given how dinner has started.

"Scott is a kind and generous man," Sandra puts in, although I notice her tone already has an angry edge to it. "Did I ever tell you the story of how we met, Dad?"

"You said you met at your work."

"That's right. A woman forgot her money to pay for a coffee, and Scott was chivalrous and paid for her. His kind heart caught my eye, and we started talking after that. And you should try his father's bakery sometime. Darryl makes amazing doughnuts and croissants. You'd love them, too, Cory." The edge in Sandra's voice grows with the last few words.

"And where would I find the money to eat doughnuts? With all my taxes going to pay for a war thousands of miles away, extra money is hard to come by," Gus grumbles.

All this time, I wait for Sandra's mother, Eleanor, to say something, but I'm not sure she's even heard the whole conversation. Sandra told me she doesn't hear well, after all, and that sometimes one must speak straight into Eleanor's ear if they want a response. But her eyes shift from speaker to speaker, so maybe she can hear a little.

"Why'd you join up, son?"

"I was drafted, so it wasn't up to me. But I thought my country needed me, so I didn't mind." It's getting tougher to stay diplomatic, but I'm trying.

"Yeah, your country needed you, all right. It needed you to get shot so that Rockefeller and the big bankers and industrialists could grind your bones into money."

"Ain't that the truth," Cory puts in before I can attempt a defense, although, honestly, I'm not sure why I'm trying anymore. I should have aborted this mission before engaging.

"This country hasn't done nothing for the poor people," Cory continues. "I mean, I see guys who work their whole lives, and the only thing they have to show at the end is enough money to buy themselves a decent coffin to die in."

I consider pointing out that Cory is wearing a tailored shirt and a silk tie while he says this, but why bother? I don't know if his cufflinks are silver, but I wouldn't be surprised.

Instead, I ask, "Cory, how long have you been at the bank using other peoples' money to make your own?"

"Almost a year now. I got promoted a few months after starting. The bank president realized I was good at my job, and he wanted someone with degrees in business and finance like I have."

"I see." I didn't think my barb was that subtle, but Cory didn't seem to notice.

"I'm not sure how long I'll stay there, to be honest. The pay is okay for now, but if a chance to move up presents itself, I'll jump at it. I plan to own beachfront property someday, but that isn't cheap. I think it's worth it, though, to make sure the neighborhood is exclusive enough to keep out the more undesirable types."

I wonder if "undesirable" refers to grease monkeys like me or Black people like Ted and his family. Perhaps he means both.

"You'll get there, Cory. People will trust you because you're honest," Gus is saying.

"That's the key to getting ahead in any business. Honesty and integrity always carry the day."

"If all our leaders were honest, we never would have gone to war over in Vietnam."

"Agreed, Gus. It's too bad that some people believe the politicians and take their words at face value."

From the corner of my eye, I notice Sandra hasn't tasted any of her food. Suddenly, she stands up. Jabbing her finger, Sandra proclaims, "Shame on you, Cory, for doing this. And shame on you, too, Father, for setting Scott up. I don't know if you planned this ahead of time, but you might as well have. Scott is a kind, considerate man, and we're very happy spending time together. He has far more integrity and compassion than the two of you put together!"

Sabotage

Sandra turns to depart, tugging me by the arm. "Let's go, Scott, and leave these two men to stew in their own unhappiness."

Without saying anything more, I fold my napkin, place it on my plate, stand, and follow Sandra out of the dining room.

As I walk out the front door, I hear Gus yell, "I don't want to see you here again, or else."

Fifteen minutes later, we're back at Sandra's apartment, and she's crying uncontrollably. Sandra has a roommate, but she's out on a date of her own tonight.

"I can't *believe* they did that to you. It was awful."

"Who is Cory, anyway?"

Running her hands through her hair, Sandra slumps back in her chair and mutters, "He was sorta my boyfriend for a while."

"Sorta your boyfriend?"

"He grew up down the street. Cory is a few years older than me, but for some reason, my father took a liking to him. Maybe because Cory always agrees with what my father says, no matter what it is. But we knew each other growing up, and after I graduated high school, we dated for a little while. At least, I guess you'd call it dating." Sandra shakes her head at the memory.

"What happened? I mean, I can see he's a jerk, but maybe he used to be different?"

"No, not very different. Oh, I regret it now, all right. But at the time, I sorta looked up to him."

"Cory doesn't seem your type at all."

"He isn't. But you have to realize that I never had a boyfriend all through high school. When he showed a little interest in me and seemed like he was nice to my dad, I got sucked in by his flattery and the idea that he was a bright college kid who'd really make something of himself. It didn't take Cory long to show how shallow, greedy, and selfish he was, but you don't know that until you spend time with someone, right?"

I nod. It's true.

"Anyway, Cory acts like a whole different person around my father, which is why Dad still likes him and thinks I made a mistake by getting rid of him."

"But why, though? If he's as greedy and materialistic as he seems, why does he worry about what your father thinks?"

"I don't know for sure, but I think it's because Cory relishes manipulating people. I doubt he even cares that much about what's happening in Vietnam, but he knows my dad hates the war, so he acts like he does, too."

"Over in Vietnam, I knew guys who'd polish the boots of their officers to get better assignments, so I know the type you're talking about. You can't convince your dad of the truth, though? And what about your mom? I noticed she didn't say anything at all during dinner."

"To be honest, Scott, I think Dad is hanging on to the idea that Cory and I will date again because Dad considers himself a failure. He wants me to have the money he never had and have an easier life than he has. And Mom goes along with what Dad wants. Because he's the one who takes care of her with her handicaps, she thinks she owes it to him to follow along with what he says. Most days she doesn't talk too much."

Neither of us speaks for a while.

"Please don't hate me for tonight, Scott."

"Hate you? Of course not. You're the person who stood up for me."

"No, I mean please don't hate me for how my dad acted. I don't know what to do. I'm so angry and devastated about how tonight went."

I pull Sandra closer and kiss her forehead. "It wasn't what I was hoping for, either, but you aren't to blame."

"You probably think my father is an awful man, and tonight he was, but please don't think he's that way all the time. He's sacrificed everything, including his health, to put food on the table and clothes on the backs of my younger sisters and my mom. That makes him angry, and sometimes the anger just takes over."

"I understand that. At least, I think I do. But if he doesn't change his attitude about me later, what can we do? If he dislikes me just because I went to Vietnam, that's not something I can change."

"I know."

"What do we do, then?"

"He'll come around. I'll get him to come around."

I look at Sandra. Her body is tensed and she's quivering slightly. She doesn't look at all convinced that her father will come around.

Chapter 22

Misery Loves Company

When I get back to my apartment that night, Ted's got my old bottle of Scotch on our coffee table.

"Tough night for you, too?" I ask him.

Ted is like me—when the alcohol is anything stronger than beer, that's a sign something's badly wrong.

"Meeting Sandra's folks didn't go so well, I take it?" he asks.

"Disastrous. Her dad hates the war and thinks soldiers are tools of the bankers and industrialists. Plus, he invited Sandra's old boyfriend for dinner. The guy is a jerk, but apparently he has a hold on Sandra's father."

"That's about the most ridiculous thing I've ever heard of. Well, maybe not more ridiculous than some things we saw in the Nam, but it's still ridiculous. Well, here," Ted says, pouring a glass of Scotch and handing it to me. "Drink up, man."

"Weren't you and Tanya gonna go to the Lakers' game against the Cincinnati Royals tonight? I thought you told me her father got you tickets because neither of you had ever been to watch pro basketball."

"Yeah, we were gonna go, right up until I decided I'd had enough of Tanya and broke off the date."

"Wow. You two are done, then?"

"Yeah. I got tired of her getting on my case, saying I need to be more motivated and get a job that pays more, that sort of thing."

"Dig that, Ted."

"I did what I should have done, right? I *like* fixing things, and I'm good at it. That's not the only thing that bothered me about Tanya, but it's the biggest one. I didn't appreciate her nagging me and telling me to quit something I enjoy so that I could fit her perfect image of a boyfriend."

"Sounds like my last three dates before Sandra."

"I needed a while to realize it, but yeah, sounds like it."

"I'm sorry, Ted. The times you brought Tanya over here I liked her, but I guess I didn't see all the sides of her personality."

"What're you going to do about Sandra's dad?"

"What can I do? She thinks she can bring him around. If she doesn't, well, then I don't know what'll happen."

"Meeting that woman was the best thing to ever happen to you, Sticks. Well, other than Elaine, I mean. Don't give up without a fight on this one."

"Yeah, I dig that."

Ted leans back and sighs, throwing up his hands and then letting them fall to his sides. "Damn, Sticks, I wish this country wasn't so angry all the time. Seems like people are always getting mad these days. Either it's the Nam, or angry folks killing Dr. King or some politician like RFK, or something else, but people seem so upset. We went over there to fight and did the best we could. Why would Sandra's dad hate you for that?"

"She tried to explain it, but it's complicated. He seems likes he's angry at the whole world, and the war gives him a convenient reason to show it and vent the anger. I don't know. Maybe I've got him all wrong, but that was the feel I got."

"I hope that things don't go with him like between your sister and your mother. Did they ever patch things up? You never talk about that."

Now it's my turn to sigh deeply. "No. Neither has spoken to the other in months, and neither wants to budge. I hope that the Christmas season will finally get them back together, but I don't know that even the holidays will be enough this time."

"Well, Sticks, I'm gonna pray on that for you. I don't do a lot of prayin' these days. Hell, after some of the things we saw in the Nam, I don't even know how religious I am anymore. But I'd really like to see your family happy and getting along like mine does. I know my folks don't always approve of what I do, but they don't let their disappointment get the better of them. Maybe it's because of how long they've been teachers—they know that disappointments happen but that a new day always follows."

"You know what? I'm gonna act on that thought. Today is a Friday, and so tomorrow I'm going over to Lisa's apartment and talk some sense into her. Then I'll go to see my mom and do the same. This being angry at each other for months on end is ridiculous."

"I like that idea. You usually stay out of their arguments, so maybe you're the person to end them. Be careful, though. From what you've told me, it won't be easy."

"No, it won't. But maybe the problem is that I've been staying out of things too much, and I should be more active instead of waiting on one of them to take the first step. You think so?"

"It's hard to say, Sticks, but you might as well try at this point, right?"

I spend that night thinking of how to get through to Lisa and Mom. With Lisa, I know she'll be reasonable and open to discussion. Our relationship is solid, and she knows I'm not attacking her when I suggest things. With my mom, well, I may need a different strategy. So, I decide to visit Lisa first because I think speaking with her will be easier for me.

Once I've decided that, however, I think back on the end of the mission where my Chinook was shot down. Hearing about Ted and his decision to stop seeing Tanya just got my mind thinking about him, I suppose. Whatever the reason, I can see the last few minutes of that mission as if I were still there.

I've got Ted's arm over my shoulder, and we're limping away from our wrecked Chinook. Ted and I haven't gotten far, though, when the F-100s appear in the sky, hurtling toward our position. A quick glance reveals that the last of the Chinooks just got airborne. We're stranded in the village. Another glance and I realize we've only got one chance to survive.

"This is gonna hurt like hell, Ted," I tell him while I drag him inside the nearest hut in the village. Some were built on stilts and poles, elevated off the ground, but not all. This one wasn't, and I think I know why.

While Ted groans and curses beside me, I find what I'm looking for. A grass mat covering a pit. I've been in the Nam long enough to know that some villagers dig shelters underneath their homes specifically for times like this. It doesn't necessarily mean they're with Charlie—it simply means they want shelter for when someone targets their village. The pits are for survival.

One of two things will happen to us. If the airstrike drops napalm, we're likely to die a horrible death. If we're in the blast zone, it'll keep burning once it reaches us. Hiding underground won't help because napalm is a jelly-like liquid, and it'll fall into the pit and cover us. We'll burn up watching the skin melt off our bodies.

We might live if the planes drop cluster bombs. Those are small explosives that are released from a larger container while in the air. They spread out as they fall, exploding over a wide range of ground.

Just as Ted and I dive into the pit, we hear the detonations around us begin, and the debris flies. One blast knocks the hut away from over our heads. It's cluster bombs. I can feel the heat and the shockwave from the explosion wash over us, even in our underground shelter.

I look up to see dust clouds billowing around us, filtering the sunlight into an eerie brown-gray. My ears ring from the force and noise of the blasts.

Just when my hopes kindle, I see the small metal sphere falling toward us through a break in the dust clouds, sunlight glinting from its exterior. I cover my face, as pointless as that is, and try to duck away.

The sphere hits the ground not five feet away from us with a loud thunk, then rolls into our pit.

But the bomblet doesn't explode, and we aren't obliterated beyond recognition in a village ten thousand miles from home.

A dud. We're saved when a bomb doesn't detonate when it's supposed to.

Looking up, I can see the dust cloud blocking the view overhead once more. If it'd been napalm, everything above us would be a fiery inferno, and we would already have charred to a crisp.

"We did it!" I gasp while trying to suck in air. But Ted's shaking.

"Don't panic, man! It's a dud!" I yell to him.

"It's right there, Sticks," he says, pointing at the bomblet resting three inches from my body.

"Yeah, it's a dud. It didn't explode. We're okay!"

I can see Ted's teeth chatter when I look in his face. "Don't touch it!" he shouts.

Slowly, barely daring to breathe, I push out of the underground shelter and help Ted to his feet. Although dust floats in the air everywhere, the noise of firing is gone. Either the airstrike blew Charlie to bits, or he's decided to fall back.

"Let's look for help, Ted. We need someone to get us out of here."

Then I see it. A Chinook has circled back over the battlefield, the force of its propellors parting the clouds of dust around us.

As it touches down, I prop Ted's arm over my shoulder, and we limp toward the helicopter. A few men jump out, and one helps me with Ted.

"Careful, his leg's hurt," I yell to be heard over the noise of the Chinook's engine.

"Got it!" the other GI shouts.

"What'd you come back for?" I ask him.
"We heard an officer was still on the ground."
"Try by the well. That's the last place I saw him."

Chapter 23

I Try Diplomacy

Before going to see Lisa on Saturday, I stop by Elaine's grave to talk with her. I stand with my hands clasped behind my back, looking down at her resting place.

"It's been a while since my last visit, I know," I say to the headstone. "But I've been spending time with a lady named Sandra. She has a lot in common with you. I think you'd like her, if you could meet her.

"I've got some bad news, though. Your brother Glen dropped out of high school and enlisted in the Army, like he said he'd do. I made a couple more tries to talk him into staying to graduate. You told me that's what you wanted. Your mother, too. But it didn't work. I couldn't get through to him or get him to reconsider his plans. I'm sorry about that, but I tried my best."

In the past, I often cried when speaking to Elaine. My sadness compounded with the feeling that it was absurd and pathetic to speak to a dead person, which only made me feel worse. But I finally realized I'm not the only person who does that. Every soldier deals with war differently, and every person deals with grief in their own way, too. Sandra told me that after I mentioned I visited Elaine's grave at times, and I've found that she was right.

So, today, I stand solemnly, but I don't cry.

"I wanted to get Glen to reconsider, really I did. One time, I even had Ted come along with me, but it wasn't enough. Glen believes in what he's doing. I'll admit I haven't spoken with your parents since then, so I don't know how he's getting along now, but I hope he's okay.

"You'll also want to know that my drinking is back under control. I feel so much better, too. You'd be proud of me for that. I didn't do very well after I lost you, but I think I'm getting better finally. You'd like the person I am again now.

"I still miss you though, Elaine. All the time. Your smile, your laugh, your eyes, your touch—I wish I could see all of them again.

"But Sandra is a good person, a really good person. If you could meet her, I think you'd be happy for me.

"I need to go now. Lisa and my mother need me to help them out. They've been angry with each other for way too long. I probably should've done this a long time ago, but I was struggling so much myself with the thought of losing you that I couldn't do it. But now I'm ready. I think. I hope. Ready enough to try, anyway.

"I still love you, Elaine, and always will. I'll be back to visit again when I have a chance."

After calling to make sure she's home, I pull up to Lisa's apartment a little before noon on Saturday. I don't visit her place often, partly because I'm never sure if she'll have a boyfriend around or not. But Lisa assured me that today was a good time to visit.

Looking inside her place, the décor is tasteful. She has a brown reclining chair, paintings of the ocean, ships, and a surfer framed on the wall, and a polished kitchen table that's new since my last visit. A vase with daffodils is on the table, and the countertops in the kitchen are immaculate.

"Is that incense I smell?"

Lisa nods.

"You getting spiritual on me?"

A laugh. "No. I'm covering up the smell of the pancakes I burned for breakfast."

"I didn't know you liked pancakes."

"I don't make them often, which is probably why I did it wrong and burned them."

"You've got a new hairdo. What do you call that one?"

"The bombshell. It's pretty new, but I like it. How about you, Scott?"

"That's what it's called? It seems a little ironic you'd pick that one, given how you feel about Vietnam."

She smiles. "Good point. I hadn't made that connection. But it's only a name."

"Incense aside, I like your decorations."

"Thanks, Scott. The table was an early Christmas present from Dad. He came over one day and decided that my old table, the hand-me-down one with the folding sides, needed to go."

"The bakery must be doing well, then. He usually wouldn't do that. How're things with him? We haven't talked in a week or two."

"About the same as always. The bakery is busy this time of year. How are Ted and Tanya doing?"

"Ted's okay, I guess. I can't speak to how Tanya's doing."

"You mean they aren't a couple anymore?"

"No. To make a long story short, Ted thought she was too bossy. Tanya was getting on his case about finding a better job and things like that."

"You want a beer, Scott?"

"Nah, I'm okay. It's a little early for drinking, anyway."

"Don't mind if I do," Lisa replies, opening a bottle and joining me at the table. "That's too bad about Ted and Tanya, though. I thought they were a good pair, but then again, what do I know about relationships?"

"Yeah, it is, but Ted's handling it well. He went on a little bender last night, but not bad, and he was working on a model airplane when I left. He'll be all right. He does love his models."

"I'll try not to bring it up with Tanya in the office this week, then. I'm sure she's disappointed. You don't suppose, eh, no, probably not."

I Try Diplomacy

"Suppose what?"

"Well, I was thinking about what you said from her perspective. You said Ted thinks Tanya was nagging him. What if, instead, he felt threatened because she's more successful than him. You think?"

I run the idea through my mind before rejecting it. "I doubt it. Ted's about as down-to-earth as guys get. I mean, he repaired helicopters in Vietnam and saw combat. You think he'd feel threatened by a woman who works in an office after all that?"

"I was thinking he'd feel threatened *because* of that. Hear me out. He's been in war, so he's thinking he can handle anything. But then Ted meets a woman who has a professional job and is on her way up. That becomes a threat because his status as a man normally puts him in a position of privilege. So, subconsciously he rejects her because she challenges his primacy he thinks he's earned by fighting in a war."

"That sounds ridiculous. Ted isn't a macho type like that. He's a quiet guy who doesn't like to be hassled. If he called off the relationship, then he had a good reason to do it. Trust me on this one."

"Okay, if you say so, then I trust you. But you might try seeing things from Tanya's perspective, too."

"You don't even know that's what Tanya's perspective is, do you? Didn't you just say you hadn't talked to her for a while?"

"I haven't spoken to her in a couple days, but lots of women have that experience or one similar to it. Trust *me* on that one."

"Okay, you may have a point, generally speaking," I say with a smile. "I don't think it fits with Ted's personality, though. Not at all. But now that you mention it, I did meet someone lately who fits your description almost exactly."

"Oh?"

"Well, you see, I went over to meet Sandra's parents at their house yesterday evening. We were supposed to have dinner together."

"Supposed to have dinner? What happened?"

I pause and scrunch my mouth around while thinking of how to describe the evening. "Well, this is going to sound nuts, but here's the chain of events. Sandra and I went to Disneyland together a few weeks ago. I told you about that, right?"

Lisa nods. "You told me you two were going as friends, though."

"We were at the time. But she's the first woman I've met since Elaine whom I feel comfortable around. So, to make this part of the story brief, we're dating now."

"That's great!" Lisa proclaims, raising her beer in a toast.

"Yes, it is. We're very happy together. But her parents, or maybe I should say her father, decided that if we were going to Disneyland together, we must already be a couple, so he insisted I come to his house for dinner. That was last night.

"Trouble was, he hates the war every bit as much as you do, and like you, he also thinks anyone who fights is a stooge of the government. But the difference between you two is that you realize that not everyone who joins the Army is a bad person. You see a difference between someone being manipulated and someone being bent on destruction. I don't think that he does."

"He said all this at your first meeting? Damn, even I have more tact than that. Even Mother has more tact than that. Well, maybe not, come to think of it."

Ignoring the last comment, I go on. "You might not believe it, but that wasn't the worst thing. He also invited another guy to dinner, a guy who Sandra dated for a little while."

"You're kidding." Lisa stares at me incredulously, waiting for the punchline to reveal I'm pulling her leg.

"I wish that I was, but no, he really did that. According to Sandra, they dated for a little while because they grew up in the same neighborhood, but she realized before long that she didn't like him at all. He's shallow, materialistic, and stuck on himself. But somehow, the guy has the confidence of Sandra's father, and the old man still wants to see them back together."

"That's nuts. If you weren't my brother, and I didn't know you were honest, I'd swear you made that up."

I shake my head. "If only I had."

"So, what does that mean for you and Sandra?"

"We don't know. She told me she would go to work on her dad and try to get him to accept me eventually. I'm not too confident it'll work, though. On our way out the door he shouted he didn't want to see me in his house again, or else."

"Or else what?"

I shrug. "Neither of us stuck around to ask."

"I still can't believe that. What kind of man goes out of his way to insult his daughter and threaten her boyfriend after meeting him for ten minutes?"

Another shrug.

"Was he drunk? High?"

"It didn't look like either one to me. But does the reason even matter? He's decided I'm no good. I don't think it makes any difference if it was a fair decision or not."

"Shit, Scott, I'm sorry to hear that. You can't seem to catch a break when it comes to women."

I slap the table in frustration. Not too hard, but enough that my hand stings. "I think I really like Sandra. Her personality is like Elaine in some ways, but it's different enough that Sandra doesn't remind me of Elaine constantly. I don't want to lose her—not like this. Not because her old man thinks all GIs are awful."

"Would Sandra defy her father for your sake?"

"Geez, I don't want to see that happen. What good would come of that?"

Lisa has no response, and I realize my comment must've struck a nerve. I tell her, "That's not the only thing that has me mad. I'm not sure I can do the real thing I came over here to do, though."

"What's that?"

"I was going to convince you to make up with Mom."

The statement hangs in the air for several moments. Outside light streams through the windows, but it seems as if the room has gotten a shade dimmer.

"She's impossible," Lisa finally says after twisting her beer bottle in a circle a few times.

"I disagree. Difficult at times, for sure. But she has a lot of good traits, too, like you do. The trouble is, the way I see it, neither of you are able to agree to disagree. Not when it comes to Vietnam, at least."

When I see Lisa open her mouth to protest, I put up my index finger to signal I need to finish. "Hear me out. I know that you think you're the one with facts and she's just repeating the party line of the government. Maybe you're right about that. I know you've graduated from college, and I know you know how to do research. But Mom'll never believe those things. She just won't. It's not in her psychological makeup."

"That's her problem, not mine, if she can't handle a little cognitive dissonance."

"Yes, it is. Or, at least, it should be, except she thinks the exact same about you. She takes certain things as absolute fact and believes you'll never see the truth. Because of that, Dad and I don't get to enjoy seeing our family together. I can't imagine that a longstanding argument feels good for you either, does it? Does it make you happy to have negative thoughts come up whenever something reminds you of Mom? Remember, Lisa, when you and I planned their wedding anniversary party last year? Mom gave you the biggest hug. You remember that?"

She nods.

"Don't you miss that? Wouldn't that be better than getting upset whenever you think back on those memories, just because Mom is in them, and then throwing up a mental wall of separation to push the good thoughts away?"

"How do you know about that? Did you learn to read minds in Vietnam?"

I Try Diplomacy

"No. But one of the things you learn in boot camp is how to feel about killing another person. I don't think anyone arrives in boot camp enthusiastic about seeing bullets rip through someone else's body. In the abstract, maybe, but when someone actually sees it happen for the first time, it's horrible and shocking. So, then, how does the Army teach soldiers to overcome that shock at seeing another person shredded to bloody pieces? It teaches them mental separation. The VC is the enemy. The VC is communist. You're killing rats, not people. They'll do the same to you."

It's not often I get intellectual with my sister. Usually, she knows more than me because she's been to college and I haven't. But for once, I realize I've got her attention. And one difference between my sister and my mother is that Lisa will listen to a reasoned argument if she doesn't feel threatened by the person making the argument.

"My point is, soldiers learn to have this mental wall, and the Army does such a good job of reinforcing it that GIs can't help but believe the VC really *are* murderous, evil savages who'll tear their heart out and feed it to the dogs. Looking back now, I realize that's not all literally true. But I know guys who'll swear to it and who'll probably hate the Vietnamese until the day they die. They'll never learn to take down that mental wall of hatred.

"I feel like you're going through a version of that. Am I right that whenever you think back on things we did as a family, you tend to remember the negative things, and they all lead to the conclusion that Mom's always been unreasonable, obstinate, and stubborn?"

Lisa gives a very slight nod.

"That's part of what Vietnam was like. Anytime something went wrong or made our jobs as soldiers tougher, it was Charlie's fault. Well, sometimes we blamed our officers, but we could always find a way to link every problem to Charlie, and most of us did. As a result, any horrible thing we did was okay because, ultimately, Charlie had caused it.

"I realize I'm just your little brother who doesn't know much, but that's what I see going on with you and Mom. Every experience, every memory, confirms the negative and builds the mental wall higher. And from experience, I can tell you those emotions can warp the personalities of guys who otherwise are normal guys. I'm your brother, and I don't want to see that happen to you. Or to Mom."

"Sometimes I wonder if it's too late for that," Lisa admits quietly.

"I'm going to visit Mom next to talk some sense into her. I'll have to use a different approach, though. One reason I came here first was that I know you'll listen to logical ideas when they come from me. With her, I might try something more emotional. But it'd sure help me a lot if I could tell her you're considering a change of heart. What do you say?"

Chapter 24

A Finesse Mission

"How've you been, Mom?"

"Scott, nice of you to drop by on a Saturday. I'm about to leave for a church meeting."

"I would've thought that those happened on Sundays."

"Well, this is more of a social church meeting, if you know what I mean. Then, I want to go shopping for a little while."

I nod and smile. "New hairstyle?"

"It's nice of you to notice. Yes, I told my stylist to give me a chin-length cut with swoop bangs. She does a wonderful job, don't you think?"

"Absolutely."

"I wanted something new, but nothing girlish like a pixie cut or silly like a bouffant. Who needs a bouffant, anyway? I'm already six feet tall."

I'm thinking to myself I have a chance today. If Mom's in a good enough mood to joke about her hairstyle, maybe I've caught her at a good time. Besides, the sun is shining, it's nearly Christmas, and I can see a few gifts wrapped in red and green paper under Mom's Christmas tree.

"Can you spare a few minutes to talk before you leave?"

"Something important?"

"Yeah, I'd say so."

"Your dinner last night didn't go well? Or did it go really well, and you wanted to tell me that?"

"The first."

"I'm sorry to hear that. One of these days you need to have Sandra over here, so that your father and I can meet her."

"Dad already knows her. A little bit, anyway. Sandra's employer sends her to buy things from Dad's bakery sometimes. But you're right, it'd be nice if you met Sandra before too much longer. I think you'll like her. A lot. She's not a hippie, and I've never heard her mention the words 'flower power.'"

Mom chuckles. "If your dad approves, then I'm sure she's a nice lady. What went wrong last night, though?"

I sigh. Even now, after telling both Ted and Lisa, thinking about last night steals my energy and enthusiasm.

"Everything, to be honest. Sandra's dad, well, let me say that the two of you wouldn't get along very well. As much as you support the war, he hates it that much."

"What an idiot. Is he a Red or something?"

Although my mom's knee-jerk assumptions bother me as much as ever, I decide to use them to my advantage today. Unless things change substantially, the chances of her ever meeting Gus Larson are close to zero, anyway.

"No, not a Red. Just an angry old guy. But he was pretty rude to me last night, and even Sandra is furious with him for how he acted."

"Good for her. I think I like her already."

"Gus's attitude would've put one of Lisa's old boyfriends to shame, come to think of it."

For once, my mother has nothing to say.

"She's not dating anyone right now, so you don't have to worry about her moving to San Francisco or joining a free love commune."

Mother still says nothing in reply. That's not good. My joke was supposed to put her more at ease, but her shoulders are still tense, and she's staring at me like she doesn't know it was a joke. Maybe this won't be easy, after all.

"Oh, come on, Mom. That was a little bit funny, wasn't it?"

"You've spoken with your sister lately?"

"About an hour ago. She told me something you might want to hear about."

"I can't imagine what that would be," Mom states in a polar tone.

I ignore the icicles hanging from Mom's words. "Lisa wants to see you."

"She wants to see me dead, you mean."

"No, she really wants to see you and talk to you."

"For what? To spout more communist nonsense to me?"

I'm almost ready to shout in frustration, but I unclench my fists, focus on breathing evenly, and hold it down.

"Mom, just relax some. I'm trying to help you out here. I told Lisa it was killing me that you two haven't talked in so long. I convinced her that it was time to bury the grudges. It's possible that she's ready to do it. But you know Lisa. She won't come around all the way if she doesn't think you'll move to meet her."

"I'd be happy to do that—as soon as she apologizes to me. Your sister knows that. She's known it for months."

I want to palm my forehead now, but that would ruin everything. I knew guys in Vietnam who got medals for missions easier than this. Luckily, I anticipated that Mom would say something like that.

"How about if you both lay aside the idea of demanding an apology to start with? She's convinced that she's right. You're convinced that you are. That's the first barrier to you two reconciling, right? So, instead of head-butting each other like rams, why not move around the barrier instead?"

"I'm not sure what you mean by that."

"Isn't there something you and Lisa can talk about that doesn't involve Vietnam or your arguments? Something you can do that'll remind you of the good times you used to have together? Christmas isn't that far away. You two always liked to drive around and look at the lights together. Remember that? Then you'd go and get ice cream because nothing ever freezes in L.A., and that was as close to snow as you were going to get."

Maybe it's me, but I'd swear Mom's shoulders relax a fraction of an inch.

"Or remember the time that you sewed her a Halloween costume yourself? You convinced Lisa she was Dorothy from *The Wizard of Oz*, and when she got home from trick-or-treating, you had the ruby red slippers for her. The two of you stayed up watching the movie on television the next time it came on, too."

"And I made you be the scarecrow, so that Dorothy would have a friend."

"It took months before Lisa stopped joking that I'd lost my brain."

I think Mom almost smiled after that one.

"Before Lisa's first high school dance, the two of you spent, what, two hours making sure her hair looked perfect?"

"Yes, it was two hours. And then they went swimming after the dance, and all our effort got wasted." Mom shakes her head, but she's up to a half-smile now.

"My point is, you did lots of fun things together over the years. I remember the hug you gave Lisa after your anniversary party last year. The smile on her face was so big because you and Dad looked happy and had a wonderful time. My thought is that if the two of you can agree to say nothing to each other about Vietnam, but focus on those things that bring you together, you can start seeing each other again. It's time, isn't it? Christmas is a week away. I don't want to celebrate one Christmas with you and another with Lisa. That doesn't feel right to me. Does it feel right to you?"

Mom doesn't reply, but I think she's wavering. She's looking down, studying the floor and working her mouth like she wants to say something.

"I think I can get Lisa to agree if you will. How about it, Mom?"

Chapter 25

Secret Plans

"This is terrible, Scott. Things are worse than ever," Sandra tells me over the phone.

"What now?"

"I don't know what happened after we left dinner, but somehow Cory convinced my parents he wants to date me again. Both of them. My dad is putting pressure on me to do it."

"Damn. I know you never would, but what are you going to do?"

"I told them no way, but they're convinced it's for my own good. They won't let the idea die."

"What will it take to get them off your case and let you live your own life?"

"Beats me. You'd think they'd want that. But when I talked to Dad on the phone yesterday, he tried guilting me into seeing Cory again."

"Does he really despise me that much?"

"It doesn't make any sense, Scott, I know. Besides the fact that he hates Vietnam, he likes Cory because we grew up in the same neighborhood. Dad knows Cory and trusts him, and that means a lot to someone like my dad. He's never had many people he could count on, so when he thinks he's met one, he latches on. Dad's circle of people he spends time with has gotten smaller over the years, and his isolation shows at times like this."

"Even to the point of trying to put you in a cage and control you."

I hope the silence on the line signals agreement.

When it continues, I ask, "You still there, Sandra?"

"Yes, of course. I just don't know what to say or do. You're right about my dad. I wasn't quiet because I was upset with you. But I don't know what to do."

As much as I want to, I know I shouldn't throw down an ultimatum and demand anything from Sandra. Why can't her dad let up and allow his daughter to be her own person?

"I wish we could prove to him that Cory isn't who he thinks Cory is. What would it take to do that, do you think?" I ask after a few seconds.

Again, Sandra hesitates. "I have no idea. To be honest, I think Cory is trying to spoil my relationship with you as retaliation for me not wanting to see him anymore. That'd be just like him."

"Well, geez, Sandra, let's not allow that to spoil our fun tomorrow. Tomorrow is New Year's Eve, after all, and you're still coming to the party at my apartment, right? Ted will be there, plus my sister and a couple other people, but that's all."

Another lengthy pause. "Sandra?"

"I can't be there after all. I need to babysit my sisters."

Now I'm steaming. It takes all my self-control not to shout into the phone. I'm squeezing the receiver so hard, I fear the plastic will crack. As measured as I can, I tell Sandra, "You said you would be there. Is this another scheme from your father?"

"No, this wasn't planned. He got a new job as a cashier at a liquor store after the grocery store let him go. The store needs a full staff on New Year's Eve. You can imagine why."

I smack the receiver against my forehead in frustration.

"What was that, Scott?"

"Me seeing how much force the phone could withstand."

"Huh?"

"Never mind. I'm so disappointed, and I know it's not your fault, but I really wanted to spend the evening with you."

"I'm sorry. I don't know what more to say. As much as I want to be there, someone needs to watch my little sisters," Sandra tells me in a plaintive tone.

"I don't suppose, no, that wouldn't be a good idea."

"You were gonna suggest I come anyway and bring them along?"

"Yeah, but I know it's not the right place for girls that age. Damn. Well, I'll probably spend January 1 watching college football with my dad like I always do. You want to come over to his house? After you had dinner with us the day after Christmas, I think he likes you almost as much as I do."

"I'd love to stop by after my shift at the coffee shop. Your parents treated me like royalty."

"They recognize a good thing when they see it."

"Do you have the same bet with your dad as always?"

"Yeah. If Southern Cal wins, I wash his car twice. If Michigan wins, he puts two plastic pink flamingos in his yard for a month. I won last year, though, so maybe this year will make two straight."

"All right, I'll meet you at your parents' house around dinner time. See you then."

I almost do it. I almost tell Sandra "I love you" over the phone. Maybe I should. It's not my style to move so quickly on things like that, especially given that I've never said those words to anyone besides Elaine. But I've also realized that when you know you've met someone special, you should treat them like they're special.

In the end, though, I lack the guts to say it. Instead, I tell Sandra, "I'll see you tomorrow. I'm really looking forward to it."

The party at our apartment is somewhat less than raucous, but that suits Ted and me. I'm surprised that Lisa agreed to join us when I asked, but she claimed she had nothing going this year and was happy to spend the time with me.

So, we're sitting on my couch, glasses of champagne in hand, as midnight approaches. The television is on, but it's mostly background noise because everyone else is around our card table, eating popcorn and playing poker for small stakes.

"Well, Scott, I guess I owe you one," Lisa is telling me.

"Christmas went better than I thought it would. I know you and Mom didn't say much to each other, but at least you were under the same roof without arguing."

"It's a start. And I've got you to thank for that."

"Nah, I did what a brother should do for his sister. Truth be told, I probably should've tried something sooner. Dad kept telling me you two would work things out when you were ready to, but maybe this once I shouldn't have listened to him and trusted myself instead."

"I'm disappointed that Sandra isn't here. Getting to know her better is important to me."

"Well, if you want to see Mom again already, Sandra's coming over to our parents' house tomorrow. I always spend the day watching football with Dad, remember, and she's going to join us for a little while since she couldn't be here tonight. You can meet her then."

"That doesn't sound bad. Maybe I will. Around lunch time?"

"Maybe try dinner time. Sandra has to work the afternoon shift."

"I don't suppose her father's attitude has improved any with the holiday season?"

I shake my head and sigh.

"That makes me feel bad for you. Really, it does. From what you've told me, the two of you are a great pair who deserve each other. Still, maybe things will work out okay given enough time. Mom and I are proof that they can, I suppose."

"Maybe I told you about this, maybe not, but apparently the old boyfriend has told Gus that he wants to get back together with Sandra. She thinks he's doing it out of spite to ruin her relationship with me."

"Sounds like a man I dated a few months back. He struck me as a guy with a jealous streak, too—the type who wouldn't be pleased to see a former date find happiness without him." Lisa shakes her head. "Shallow, stuck on himself, yeah, I know that type. I seem to be a magnet for them."

I laugh. Perhaps I shouldn't, but it's my sister, and I know it doesn't bother her. She laughs at most of her mistake relationships, too.

Lisa goes on. Sometimes, she gets on a roll talking about some of her old boyfriends, and now is one of those times. "Geez, that guy was conceited. You know what the craziest thing about him was? He kept records of the women he dated and how many dates it took before they slept with him. Can you imagine?"

"How do you know about that?"

"I found his book one night after he got drunk. Even though I was almost sure I wanted to dump him, he kept bragging about his house, so I thought I'd go and see what all the fuss was about. Probably he meant to make me his latest conquest, but I'm not that easy. I might date a lot of men, but I have standards."

I don't know if I'm supposed to laugh at that, too, so I let Lisa continue.

"Anyway, I let him drink while pretending I was getting drunk, too, and finally he mentioned this book he kept. I couldn't believe anyone would do that, much less admit it to a woman, but sometimes alcohol can be a useful tool. I excused myself to find the bathroom but ducked into his bedroom to find this book instead. I figured if he kept it anywhere, it'd be there."

"Damn, you've got nerve."

"Well, what was he going to do to me if he found me? Tell me to get out? I was gonna do that anyway," Lisa answers with a laugh and a big grin. It's also her grin that indicates she isn't done with the story yet, so I grin back and wait for her to finish.

"It didn't take long to find the book in his closet. Once I realized I had the right book, I heard him stumbling around and figured I'd better get out of the bedroom so that I could go home."

Now I'm laughing nonstop. Partly because I didn't know my sister would do something like that and partly at the absurdity of the whole story.

"Yeah, Cory and I dated a handful of times before I realized he thought he was God's chosen one, and after that night, I called him and told him we were done."

My laughter ceases abruptly. "Wait, what did you say his name was?"

"Cory. Cory, what was his last name? Hatfield, or Smithfield, maybe? I think it was Hatfield. Why are you looking at me like that?"

"Cory is the name of Sandra's old boyfriend. You don't suppose, no, what are the odds it's the same guy?"

"Not very good, but let's compare notes. Did Cory tell you what he did at dinner?"

"Yeah. He said he was already a bank manager. That surprised me. I mean, the guy looks like he's only shaved twice in his life."

"The guy I dated had just got promoted to bank manager."

"You don't say."

Lisa shakes her head. "I'll be damned. And the other thing you said, about him looking really young, well, that's the guy I dated, too."

"Blond hair, medium length, parted on the side?"

Lisa nods while I describe him. Then my face falls.

"What?" Lisa asks, her brow crinkled.

"What if Sandra's in the book?"

"Oh my."

"I'm hesitant to ask, but did you read any pages?"

"No. I mean, I glanced at one of them. It was written like a diary, but it made me feel icky to read it. I decided I wasn't there to play voyeur, and I put the book back."

I sit there, not moving.

"Scott, you're looking at me with a funny look. What now?"

"I just thought of something."

"Yes?"

"You said you owe me for helping with Mom, right?"

Lisa nods.

"I want to call in that favor right now."

"How? Cory was a conceited jerk. We both know that. The less we have to do with him, the better, right?"

"We're going to use his vanity against him."

After a moment, Lisa replies, "I think I know where this is going, and I'm not sure I like it."

"I want you to call him up and ask to meet him again."

"Unlike Cory, I don't keep a book with records of my dates. That phone number got tossed in the trash months ago."

"Sandra will have it."

"Damn. You're too smart."

"No, you aren't getting out of this that easy," I say with a smile. "You'll call him up, say you were wrong to dump him before, that he's the smartest and handsomest man you've ever dated, and blah, blah, blah, to puff up his ego and make him think you're crawling back to him on hands and knees. Cory won't be able to resist that."

"But why? Will this somehow prove to Sandra's father that he isn't interested in Sandra, after all?"

"It might if you steal his book."

Lisa looks me in the eye. "My God. You *are* thinking what I was thinking."

"Stealing the book shouldn't be hard. You know where he keeps it."

To my surprise, a grin spreads across Lisa's face.

"You know what, Scott? I love your plan. Anyone obnoxious enough to keep a diary about how many women he sleeps with deserves to be exposed. Especially when he's also a jerk who tried to tell me how sorry I'd be without him. And double especially when he's trying to ruin my brother's relationship with a sweet woman like Sandra."

"I thought it'd be your type of mission."

"Hell yes, it is. Didn't someone once say that there's no more deeply moving religious experience than cheating a cheater?"

"You'll really do it?"

"It'd be my honor. Except I can see one potential flaw, little brother."

"What's that?"

"What if he didn't write anything about Sandra in his book? Then we've got nothing except a gross recapitulation of Cory's love life."

"I'm a step ahead of you."

"Oh?"

"We'll get you a Polaroid instant camera. A couple photos of you and him out at dinner somewhere, or drinking champagne in his house, or hugging, or whatever, should also prove that he's faking his interest in Sandra to spite her."

"I'm never gonna underestimate my younger brother again."

I'm grinning at Lisa when, in the distance, I hear the faint pop of fireworks. Glancing at the clock, it's still about twenty minutes to midnight, but it seems a few neighbors are getting anxious to see in the new year.

"Are you ready for this right now?" Lisa asks me.

"I hope so," I venture while looking toward Ted. He, too, turned to look at me when he heard the fireworks. "I'm hoping that with my friends around me maybe the big fireworks won't set off the flashbacks this time."

Chapter 26

The Mission

"Lucky for you that you're my little brother, and I love you."

"You got them, Lisa?"

"I've got everything, Scott. Photographs, diary pages, and a headache from spending an evening with Cory."

I laugh at the last part. "Let's see what you've got."

"These photographs ought to be ample proof, right? I met Cory at his house after a few drinks at a bar. I mean, look at this picture we had someone take of us at the bar. He's practically fondling my breast right there in public."

"You're a good soldier, Lisa. A real good soldier. These ought to be perfect, especially combined with the diary pages you stole."

"What do we do now? What's your next move, Sergeant Sticks?"

"Something simple, I think. You can pretend you're someone Sandra works with, or pick another cover story that suits you, and then find a reason to meet her at her parents' house. She brings up Cory's name on accident, you mention the 'date' you just had with someone named Cory, and the details come out from there."

"Hmm, not very subtle, but I suppose it'll work. How much have you told Sandra about our plan already?"

"Most of it. I figure you two can work out the finer details. Oh, but she doesn't know about the diary."

"That's a pretty big detail."

"Yeah, but what if she's in it, Lisa? Sandra gets self-conscious about herself already. I don't want her to find out about the diary unless we have no other choice. That could really send her emotions into a tailspin, don't you think? Unless . . ."

"Yes?"

"Well, have you read them? If Cory never mentions Sandra, then we're okay."

"No, I haven't read the diary. I was going to leave that to you."

"Me? I don't want to read that."

"Neither do I. It sounds yucky and sick to write about the women you sleep with. I don't want to read those pages any more than you do, Scott."

"But you'll need to do it. How else can you frame Cory properly?"

"You could read them and tell me what they say. Sandra's your girlfriend, after all."

"It'll work better if you do it, Lisa."

"I already spent an evening with this loser. Isn't that enough?"

We sit looking at each other for several moments.

"There's only one way to settle this," Lisa states finally.

"Oh?"

"Rock-paper-scissors."

"Agreed," I say after I finish laughing.

"Ready? One, two, three!"

We look down. I've got rock. Lisa has scissors.

"Damn," she whines. "Okay, I'll do it."

"Thank you, Lisa. For everything."

"You think the old guy will come around after this?"

"From this alone, probably not. It won't change the fact that I was in Vietnam and Gus hates the war. But it should eliminate Cory from the picture, at least, and that's a start. Not to mention that you get a little revenge, too, for Cory trying to guilt you after your breakup."

The Mission

"Do I get a medal for all of this? Last night really was rough. I felt like ants or fleas were crawling on my arms all night. That's how gross I felt, sitting there talking to Cory for five hours. I had to remind myself not to stare at a clock and keep faking some interest in him."

"I can make a medal just for you. We can call it the 'Atta Girl Star.' I'll even let you choose the color of construction paper I use when I cut out the star. How's that sound?"

"Good enough," Lisa laughs. "But it'd better be big—big enough to light the bonfire I'm gonna burn all this stuff in when everything is over."

Chapter 27

A Final Visit

"You would've turned twenty-three today," I say to Elaine, standing near her headstone. "I brought you an extra rose as a present. Rose is your middle name, after all, so it seemed appropriate."

It's a rainy October day in 1970, and I stand beneath a black umbrella, looking down. It's a scene like one finds at the end of a sad movie—the hero saying goodbye to a loved one while a steady rain falls, the gray sky making the scene even sadder than it already is.

Even though I always feel sorrow when I visit Elaine, today I feel something else. I need a while to get myself together and speak the words, but eventually I say, "I've made up my mind about something important. I want to tell you about it. It's silly, I know, to come here to speak to you about the things I do, but it makes me feel better. I think you'd be happy for me, though, if you could say so. I'm going to ask Sandra to marry me.

"We haven't dated as long as some people—about ten months. But I feel really happy and at peace with her, and I think she feels the same. You would like her, too, Elaine, and even though that shouldn't matter, it's important to me to think that you would.

"I know I don't need to ask for your blessing to be with Sandra. You already gave it before you died. But it still matters to me to tell you. I'll always love you. You'll always be my sweetheart, my true love. Sandra is a great woman too, though—the only woman I've

A Final Visit

ever met besides you who makes me want to be something better than I am, just so I won't let her down. Those people don't come around very often, and I won't let Sandra slip away."

I stand in silence for a few more minutes. I've told Elaine what I came to say. Yet, for the first time when visiting her grave, the inner calm feels stronger than the inner torment. I'll never be completely whole without Elaine, but this is as close to whole as I've felt in a long time. Sandra has a lot to do with that, for sure, but I think I've grown, too. Or, maybe it's best to say that because of Sandra, I have a reason to want to feel whole again. I guess that's what people mean when they speak of having a purpose in life.

Like I always do before departing, I kneel beside Elaine's headstone, touch two fingers to my lips, and leave her with a kiss.

Scott's Postscript

Sandra and I got married in the spring of 1971. It was a modest wedding—neither of us wanted or could afford a huge production.

Ted was the best man in the wedding party. His parents and sister Rachel came, too. Even though my dad insisted on helping cater the wedding, I made him promise to have some of Gloria's molasses cookies. I do love her cookies.

I felt a little surprised to see them, but Elaine's parents attended as well. They said they felt overjoyed to see me happy and in love. When I asked them, Mildred told me their son Glen had decided to sign up for a second tour in Vietnam already. Maybe the Army was the right place for him, after all.

Sandra's younger sisters made the most beautiful flower girls. They looked so cute with white ribbons in their hair, tossing petals this way and that.

I didn't know if he'd do it, but Sandra's father Gus did come to the wedding. After Lisa and I proved Cory a fraud, he finally relented and allowed that I wasn't wholly without merit.

Cory did write about Sandra in his book, and it wasn't complimentary. He referred to her as a naïve butterball who was beneath his standards but fun to manipulate. To him, she was practice.

Lisa and I didn't want Sandra to read that about herself, so instead, Lisa went "undercover" again, as she called it, and posed as Sandra's friend for a visit to Gus's house. When they departed, she left the relevant pages of the diary on the kitchen table, along with a couple Polaroid pictures of herself with Cory and a note explaining everything.

It worked. I wouldn't say Gus ever liked me, even after that, but he realized who Cory really was and ostracized him like Cory deserved all along. Then Lisa asked to get the diary pages back and burned everything that she'd taken.

The reason I write of Gus in the past tense is that he died of a heart attack shortly after the wedding. He was only a little over fifty, but it seems that a lifetime of hard work, stress, and struggle caught up with him. I feel bad for Sandra for losing her father. Maybe I'll feel bad about it myself later, but at the moment, I feel some relief, too. Is that a shortcoming of character on my part? I hope not.

Sandra's mother and sisters now live with Sandra's aunt. I later found out that the aunt and her husband had offered to help with the daughters on multiple occasions, but Gus had always been too stubborn to accept.

Lisa and my mother are mostly on good terms again. Their relationship isn't perfect, but they haven't had any more blow-ups about Vietnam. Because my parents both adore Sandra, Lisa redeemed herself considerably in Mom's eyes when Lisa helped me prove Cory a fake. We never told her exactly how Lisa did it, mind you. Our methods would probably not meet with Mom's approval. But Mom delights in having Sandra as her daughter-in-law.

I wish I could write that Lisa now has a steady boyfriend and has settled down, but not everything works out perfectly, I guess. She's become more selective about who she dates but hasn't found the right man yet.

This frustrates her, I know. After all, she's a smart woman in her twenties with a quality job. Lisa isn't shy about her views, whether it's the war in Vietnam or the ways in which society tries to control women, but I've met several of her boyfriends, and she's never obnoxious when I'm around. I really can't say why things never work out for Lisa. She thinks most men find her achievements and intellect threatening. Maybe she's right. I don't know.

Ted remains the same quiet and low-key man he's always been. His fleet of model cars and planes keeps growing, as does his record collection. We still go to Inglewood to visit his parents for dinner about once a month. Sandra agrees that Gloria's molasses cookies have no equal. She even tried to get my dad to sell them in his bakery if Gloria would share the recipe. Gloria agreed, but my father, true to his nature, decided he wasn't comfortable profiting from someone else's ideas. Even after Gloria insisted she didn't mind, he politely turned her down. So, now that idea is on hold until Sandra finishes college and opens her own café, where she promises to feature Gloria's cookies.

A few months back, I left the garage where I'd worked since returning from Vietnam. I didn't think I'd do it two years ago, but I decided to join Dad in his bakery after all. A guy does have to get up early to be a baker, but that's no problem for me after Vietnam.

Why did I do it? I still sometimes wonder that myself. But at heart, I think it's because I saw what too much work and stress did to Sandra's father. My own father is at no risk of becoming angry with the world like Gus was, but he's worked five and six days a week at his bakery for nearly twenty-five years. I'd like to give him a little relief from that. He's earned it.

Besides that, seeing my mother and Lisa finally make up reinforced for me how important it is to have family members active in your life. Carrying on the family business is one way I can do that. Although Dad remains the boss while we're at work, once the day is over, he teaches me about managing the business, how to relate to the customers, and the rest. Now that I can see how his bakery works from the inside, the more I admire him for how thoroughly he understands what he's doing.

I still have nightmares and flashbacks on occasion. As time has gone by, I've learned what things set me off, like sudden, loud noises and depressing setbacks. The noises I can sometimes avoid, but everyone has rough days, and I still struggle at night when those happen. I've learned that I can manage these problems, but I doubt

I'll ever be free of them. That part of fighting in Vietnam will stay with me forever, it seems.

Sandra is at her best during those nights. It took Elaine a long time to grasp that my nightmares weren't temporary issues and that they don't truly have a cure. She understood that eventually, but the realization took quite a while to set in. Maybe that's because I wasn't sure myself how long they'd last. But Sandra doesn't see the flashbacks as problems to be solved or flaws that must be remedied. She puts her arms around me, talks me through the episode, and always listens, no matter what ungodly hour of the night it is.

All in all, I consider myself a lucky man. I married someone who loves me for who I am, not for who she wants me to be. I try to return her love, and I support Sandra's goal of getting her college degree and opening a café.

That isn't to say our lives are easy, or that we never fight. Both of us work hard, and we don't always look at every issue the same way. But one lesson we learned from watching our parents is to not take disagreements personally. Normally, people try to learn from the good things their parents do, but after the arguments between my mother and Lisa on the one hand, and the anger of Sandra's father on the other, we've seen lots of examples of what *not* to do in a healthy relationship.

The war in Vietnam continues. Although my role in the war is over, I still follow what's happening. Despite the fact that the U.S. government instituted a new lottery draft in 1969 to raise manpower, as of 1971, I see no end in sight. A few days ago the *New York Times* published a series of stunning exposés that people are referring to as the Pentagon Papers. They contain damning records of the many ways that the U.S. government has been lying to people about the war in Vietnam for years. The public reaction has been a mix of shock and anger.

The longer things go on in Southeast Asia, the more I think my father was right in his views about Vietnam. Perhaps not enough of the soldiers feel their sacrifices are worth it, and that's why the U.S.

hasn't won after seven years of war. I don't know if that's true, but maybe it is.

I admitted this to Lisa one time, and she tried again to drag me to one of her anti-war meetings. Even after the Pentagon Papers appeared, I still won't do it. Maybe that's because after my own experiences, I care more about what happens to the individual people who fought overseas than about the morality of it all. I see homeless veterans on the streets from time to time, and I never turn them down when they ask for spare change. Maybe they take the money to get beer. I don't mind that. Sometimes I talk with them for a bit and ask them where they served, when they were overseas, and so forth, like I did with Edward Davis on the night Sandra found me drunk.

After I go my way, I have a tough time not crying. Many of those homeless guys weren't that different from me when they joined up. Not all of the guys I talk to were drafted—some volunteered because they felt it was the right thing to do. But something went wrong for them. Some didn't have a stable family to come home to. Others brought the war home with them and couldn't cope with being civilians. A few have injuries that keep them from doing steady, productive work. A couple times when I've mentioned my flashbacks, I've seen the light of recognition in their hollow eyes.

Not much I can do will help those people directly, I realize, but I try to let them know that I don't see them as failures, even if everyone else seems to. It's not much, but it feels better than looking the other way when I walk by. Seeing homeless veterans also reaffirms the importance of what Sandra wants to do when she opens her coffee shop. She still wants to make it friendly to handicapped people, and I support her plans fully. That won't change the world by itself, but it's something.

At the moment, the thing that scares me most is that Sandra is pregnant, and I'll be a father before too much longer. I doubt I'm ready for that, but is anyone ever truly ready? Sandra and I don't know yet if it'll be a boy or girl. Whichever we have, I plan to lean heavily on my dad for advice. If I'm half as good at fatherhood as he was, the baby should turn out fine.

My dog Pete lived to see me marry Sandra and moved with us to our new place together. I don't know if he'll make it long enough to welcome our baby into the world, too, but one never knows.

Although having a baby makes both of us nervous, Sandra and I look to the future with promise. Sandra has decided not to drink any alcohol while pregnant, fearing to repeat what happened to her own mother. I joined her out of solidarity.

Every now and then, I still visit Elaine's gravesite to pay my respects. Sometimes Sandra joins me, but mostly she lets me go alone. I tell Elaine that I still miss her, but I'd think she'd be happy to see where I'm at now. I'm confident that she'd like Sandra and approve of us being together. Before I leave, I always place a rose by the grave marker and thank Elaine for our years together.

Sandra even volunteered that if our child turns out to be a girl, we should name her Elaine, but I said that wasn't necessary. My memories of her don't require a constant reminder, and if we do have a daughter, I want her to grow up without the shadow of Elaine's tragedy hanging over her. Being young is hard enough without that association adding its weight.

Mostly, Sandra and I spend our free time walking Pete at the park, watching her favorite TV shows, and planning what she'll need to own her business someday. My dad helps considerably with this, since I need to learn how as well if I'm ever to run his bakery. He's a patient teacher, and thanks to him, both Sandra and I know a vast array of things we might've learned the hard way otherwise.

So, to the extent that any of us can claim our story has a happy ending before it's over, ours does. Sandra and I keep our faith that life has wonderful things in store for us, even if we've learned that tragedy can strike along the way. But we've decided that the best way to handle tragedy is together, standing side by side, with each other to lean on.

Sandra's Postscript

My husband Scott died in 1983 at the age of thirty-six. Our final few years together were difficult ones at times. It's not quite true to write that Scott died an angry, bitter man like my own father, but neither did he die content and at peace with himself.

One sad irony is that he died of the same disease that killed Elaine—cancer. Another is that, like Elaine, he died well before he should have. But that's where the parallels in their deaths end.

Shortly after our second daughter's birth in 1974, Scott began to complain of fatigue and told me that sometimes his vision was blurry. He also started to lose weight, even though he didn't have much extra to begin with. It took doctors months to make a proper diagnosis, but eventually they told us Scott suffered from type two diabetes.

The reason it took them so long to arrive at that conclusion was that Scott showed none of the signs typically associated with adult diabetes. He wasn't overweight, his work at the bakery kept him active, and his family had no history of the disorder.

One day Scott and his doctor were talking about the end of the Vietnam War, and Scott mentioned that he'd flown in helicopters that sprayed Agent Orange. That had been the clue that allowed the doctor to finally make the proper diagnosis—Scott had been exposed to Agent Orange on numerous occasions.

Neither Scott or I felt surprised, therefore, when a follow-up exam revealed the presence of cancer. The doctor gave us scientific literature describing how Agent Orange contains dioxin, a toxic chemical linked to adult diabetes, cancer, and a host of other problems, including severe birth defects in children.

This explained so much. Although our first daughter is normal in most ways, her eyesight is unusually poor. Neither Scott nor I connected that to anything, however, because she can manage with glasses. Our second girl, however, who only arrived a few months prior to Scott's diagnosis, was born with deformed legs and toes and cannot walk without crutches and leg braces.

To his credit, Scott tried. He tried to bear the misfortunes with dignity and composure. He told me that Elaine had taught him how a person should handle tragedy. But he couldn't help his feelings of anger and betrayal. You see, when he'd flown in helicopters in Vietnam, he'd been told that Agent Orange was safe to handle and that exposure was harmless. Both the U.S. government and the military leadership had said so. Only later had the public learned that those statements were lies.

The last few months were the most difficult. Scott's bitterness increased as his days grew shorter. Even though he tried to keep a brave face for our girls, he was in a great deal of pain, physical and emotional. Sometimes he got angry with me, too. He always apologized immediately, and I knew the reason behind his anger, but that hurt.

Scott joined the class action lawsuit brought against the U.S. government in 1979 by soldiers exposed to dioxin, but he did so half-heartedly. He never lived to see the result, which came in 1984 and turned out to be a $180-million-dollar settlement. Given the vast number of veterans who were part of the lawsuit, each one who could prove disabilities related to Agent Orange got, on average, about $3,800. I think that's the right number, anyway. That's what the life, death, and suffering of those veterans was worth to the U.S. government and the chemical companies that lied to the public for so long.

Scott's sister Lisa was our biggest support throughout. I'm sure that she felt vindicated that most of the things she believed about the horrors and lies of the Vietnam War turned out to be true. But I never heard her say anything about that to Scott after his illness began.

Lisa came over to help with our daughters twice a week when Scott became too tired to keep up with growing children. She bought groceries, took our girls shopping for clothes, and treated them to ice cream every Friday evening. We owed her so much, but she adamantly refused any compensation. Lisa always said that since she didn't have a family of her own, our family was her family.

Darryl and Susan took Scott's death hard, as one would expect. I've never cried like I did the day I watched Darryl sign the papers selling his bakery so that he'd have money to help with the medical bills of our youngest daughter.

Surprisingly, both spoke at Scott's funeral. Darryl spoke with pride about the man Scott had been and the joy he took from running the bakery together. Susan excoriated the people who'd lied to Scott about the risks of Agent Orange and blamed them for his death. That shocked me. I'd never heard her speak in bitterness about the U.S. government before, and I don't think anyone else present had, either.

Maybe I should've seen Susan's change of heart coming, though. The year before Scott's death, 1982, I traveled to New York City for the great demonstration against nuclear weapons held on June 12. One million people gathered in Central Park to protest the Reagan administration's desire for a nuclear weapon build-up and to rally for nuclear arms reductions instead.

Scott wanted me to go, but neither of us thought that Susan would approve. To our surprise, she volunteered to watch our girls since Lisa wasn't available. Susan never went so far as to say she liked what I planned to do, but neither did she attempt to talk me out of it—something she undoubtedly would have tried to do when I first met her.

My career as an anti-nuclear activist was not a long one, however. I support the cause today as much as I ever did, but raising two daughters, one badly disabled, on one's own leaves little time for activism. Between cooking, getting the girls ready for school,

Sandra's Postscript

and working as a waitress at an upscale restaurant, most of my days are spoken for. I still want to pursue the dream Scott and I began with when we married—owning my own café. But that dream is on hold until the girls grow up.

When I realized that Scott didn't have much longer to live, I asked him if he'd like to be buried near Elaine's grave. Even though I was his wife, and we loved each other deeply, I know it was only Elaine's bad luck that made our relationship possible. But Scott said no, I was his wife, and he'd like for his body to rest beside mine.

Ted came to the funeral service, of course. He eventually got married himself, and he has two sons. After the formal service was over, he took his boys by the hand and led them to the casket. Through his tears, Ted told them that if they grew up to be as good a person as Scott had been, he'd be very proud of them. That started my own tears flowing again. Then Ted whispered something to Scott that I couldn't hear, gave him a trembling salute, and gave each of his sons a big hug.

I'm proud of who my husband was and who he tried to be. He should have had the chance to do so much more in life, to see his daughters grow to be women and have their own families. But destiny had other plans for Scott. Even now, three years after his death, sometimes I still expect to hear him come through the door in the evening after a day at the bakery. Although I sleep better without his nightmares waking us up, I'd trade sleep a thousand times to have him back.

What worries me most is seeing our children grow into teenagers without Scott to help them. I try to teach them the values that Scott lived out—compassion, decency, and kindness. Sometimes, though, I feel like they inherited a bit of their Aunt Lisa's rebellious streak. But, then again, what kind of mother would I be if I didn't worry about my daughters at times?

In another way, though, both Scott and I were happy that we had two daughters together. After what Vietnam did to him, both during his service and after, Scott was glad we'd never have a son get drafted and possibly go through what he'd experienced.

It's strange how life works, I suppose. When I first met Scott, my father was angry with me for dating a soldier. By the end of Scott's life, he sometimes spoke about war and the Army in the same way.

But I also have happy memories of my time with Scott. He'd never want the last few years to overshadow the love we shared for a decade or any of the fun things we did together. He once told me that if he let that happen, then cancer truly would have defeated him.

Although it's fallen to me to finish the story of Scott's life, I hope I've given a fair account of the years since our marriage. I wish our story had a happier ending, but life doesn't always cooperate.

Goodbye, Scott. Thank you for the man you were and the example you tried to set for our children.

Sandra Reynolds

May 9, 1986

Thank You!

I'd like to thank everyone who purchases *One Kind of Hero* for reading my book. If you enjoyed it, I would be grateful if you'd leave a short review of the book on whatever website you purchased it from. Favorable reader reviews are very important to authors like me. They help tremendously in attracting new readers and spreading the word about existing books that you think others will enjoy.

Thank you!

If you want updates on future books, please join my Reader's Club mailing list at https://robbauerbooks.com.

I also write a blog where I discuss important historical topics and review books. You can follow at https://robbauerbooks.com/join-my-history-blog/.

About the Author

I'm Rob Bauer, author of historical fiction and nonfiction books and owner of Rob Bauer Books. I hold a PhD in American History and was a Distinguished Doctoral Fellow at the University of Arkansas.

My fiction has two purposes—entertaining readers and explaining historical injustice. Although I enjoy adventure and humorous books as much as the next reader, I'd like my books to stand for something a little bigger. All my studies in history put me in a position to do that. Whether I'm writing about how racism damages the individual psyche, the deportation of the Métis people of Montana, the South's prison labor system, or the utter terror of the Belgian Congo, with my books you'll find yourself in powerful historical stories.

I also write nonfiction about baseball history because I've always loved the game, its history, and its lore. I sometimes joke that baseball may be the one thing in life I truly understand. Although I love the statistical side of the game, if you don't, never fear because my histories go light on the statistics and heavy on what baseball was like in the past. They're stories about baseball, but stories with a point.

The history blog on my website offers posts on a variety of interesting historical figures and events. I'd love to have you follow along.

When I'm not working on my next story or writing project, I enjoy spending time at the beach. And, oh yeah, I still read a history book or two. When I'm not watching baseball.

Acknowledgments

I also want to thank the people who helped make this book possible, especially Jim Soular for his help with editing. Thank you to Mike Bosso, Jennifer Lodine-Chaffey, Rea Johnson, Wendy Wallace, and Paula Mason for reading and making suggestions. I also appreciate Kyle Lockwood and Jim Soular's assistance with some of the Vietnam scenes in the story. You helped in making this story into the best I could write.

Made in United States
North Haven, CT
14 March 2025

66806876R00143